I0764537

Published by
Computer Classics ®
Nashville, Tennessee

This is a work of fiction. Names, characters, places, and incidents are used factiously. Any resemblance to actual persons, living or dead, events, or locals is entirely coincidental.

I am Napoleone Bounaparte
Is published in e-book format by
Computer Classics ®
www.computer-classics.com

Library of Congress Control Number: 2011907023
ISBN: 97809836019-0-6

I am Napoleone Bounaparte

Never interrupt your enemy when he is making a mistake.
- Napoleone Bounaparte

Edward Ronny Arnold

Computer Classics ®
Nashville, Tennessee

Introduction

Everyone has heard stories of men and women who become insane and believe they are famous and infamous figures from history. On the female side there is: Cleopatra, Josephine, Martha Washington, Betsy Ross, and most recent Marilyn Monroe.

On the male side there is: George Washington, Abraham Lincoln, Wyatt Earp and Billy the Kid.

These people are portrayed in a comical form. The man who believes he is George Washington is seen attempting to cross the Delaware River, standing up in the boat, as portrayed in the 1851 painting by Emanuel Gottlieb Leutze, *Washington Crossing the Delaware.* Betsy Ross sews a flag and Abraham Lincoln constantly repeats the Gettysburg Address.

While these presentations bring laughter, no one can tell, exactly, when the concept began. No one can point to a specific case or a specific person. It is as if, these characterizations came out of nowhere and have no basis in fact.

Everything has to have a beginning and these characterizations appear to have begun one hundred years ago in the year 1910. Shortly before World War I, stories began to surface of people who became "fixated" with a historical figure. These people were diagnosed as having an inferiority complex. The most famous is the man who went insane and believed he was Napoleon Bonaparte. This man is often characterized wearing a French military uniform and placing his right hand into his coat as depicted in the 1812 painting by Jacques-Louis David, *The Emperor Napoleon in His Study at the Tuileries.*

While this is the most famous case of a fixation, it is also the first. While there is no discernable evidence such a thing ever occurred; the question is often asked, if such a thing never occurred, why is there a story?

Before this reported incident, such a thing had never been heard of. People would be declared insane and ramble about different things but no one actually believed they were Napoleon or any historical figure.

The story continues to be repeated in college abnormal psychology classes. What is repeated is the story is true and more bizarre than believed.

The basic story is a man was taken to a hospital with a burning fever. When he recovered, the man said he was Napoleone Bounaparte. Many rumors are attached to the story.

One rumor is the man only spoke two languages, French and Corsican.

One rumor is experts in French history were recruited to prove the man wrong, they couldn't!

One rumor is the man knew everything about Napoleon but the Battle of Waterloo, his exile and how he died.

One rumor is the man was blind. He was blind from birth.

One rumor is he was allegedly descended from Napoleon.

One rumor is several of his examiners attempted to free him.

One rumor is the people who examined the man were, themselves, placed in a mental institution.

One rumor is the Catholic Church performed an exorcism that failed.

One rumor is French soldiers attempted to free him and German soldiers attempted to kill him.

One rumor is soldiers in France began raising an Army to attack America and free their emperor.

One rumor is the man was actually a political prisoner and officials of the United States Government created a series of false stories to hide him.

One rumor is the man was in command of the American Army during World War I.

One rumor is the man lived in a secret room underneath the White House.

One rumor is the man is buried in the Arlington National Military Cemetery under a false name.

The rumors are as strange as the story. No one can say for sure which city hospital he was taken to. The stories differ: New

York, Boston, Memphis, San Diego, Dallas, New Orleans, St. Louis, and more than a dozen others. The one city repeated most often is New York.

No one can say for sure which year the man was taken to the hospital. The stories differ: 1908, 1909, 1910 or 1911. The year repeated most often is 1910.

The only thing consistent about the story is the man's age, about twenty-nine or thirty.

Separate, these rumors seem disjointed and make great foible for classroom breaks; together they form an amazing and intriguing story. Perhaps the most unbelievable rumor is the one that is infrequently whispered. The one rumor that is whispered, and never spoken aloud, is the most fantastic… the man who went insane and said he was Napoleone Bounaparte was never proven to be insane. An official of the United States Government created false stories to hide what they believed was fact; Napoleon Bonaparte had been reincarnated. This official was the twenty-seventh president of the United States William Howard Taft.

The puzzle no one could solve was how did someone who died in 1821, at the age of fifty-one; suddenly reappear eighty-nine years later in the body of a twenty-nine year-old blind man?

Chapter One

He opened his eyes to see darkness.

It was dark. Not darkness in the sense of nighttime; enclosure in a room without candle; a cloudy night on the sea, looking outward from the ship's deck; a starless, moonless night within a forest of tall pine trees; or a darkness of sleep before the awakening. It was darkness he had never seen, darkness void of all light or shades of black.

His body was wet. He was not cold, he was wet. He could feel wetness about his entire body. It was not wetness of water, a bathing or swimming, his entire body was wet.

He could feel tightness across his chest, his arms and his legs; he was bound.

He moved his hands and his fingers grasped a soft covering beneath him and to his sides. He moved his feet and he could feel his legs, chest and arms covered. The covering was wet. He was lying on, and under, cloth that was damp.

The smell was nauseating. The smell was the pungent odor of sulfur. He could smell fever. He knew the smell of the sweat of fever in Egypt. During the Egyptian campaign many of his soldiers perished from fever. The tents of the ill were filled with the same nauseating smell; the odor of sweat and sulfur.

He was hungry and thirsty. When he opened his mouth to exhale, he could smell his breath. The smell was rancid food, partially eaten, stuck to his teeth. He licked his dry lips and coughed slightly, his throat was parched.

The sound of his cough alerted a woman who was sitting in a chair in the room. She stood and walked toward his bed. He could hear the sound of movement and he felt a soft hand on his forehead.

The hand on his forehead was a woman's hand. He felt the soft skin of a woman and the woman's hair brush against his left cheek as she bent downward toward his left ear.

"You are awake," a woman's cheerful voice said in English. When the woman spoke into his left ear, he could smell tea. The woman had been drinking tea. He knew the distinctive smell of a hot tea with a lemon flavoring.

He did not understand what she said. The woman's voice was older. Her voice had the sound of a woman over the age of forty years and her manner was pleasant. She said something to him in his left ear but he did not understand her language.

"Who are you?" he asked in Corsican.

The morning, or evening, was pleasant. He could not tell the time of the day from the darkness. The woman prepared him a beverage of chicken and potatoes and she fed the beverage to him. A man entered the room and aided him to sit into a chair and the man removed the damp bedcovering and replaced them. The man bathed him with water and a milled soap; he was bathed as he sat in the chair. The man removed his damp clothing and dressed him in a cloth gown. The gown smelled of a starch and had the strong odor of a disinfectant.

The man and woman spoke to him in a pleasant tone. Their words were soft and gentle. He did not understand one word they said. "Who are you?" he frequently asked in Corsican. The people responded to his question. They responded in a language he did not understand.

It was many hours before a different man entered the room. This man touched him on his face, arms and chest. He aided him to stand and he forced him to attempt to walk, he couldn't. His legs were weak and his legs did not respond. The man returned him to the chair.

"Mr. Montpere," the doctor said in English. "We were very concerned of your health. I have been unable to determine the cause of your fever."

The doctor was holding a pad of paper and he wrote upon it. "On more than one occasion, we believed you would die but you did not. Your body was burning in a fever I have never encountered."

He turned to the nurse and the orderly. "The purpose of a fever is to purge the body of an infection. The heat burns the infection but I have been unable to determine the location of the infection or if there was one."

"Mr. Montpere," the doctor said in English. "Your body was in a high fever. The fever was burning, purging, something in your body but I do not know what that something was. You spoke in your delirium but we do not know what you said."

He turned to the nurse. "Have you determined what he has been saying?"

"No," the nurse answered in English. "It is a language I have never heard. He is not delirious. He keeps asking something but I do not know what he is saying."

The orderly moved forward. "He seems pleasant and agreeable. I have no idea what he is saying. The language may be Dutch."

The doctor smiled. "I think you can leave in three days," he said in English. The doctor leaned toward the man sitting in the chair. "I have no idea how he received these injuries."

The man's eyes were white, without pupils.

Suddenly, without warning the man stood. "I demand to know who you are!" he yelled in Corsican. "I demand to know to which prison I have been taken! When I am free, I will order my soldiers to kill every one of you!"

The man was weak from the illness and he fell backward into the chair.

The doctor, nurse and the orderly moved backward in fear from his unexpected outburst.

"That is the language he has been using," the nurse said in English.

"That is not Dutch," the doctor said in English.

The man attempted to stand again. "Je Suis Napoleone Bounaparte!" he yelled in French.

"That is French," the doctor said in English. "This man is a French soldier. He has somehow been injured and we must contact the Army!"

He turned toward the orderly. "This soldier is not going anywhere until the United States Army has had the opportunity to talk to him."

Chapter Two

The man sat in the chair thinking. He attempted to remember what had happened. He had been injured and he could not see. He frequently felt his face for powder burns but his face was not burned.

He could not remember a battle. His last memory was planning the attack on the town of Brienne. He recalled the French farm girl named Maria coming to his tent. They exchanged pleasantries, as they had done many times, and she returned to her home.

He considered poison. Perhaps she attempted to poison him. This idea was discounted quickly. Maria was a farm girl, unaware of the subtleties of politics. She would not know of the method or execution of such an action.

He was deep in thought when the door to the room opened.

"Good evening Mr. Montpere," a man's voice said in English.

He cocked his head slightly. He could hear the sound of boots walking toward him. There were four distinct sounds of boots. The sound of the footsteps was heavy, two men entered the room.

"I am Captain Lawrence and this is Lieutenant Simpson," one of the two men said in English. "We are representatives of the United States Army and the doctor is of the belief you are a French soldier."

"Are you?"

"I do not understand your words," the man said in Corsican.

A third set of foot steps entered the room. This set of footsteps was followed by the sound of wood being dragged on the floor. The sound of wood came closer to him and stopped an estimated six to ten American feet. The orderly followed the two officers into the room and dragged two chairs behind him. He placed the chairs a safe distance from the man.

The sound of two men sitting in chairs was distinctive.

"What is the name and location of my prison?" the man asked in Corsican.

"I do not understand what you are saying," Captain Lawrence said in English. "If you are a French soldier, speak in French."

"What is the name and location of my prison?" the man asked in Corsican.

"That is one language he keeps speaking," the orderly said in English. The orderly was standing behind the two chairs and he moved backward to the door. "He said something yesterday in another language. The doctor thought it was French."

"That is not French," Captain Lawrence said in English. "I do not know what language it is or if it is a language."

"What is the name and location of my prison?" the man asked in Corsican.

Captain Lawrence shrugged his shoulders. "I do not understand what you are saying," he said in English.

The man stood from the chair. He was weakened from the illness but he stood. He walked slowly toward the wall, feeling the wall, and walked to the edge of his bed.

"My soldiers will reward you well for my release," the man said in Corsican. "If you release me and return me to my camp, I will allow you to live. Refuse and you will die a most unpleasant death."

Captain Lawrence shrugged his shoulders and looked at Lieutenant Simpson. "I do not understand what you are saying," he said in English.

Lieutenant Simpson leaned forward. "All we want to know is who you are," he said in English. "We do not believe your real name is Rober Montpere. You may look French but we are told you do not speak French. We are told you only speak English."

The man felt for his bed, touched the metal footing, and sat on the edge. "If it is a game you play," he said in Corsican. "I play the game very well."

Captain Lawrence shrugged his shoulders and stood. Lieutenant Simpson stood. "Has he exhibited any violence?" he asked the orderly in English.

"No," the orderly answered in English. "There have been outbursts but no violence. He is blind. What can a blind man do?"

Captain Lawrence smiled slightly. "Keep his door locked and have someone stay outside his room at all times," he said in English. "If the doctor thinks he speaks French, I know someone who speaks French. I will bring her tomorrow and she can question him."

He turned toward the man. "Mr. Montpere," he said in English. "I am bringing a young lady here tomorrow who speaks French. It is in your best interest to cooperate."

"I will order my soldiers to hang you from the walls of this prison," the man said in Corsican.

The night was filled with infrequent outbursts. The man screamed and yelled in a language no one understood. He banged his two fists against the locked door and yelled, "Help me to escape!" in Corsican.

Chapter Three

The morning was without incident. He remained quite and agreeable. The nurse served him breakfast and the orderly bathed him and shaved his face. He appeared to enjoy the attention.

Toward the evening, he was sitting in his chair thinking when he heard the sound of a key being placed in a lock and his door opened slowly. "Good evening, I hope you have had a pleasant day," a woman's voice said in French.

When the door opened, he noticed something he had not noticed before. Although he could not see, his senses of smell, hearing and feeling had increased.

He could feel a change in temperature and the movement of air upon his face. He could hear additional sounds outside the room and he could smell a woman's perfume. The room was filled with smells he had not noticed before; flowers, soap, his waste in the chamber pot; and now, a woman's perfume.

He could not see the room but he had touched every wall and every object. In his mind, he could envision the room. He could see, in his mind, the placement of the bed, the wood cabinet, the chair he was sitting in and the, now, partially opened door.

He heard the sound of the door open wider. A sound of shoes, a woman's shoes, approached him. The woman was followed by two pair of men's boots. He could smell the presence of two men before they entered the room. The door closed as slowly as it was opened. He heard the sound of a key turn.

"My name is Astrid Marcelle," a young woman said in French. "I have been brought here to speak to you and to help you." The sound of her voice changed and the smell of the perfume changed. Her voice was loud then it seemed distant. The smell of a woman's perfume was strong, then weak.

He could not tell exactly from the direction of the room her voice was coming from. There were no chairs but one. He listened carefully as he heard the sound of the bedding. She had entered the room and sat on the edge of his bed.

"Are you one of my jailers?" the man asked in Corsican.

"I do not understand," she said in French. "I was told you speak French. I am here to help you but I am unfamiliar with your language. Can you speak French?"

"How can you help me?" the man asked in Corsican.

"That is not French," Astrid said in English to Captain Lawrence. "I am unfamiliar with what he said. It is a language. I do not know what language."

She stood. "Which city in France were you born?" she asked in French.

"I was not born in France," the man answered in Corsican. "I was born in the town of Ajaccio on the island of Corsica."

Astrid smiled. "If you do not speak French, I can not help you," she said in French.

"I can not speak in the language for fear of someone overhearing what is said," the man said in Corsican.

Astrid frowned. "Will you tell me your name in French?" she asked in French.

"You know my name," the man answered in Corsican.

Astrid frowned. "He said something and he appears to understand what I am saying but I do not understand what he is saying," she said in English.

Captain Lawrence shrugged his shoulders. "It was worth a try," he said in English. "Thank you for coming. I appreciate your time and effort."

Astrid smiled and turned toward Captain Lawrence. "It was worthy a try," she said in English. "I have no idea what language he is speaking but it is not French. Perhaps the doctor was mistaken. He has not said one word in French."

She turned toward him. "You have not spoken one word in French," she said in French. "I do not think you know the French language." She looked angered and stepped toward him, shaking her hand. "I came here to help because I was told you were a French soldier who had been injured."

She turned toward the two officers. "I do not care a horse's rear about these soldiers but I do care about a French soldier who has been injured. I do not know who you are but you are not a French soldier."

She began to walk toward the door.

"One word," he said in French.

Astrid turned and her eyes widened as she began to laugh.

"What did he say?" Captain Lawrence asked.

"French," Astrid answered in English. "He understands French."

"I only heard two words," Lieutenant Simpson said in English. "What did he say?"

"It is not what he said," Astrid answered in English. "It was how he said it. He understands." She laughed very loudly. "Get me a chair!" she said excited.

Chapter Four

Astrid spent the next four hours speaking to the man in French. Frequently she laughed and on more than one occasion, placed her hand on his knee.

On occasion, he whispered in her ear and she whispered into his ear.

Captain Lawrence felt uneasy with the conversation and he motioned for Astrid it was time to go.

He is so charming," she told Captain Lawrence. "I have never met a Frenchman who understands women and knows exactly what to say and when to say it, as he does."

Astrid leaned close to him. "I must leave," she said in French.

"Will you do as I ask?" he asked in French.

"If you insist," she answered in French.

"I insist," he said in French. "Do I have your word you will not repeat what I have asked to my jailers?"

"You have my word," Astrid answered in French.

The man smiled. "I thank you," he said in French. "France thanks you."

Astrid stood from her chair and smiled. She leaned forward and kissed him on his left cheek.

She motioned for the two officers to follow her as she left the room. As they left the room, the orderly closed the door and locked it from the outside. A chair was positioned outside the door and he sat in the chair.

Astrid was laughing as she walked down the hallway. "This was one of the most interesting days I have ever spent," she said in English as she continued to walk down the hallway. She stopped at the end and turned. "You do know that man is insane," she said giggling.

"Insane?" Captain Lawrence asked puzzled. "He was ill with a fever and he has recovered. He is not insane."

Astrid laughed. "Insane. Do you know who is in that locked room?"

Lieutenant Simpson shrugged his shoulders. "A French spy?"

Astrid narrowed her eyes and laughed loudly. "Napoleon Bonaparte!" she said in English.

Captain Lawrence and Lieutenant Simpson sat with Astrid and Doctor Taylor. They were in a dining area drinking coffee. "He is very charming," she said. "He told me many things of the court of France and his desire to take me there. He has promised to make me a duchess." She giggled.

"Is he serious?" Doctor Taylor asked.

"Very serious," Astrid answered. "He thinks it is the year 1814 and he was somehow injured before the attack on the town of Brienne. He has no knowledge of how he was injured. He can not see."

She sipped her coffee and giggled. "He asked me if I was married."

Captain Lawrence narrowed his eyes. "I saw you place your hand on his knee."

"Flirting," Astrid said laughing. "He was flirting with me and I was flirting with him. He said from the sound of my voice, I was a very beautiful, exciting woman." She smiled proudly and giggled. "Napoleon has excellent taste in women because I am very beautiful and very exciting!"

Doctor Taylor frowned. "He thinks he is Napoleon. I have never heard of such a thing. Obvious, the man is insane."

"He does not think he is Napoleon, he is Napoleon," Astrid giggled.

"I do not think he is insane," Captain Lawrence said. "The man is saying that to hide who he really is."

Astrid stopped laughing. "I agree. The man is not insane. He is pretending to be Napoleon. His French is excellent. It is an older form used by my grandparents but easily understood."

"According to his parents, he can not speak French," Captain Lawrence said.

"He speaks French," Astrid said. "He knows it too well to be self-taught. He also knows the city of Paris and the country of France. I asked him several questions about various areas and he knew those areas. I was born in France and I have been there, so has he."

"He has never been to France according to his parents," Doctor Taylor said. "According to his parents, he has never spoken French until his fever."

"His parents are lying," Astrid said. "The man in that locked room has visited France on more than one occasion and he speaks excellent French." She leaned forward. "He used the second language several times. I do not know why he used it but he answered several of my questions in a different language. He understood the French but he used two languages."

"Curious," Doctor Taylor said. He leaned toward Astrid. "Is this man serious that he is Napoleon?"

"Serious," Astrid answered. "He said he is Napoleon and when he is freed, he is going to order his soldiers to kill every one of you." She pointed her hand at Captain Lawrence and Lieutenant Simpson.

"A threat of violence is serious," Doctor Taylor said. "This man is insane if he thinks he has soldiers." He looked at Astrid. "Did he threaten to kill you?"

"Not yet," she answered smiling. "I think he has other plans for me."

Captain Lawrence looked irritated. "It was a mistake to bring you here."

"I only make the joke," Astrid said. "I have no interest in this man. He is very charming and his words are mesmerizing. I have never heard anyone speak like him. I have no interest in an insane man who promised to make me a duchess if I bed him." She laughed. "I am holding out for queen!"

Everyone laughed.

Captain Lawrence frowned. "What do we do with a man who claims he is Napoleon? We need to know who he really is and why he speaks a language his parents says he can not speak."

"Prove he is not Napoleon," Astrid suggested. "I asked him several questions about France and he seemed to know the answers. We can play his game and prove he is not who he says he is." She shrugged her shoulders.

"Seems reasonable," Doctor Taylor said. "One method of treatment of a psychosis is to confront the delusion. We can ask him questions about Napoleon and confront him when he can not answer the questions."

"Are you available tomorrow?" Captain Lawrence asked Astrid. "I can prepare questions and you can ask them in French."

"Not tomorrow," Astrid answered. "I have to work at the dress shop. I need the money."

"The Army will pay you," Captain Lawrence said. "I do not know anyone other than you who speaks French. I would like this over with as soon as possible and he seems to like you. Will you reconsider?"

"If you pay me," Astrid answered. "I am very expensive. I turned down the title of duchess."

Everyone laughed.

"I have been authorized to spend what is necessary," Captain Lawrence said. He paused. "There are certain people who are concerned with this man. There is a belief he was sent here from France. Why he was sent here we do not know. The Army needs to know who this man is."

"I will help," Astrid said. "Can you can pay me five American dollars a day?"

"Agreed!" Captain Lawrence said. He nodded to Lieutenant Simpson.

Lieutenant Simpson reached into his right trousers pocket and he removed a fold of money. He counted three five American bills and handed them to Astrid.

Doctor Taylor whistled.

"You people are serious about this," Astrid said, as she accepted the money.

"We need to know who this man is," Captain Lawrence said. "I do not think he is a French spy but we need to prove it."

Chapter Five

"Amaury Benoit, I have been searching for you!"

"You found me!"

The three men sitting beside Amaury laughed. One of the men stood and offered Astrid his chair. The four men were drinking and speaking at the Cherbourg French café near the 42nd street entrance to Bryant Park. The café was located near the Lyric Theater and within walking distance of the Criterion Theatre. This section of New York was often called Broadway. The area was busy at night but catered to a regular crowd during the day.

The café served modest meals but its main business was tables located on the sidewalk where wine, varied by taste and expense, was served.

"It is obvious we are no longer needed," one of the three men said in French. He nodded toward the other two men and they stood.

"Always, a pleasure, Commandant!" one of the three men said in French. They saluted Amaury and he returned the salute.

"Mademoiselle," the man said as he bowed. The three men bowed and walked away. They kept turning their heads to see Astrid. She was a very attractive French woman. Astrid was thirty-two years of age and thin. Her hair was long and she was wearing a blue print dress. Her reputation was well known.

Astrid smiled. She sat in the chair and smiled. "I have been searching for you because I have a message to give you," she said in French.

Amaury smiled. "If it is a message from a young lady, I have no interest," he said in French. "I will listen to the message but before I listen to the ramblings of a distraught female, may I offer you a glass of wine?"

"May I offer you a glass of wine before I deliver the message of a distraught male?" Astrid asked. She opened the purse she was carrying and placed a five dollar American bill on the table. She motioned for the waiter. “A carafe of your rosé, please?”

The waiter smiled and he brought a carafe of wine and glasses to the table. He poured two glasses and accepted the money. He counted the change and placed it on the table.

Amaury motioned for the waiter to leave and the waiter left their area of the outside café.

Amaury laughed. “It has been many months. I thought I was too poor for you,” he said in French.

“You are,” Astrid said in French. “However, there is much to be said for tall, strong and handsome.” She sipped her wine.

Amaury laughed as he sipped his wine. “You did not mention old,” he said in French.

“Age is like wine,” Astrid said in French. “The older the better.”

Amaury laughed. “What is this message?” he asked in French.

“A secret message,” Astrid answered in English.

Amaury paused. “Why do you speak English in a French restaurant?” he asked in English.

Astrid leaned forward. She placed her glass on the table and stroked her long black hair. “It is a secret message,” she whispered in English. She looked at the people sitting. “I do not think these people in the French restaurant understand or speak English.”

Amaury leaned forward. “What is it?” he whispered in English.

Astrid laughed and leaned backward in her chair. She sipped her wine and laughed. “Before I deliver the message, I must ask if you are a French officer,” she said in English.

“You know I am,” Amaury said in English. “I am a retired captain but I still have contacts.”

Astrid shrugged her shoulders. “Good enough,” she said in English. She sipped her wine. “I have been told to deliver a message to a French officer.”

“Who is this message from?” Amaury asked puzzled.

"Napoleone Bounaparte," Astrid answered in English.

Amaury laughed. He sipped his wine and smiled. "Napoleon died in the year 1821," he said in English. "He died on the island of St. Helena and he is currently in France. I do not think he ever made it to America. Where did you meet him?"

"The city hospital," Astrid answered in English. "I met him five days ago and I have been spending time with him this week. He is very charming and desperately desires the company of a willing woman." She sipped her wine.

"Napoleon was very wealthy," Amaury said in English. "He is rich enough. However, he has been dead for eighty-nine years. He was fifty-two years old when he died. Fifty-two added to eighty-nine gives an age of one hundred forty-one. That is a very old wine and some old wines turn to vinegar."

Astrid laughed. She laughed very hard. "I miss your sense of humor," she said in English. "This Napoleon is not one hundred forty-one years of age he is twenty-nine years old."

Amaury smiled as he drank the remainder of the wine in his glass. He filled Astrid's glass and he filled his. "What is this secret message?" he asked in English.

Astrid sipped her wine and she moved her glass and chair beside Amaury. "Your emperor has been taken prisoner before the attack on the city of Brienne," she whispered in English. "He has been injured and you are to rescue him from the prison."

Amaury laughed. "Is that all?" he whispered in English.

Astrid smiled and sipped her wine. "No," she whispered in English. She moved her glass and chair to the opposite side of the table. "He has given strict orders for you to kill everyone in his prison when he has been released, except me." She leaned backward and smiled. "You are to hang the two officers from the outside walls of his prison."

Amaury looked puzzled. He drank his wine. "Unusual message," he said in English. "Why has he not ordered your death?"

"He said I am the only person he can trust," Astrid answered in English.

Amaury smiled. "And you believe this man?"

"I do not know what to believe," Astrid answered in English. "There are two American Army officers who have been asking him questions. They think he is a French spy. The man says he is Napoleon and they are attempting to prove he is insane."

"He is insane if he says he is Napoleon," Amaury said in English. He looked at her very seriously. "I always respected you. I am ashamed that the American Army has paid you to keep the company of an insane man."

Astrid frowned. "Now I remember why I dislike you," she said in English. "I have been paid to ask the man questions in French and give his answers in English. Nothing more!"

Amaury shrugged his shoulders. "Why are you here?" he asked in English. "Why would you waste your time and my time with a story of an insane man?"

"Because he may not be insane," Astrid answered in English. "He has answered every question correctly. He knows more about Napoleon than you do and he is not a French officer."

Amaury smiled. "I do not think so," he said in English. "I have read all of his writings and studied all of his battles. What can this man know that I do not know?"

"The man knows the names of Napoleon's brothers and sisters," Astrid answered in English. "Do you know the names of Napoleon's brothers and sisters?"

Amaury smiled. "The names of Napoleon's brothers and sisters are irrelevant," he said in English. "The only sibling that mattered was Joseph."

"Joseph, Lucien, Elisa, Louis, Pauline, Caroline and Jerome," Astrid said in English. "He knows the names of Napoleon's brothers and sisters."

"Interesting," Amaury said in English. "This man seems well versed in Napoleon. Of what interest does this insane man have for me?"

"None, if you ignore his order to rescue him," Astrid answered in English. "The United States Army is interested in him. They have brought three professors of French history to the hospital to ask him questions. Their names are Marlow, Lytle and Angle."

Amaury smiled. "The only professor of French history that would interest me is Abner Sykes," he said in English.

"Have you seen Napoleon's sword?" Astrid asked in English.

"Yes," Amaury answered in English. "It is in the Palace of Fontainebleau and very beautiful."

Astrid smiled. "What do the words Veni Vidi Vici mean?" she asked in English.

Amaury laughed and he leaned forward and hugged her. He stood and held his right hand outward as he was making a speech. "I came, I saw, I conquered," he answered in English. "These are the words of Julius Caesar written in 47 BC. Caesar wrote these words after the short war with Pharnaces II of Pontus in the city of Zela."

He sat in his chair. "Those Latin words are engraved on the sword of Napoleon." He shook his head slightly. "My dear, beloved Astrid, every French soldier knows those words. The man who says he is Napoleon knows nothing every French soldier already knows."

Astrid frowned and she looked sad. She shuffled slightly in her chair and sipped her wine. She looked to her left and smiled slightly. "What are the other words engraved on the sword of Napoleon?" she asked in English.

Amaurey leaned backward in his chair and he looked puzzled. "There are no other words," he answered in English. He sipped his wine. "I have seen the sword and there are no other words engraved on the sword."

Astrid smiled slightly. "Professors Lytle and Marlow have also seen the sword," she said in English. "They have actually held it and they can describe the sword in detail. On the other side of the sword are engraved two additional words."

Amaurey frowned. "There are no other words engraved on the sword of Napoleon!" he said angered in English. "I have seen the sword. I have not held the sword because people are not allowed to hold it. The sword is protected in a glass case and turned to display the three words."

Astrid frowned. "It is as I have suspected," she said in French. "The two professors were allowed to hold the sword and they were allowed to examine it. He correctly described the sword's length, weight, and design and identified the maker, Biennais."

Amaurey frowned as he sipped his wine slowly. "I have discussed the sword of Napoleon with many people and there has been no mention of additional words," he said in English. "What are the two words?"

"The words Honneur et Patrie are also engraved on the sword," Astrid answered in English. "That was one of the many trick questions he was asked. He correctly described the sword and the two additional words engraved on the obverse, near the bow guard." She slowly shook her head. "Professor Angle has seen the sword in the Palace of Fontainebleau but he has never held it. He was unaware of the two additional words and he did not know the answer. Only someone who has actually held the coronation sword of Napoleon would know that answer."

Amaurey widened his eyes in disbelief.

Astrid stood and finished drinking her wine. She pointed to the money. "Keep it," she said in English. "I have plenty because the American officer named Captain Lawrence is very generous with his government's money. Stay and enjoy yourself while your emperor is waiting to be rescued."

She started to walk away from the table and she stopped. She returned to the table and leaned toward Amaury. "This captain named Lawrence is one of the two officers you have been ordered to hang from the walls of his prison," she said in English. "You can not hang him today because he left this morning to get a fourth professor."

She leaned closer to him and kissed him on his right cheek. "The fourth professor's name is Abner Sykes," she whispered in French.

She moved to his left side and kissed him on his left cheek. "Some people do not think he is insane," she whispered in French. "One of the three French history professors suggested Napoleon Bonaparte has been reincarnated in the body of a twenty-nine year-old blind man."

Astrid laughed as she leaned upward. "I will return in three days!" she said in French. "I hope to see you!"

Amaury looked puzzled. He slowly sipped his wine as he watched Astrid walk away.

Chapter Six

"Interesting."

Abner Sykes was a professor of French history at the University of Paris often referred to as La Sorbonne. He was on a leave of absence as a guest lecturer at Harvard University where he was contacted by a representative of the United States Army to verify historical events. The officer came to his office with a list of questions and their answers.

Captain Lawrence showed no emotion as Professor Sykes looked at the list of questions and the answers.

"Where did you get these questions?" Professor Sykes asked. He was sitting in his chair with his feet propped upward on the edge. The professor looked unkempt, his shoes were worn, his short beard was untrimmed and he had not bathed…he smelled.

"A college history book," Captain Lawrence answered. He leaned forward. "Most of the answers are correct but some of the answers make no sense."

Professor Sykes laughed. "Which ones?"

"Several," Captain Lawrence answered.

"Can you name one specific answer?" Professor Sykes asked. He moved his feet to the floor and stood. "The French and English translations leave much to be desired. Who asked the questions in French and who wrote the answers in English?"

Captain Lawrence smiled. "A lady I know speaks French. I wrote the questions in English. She translated for me and I wrote the English answers."

Professor Sykes smiled. "Is this a prank?"

Captain Lawrence frowned. "No," he answered. "We need someone who knows French history and someone mentioned you."

Professor Sykes frowned. "Some students like to play pranks on their professors. Some questions will be asked in class with the hope the professor can not answer them. Most of these questions are trivial and usually the professor is caught. It makes for fun in the classroom."

He placed the sheet of paper on his desk. "Every answer to every question is correct."

"No they are not!" Captain Lawrence said. "There are at least four answers that are totally incorrect!"

Professor Sykes sat in his chair. "Every answer to every question is correct!"

"Not according to the history book," Captain Lawrence said.

Professor Sykes leaned forward. "Every answer to every question is correct. Why are you taking my time?"

"We were attempting to verify the answers," Captain Lawrence answered. "I thought you may be able to confirm what we believe."

"And what do you believe?" Professor Sykes asked. He smiled slightly.

"That this man does not know what he is talking about," Captain Lawrence answered. He pointed toward the sheet of paper. "He answered every question correctly except for four. I wanted confirmation."

"I can not give it," Professor Sykes said. "Every answer to every question is correct. Whoever answered these questions knows more about Napoleon Bonaparte than most college professors."

"No," Captain Lawrence said as he leaned forward and picked up the paper. "Napoleon's first wife's name was Josephine. He gave a completely different name. That name was nowhere in the history book. The man made a mistake! Napoleon's wife's first name is not Marie."

Professor Sykes smiled. "His answer to that question was not Marie. His answer was Marie-Rose."

"Marie-Rose or Marie. What is the difference?" Captain Lawrence asked. "The answer is wrong!"

Professor Sykes smiled. "His answer is not wrong. It is correct! Napoleon's first wife's name was Marie-Rose. Her name was not Josephine."

"I see," Captain Lawrence said. "He is playing with us. Napoleon was married twice and his second wife's first name was Josephine."

Professor Sykes laughed. "This is much fun! Napoleon was married twice but neither of his wife's first names was Josephine."

Captain Lawrence looked puzzled. "He answered four questions incorrect. He gave the wrong name for his first wife and he answered they never lived in the Palace of Versailles."

"What do you base that on?" Professor Sykes asked smiling.

"It is not in the history book," Captain Lawrence answered.

Professor Sykes leaned backward in his chair. "Is it possible the history book is incorrect?"

Captain Lawrence looked puzzled. "Why would a history book be incorrect?"

"Because the person who wrote the history book did not know the correct answers," Professor Sykes answered.

Captain Lawrence looked puzzled. "These answers are correct?"

Professor Sykes stood. "Napoleon and Josephine never lived in the Palace of Versailles. Josephine's first name was Marie-Rose. Her full maiden name was Marie-Rose de Tascher de la Pagerie. She was born in the West Indies on the island of Martinique. People called her Rose but Napoleon did not like the name Rose. Napoleon gave her the nickname of Josephine. Everyone called her Josephine but that was not her name. Only a scholar of Napoleon would know those two answers."

Captain Lawrence looked interested. "Will you help us?"

"Help you do what?" Professor Sykes asked. "I told you the answers were correct. What do you need from me?"

"To prove the man is faking," Captain Lawrence answered.

"Faking what?" Professor Sykes asked.

Captain Lawrence was sitting but he stood. "A young man was taken to a hospital with a fever. When he recovered he began speaking in two languages. One language is French. We have not identified the second language. The Army became involved because the man is of military age and he speaks French. We think he is a spy and he is making up stories to hide who he really is."

"Why are you interested in asking this Frenchman questions about Napoleon if you think he is a spy?" Professor Sykes asked. "What difference does it make?"

Captain Lawrence took a deep breath. "He is not a Frenchman. The man was born in New York and he has never been to France. He says he is Napoleone Bounaparte."

Professor Sykes laughed. He laughed so hard he bent over forward and coughed. "I have never heard of such a thing. Quite a story! And you believe him?"

"No," Captain Lawrence answered. "We do not believe him but we are attempting to prove him wrong. We thought we had the proof but you said his answers were correct."

"His answers are correct," Professor Sykes said. "Which university did he attend?"

"None," Captain Lawrence answered. "He has never attended a school."

"None?" Professor Sykes asked smiling. "These are the answers of a college French history professor. Which college does he teach?"

"None," Captain Lawrence answered. "He does not have a job, a real job. He sells apples."

Professor Sykes smiled. "Where did he learn French?"

"We do not know," Captain Lawrence answered. "He only spoke English until his fever. According to his parents, he has never spoken French. He speaks another language but we have not identified it."

"How old is this man?" Professor Sykes asked.

"Twenty-nine," Captain Lawrence answered.

Professor Sykes laughed. "I think I have solved your mystery. The young man likes to read. It is not uncommon for people to be very intelligent without having a formal education. It is obvious that he is interested in Napoleon and he has read many books. If you will check his home you will find he spends most of his time reading. You will find a history book in his home." He leaned forward and smiled. "But not the history book you used to answer these questions."

"That is the biggest mystery," Captain Lawrence said. "He can't read."

Professor Sykes looked puzzled. "He is illiterate? An illiterate person did not answer those questions. Whoever answered those questions is well versed in French history."

Captain Lawrence smiled slightly. "When he was taken to the hospital, he had a fever and what appeared to be a war injury. That is the main reason the Army became involved because it was initially believed the man was a French soldier who was injured on American soil. It has been determined that the injury to both eyes is a birth defect. The man is blind. He was born blind and he can not read or write."

"Curious," Professor Sykes said. "Perhaps he has been tutored by someone well versed in Napoleon. It is possible someone has been teaching him."

"Possible," Captain Lawrence said. "I was hoping you could come with me and speak to him. You could ask him questions. It is possible he will explain everything and this mystery is over. The Army will pay you for your time. It will only take one day and all of your expenses will be paid."

"Where is this young man?" Professor Sykes asked. "My last class is on Thursday. I could leave Thursday afternoon and return Sunday. That should be more than enough time to meet him and discover his source of knowledge."

"He is in the New York City Hospital," Captain Lawrence answered. "I can pick you up here Thursday. There are three other professors who will be joining us. Together, we should unravel his story."

"What three professors?" Professor Sykes asked.

"Professors Marlow, Angle and Lytle," Captain Lawrence answered.

"Nathan Lytle?" Professor Sykes asked surprised. "I know Nathan." He paused. "I have never met professors' Angle and

Marlow but Professor Lytle is also a psychiatrist. Why do you need a psychiatrist?"

"The man says he is Napoleon," Captain Lawrence answered. "We are getting a team together to prove this man wrong." He paused. "There is still a possibility he may be a French spy and his parents are covering for him. No one would suspect a blind man of being a spy. This is a very quiet operation and you are not to tell anyone of the details. Agreed?"

"Agreed," Professor Sykes answered. "I think this mystery can be solved very quickly. I was interested but now I am intrigued. I have never met professors' Angle and Marlow but I have heard Professor Marlow is an expert in French history. I have not seen Nathan in more than one year. The reunion will be most enjoyable."

"I was told you were an expert in French history?" Captain Lawrence asked.

"Many consider me so," Professor Sykes answered. "There are experts and there are experts. Professor Marlow perhaps knows more than the three of us. It should be quick and simple."

Chapter Seven

Professor Sykes arrived at the hospital late Thursday night. The trip from Boston to New York was tiring. Captain Lawrence drove him to the hospital in a new car, a Badger. He rode in the front seat most of the distance but he gradually became tired of sitting. Captain Lawrence stopped the car and he lay down on the backseat. It was not cold but he covered himself with a blanket. He was still asleep when they arrived.

The New York City Hospital was an old hospital. It was well kept but busy. Electric lights had been installed in the main areas but kerosene lanterns were still used.

They entered the hospital and Captain Lawrence took him to a patients' room that had been converted into a conference room and reference room. When he entered, professors' Angle, Marlow and Lytle were sitting at a table, busy speaking.

Professor Lytle immediately stood and they shook hands and embraced. "Wonderful to see you," Professor Lytle said. "This is one mystery we are going to solve."

"Solve?" Professor Sykes asked puzzled. "You have not solved it yet?"

"Professor Marlow," Professor Marlow said, as he stood and introduced himself. "We have not yet solved it."

"Professor Angle," Professor Angle said, as he stood and introduced himself. "One mystery begins another mystery."

"We are hitting brick walls," Professor Lytle said. "Every question we have asked him so far, he can answer. He has a delusion that he is Napoleon. The problem is he knows everything about him. It is almost like you are speaking to Napoleon."

"Obviously he is not Napoleon," Professor Angle said.

"Obvious," Professor Marlow said. "The curious question is how does he know all of these answers? Have you read the list of questions and his answers?"

"Yes," Professor Sykes answered. "Amazing". He smiled and looked at Captain Lawrence. "When do I meet him?"

"Not just yet," Professor Marlow answered grinning. "We were discussing a possible role you could play in this mystery."

"Yes," Professor Angle said. "We have not yet determined what his game is. He is pretending he is Napoleon. He acts like I would imagine Napoleon would act and he is pretending the year is 1814."

Professor Sykes looked confused. "I have many questions to ask him. Do you have a list of questions for me to ask?"

"Oh yes," Professor Marlow answered. "We need someone on the inside to ask him questions."

"What inside?" Professor Sykes asked confused. "We are on the inside." He turned to Captain Lawrence. "Is he outside?"

The professors laughed.

"He is pretending he is Napoleon," Professor Marlow answered. "He has met every one of us but he has not yet met you."

Professor Sykes narrowed his eyes.

Professor Marlow laughed. "He has been asking for things and to play his game, we have been giving him those things."

"What things?" Professor Sykes asked slowly.

"Wine, food, brandy," Professor Marlow answered. "Everything he has asked for appears to be from the 1800s. He seems to know what types of food and beverage Napoleon would have eaten and drank."

"He likes Courvoisier cognac," Professor Angle chuckled.

"The Cognac of Napoleon!" Professor Lytle chuckled.

The professors laughed.

"We caught him in one thing!" Professor Angle said excited. "He claims he knows nothing about Napoleon after the year 1814. Napoleon did not taste Courvoisier cognac until his exile to St. Helena in 1821. The story is he took several barrels of the cognac with him and shared it with the English officers. It was they who named it the Cognac of Napoleon."

"Not correct," Professor Sykes said. "That story is a rumor and unfounded. Napoleon visited the Emmanuel Courvoisier wine and spirits company in 1811. The company warehouse was located in the Paris suburb of Bercy. It is possible he sampled the cognac in 1811. He would know the taste and the name."

The professors looked puzzled.

"If that is correct, he would know the taste and the name," Professor Angle said.

The professors shrugged their shoulders.

"What about me?" Professor Sykes asked. "What is this project?"

"The main thing he has been asking for is a servant," Professor Angle chuckled.

Professor Sykes laughed. "You want me to be his servant?"

"Just for a day," Professor Marlow answered. "Pretend you are his servant. This will give you the opportunity to ask him questions."

"Every time we meet, it is formal," Professor Angle said. "We sit in chairs and ask him questions. He answers and then we leave. We come back and ask him more questions, he answers, and then we leave. We need someone to stay with him. We think he will make an error and speak in English. He will say the name of someone or perhaps the title of a book. If someone is with him we can learn how he knows the answers."

"He says we are his jailers and inquisitors," Professor Lytle said.

"What do I do?" Professor Sykes asked.

"Pretend you are his servant," Professor Marlow answered.

Professor Sykes was to speak when Captain Lawrence interrupted him. "Everyone in this room knows what I am about to say but you may have not heard it."

"There are rumors of problems in Europe," he continued. "The Army became involved when it was suspected this man was a French spy. It is possible he was sent here. If he was, we want to know who sent him and why."

"You said he had never visited France," Professor Sykes said.

"We have not yet ruled that out," Captain Lawrence said.

"His French is too good to be self-learned," Professor Angle said. "The accent is an older type French language but easily understood. His phrases appear, as close as we can tell, from the 1800s."

"He carefully words his answers," Professor Marlow said. "His speech is deliberate and very precise."

"It is possible he will slip up and use a phrase that was not used during the 1800s," Professor Lytle said. "He will have outbursts and we are too far away to hear everything he says. If someone was in the room, he may say something and we can then challenge him."

"I only have two days," Professor Sykes said. "I can not stay with him for two days. I am tired and I need sleep. I do not want to be alone with him."

"He will not harm you," Professor Lytle said. "He is blind and he just sits, thinking. I have some sleeping drugs that you can give him. It will make him sleep for four to six hours. That will give you time to leave and rest. It should all be over before two days."

"OK," Professor Sykes said. "Do you have something for me to wear that will fool him?"

"No, but we will find something," Professor Lytle answered. "We will brief you on what we know."

"The man's first name is Rober," Professor Angle said. "He was brought to this hospital …"

Chapter Eight

"I look silly!"

Professor Sykes was looking at himself in a full-length mirror. He was wearing a type of coat that was made of velvet. The trousers were short knickers, ended below his knees, and also made of velvet. His shirt was a woman's blouse. There was lace on the collar and the sleeves. The blouse was white and the color of the coat was red with the shortened trousers being a bluish green.

The professors laughed.

"He can not see but he can feel," Professor Marlow said. "It will feel like a servant's uniform."

Professor Sykes shrugged his shoulders as the two exited the room and walked down the hallway. They stopped at a door.

A male orderly was sitting outside the door in a chair. He stood and laughed at Professor Sykes. "He has been quiet," he said. "No outbursts today."

He knocked on the door.

"Enter," a man's voice responded in French.

The orderly unlocked and opened the door for professors Sykes and Marlow to enter.

The room was larger than a standard patient's room. It looked like two rooms had been combined. One section had a large bathtub and a food preparation area. There were six chairs and a large settee placed toward the center. The bed was large.

Professor Sykes narrowed his eyes. A young man was sitting on the settee. He was dressed in a type of woman's gown. The gown was too large for the man and the sleeves ended in a type of roll. The roll was larger than the sleeves and the gown looked more like a robe.

The man was looking toward his right and his head was seen at an angle. The man stood and Professor Sykes gasped.

The man looked dead!

The man's eyes were without pupils and both eyes looked like they had sunk into his skull. His hair was black and cut short. The one thing that surprised Professor Sykes, more than his eyes, was his height. He was not short in height.

Professor Sykes expected someone short. This man was not short. He appeared to be almost six feet in height. Napoleon was short. His height has been recorded at five feet two inches. Because of Napoleon's stature, he was nicknamed the Little Corporal.

Professor Marlow smiled and he spoke in French. "We have granted your request. This man is your servant."

The man moved his head slightly. "Approach," he said in French.

Professor Sykes stepped forward. The man reached outward and touched the coat and the blouse.

"What is your command?" Professor Sykes asked in French. He bowed slightly.

"Nothing at this time," the man answered in French.

"Your servant will notify us of your requests," Professor Marlow said in French. "We will grant it if we can."

He nodded to Professor Sykes and walked to the opened door.

"He will not harm you," the orderly said in English, as he closed and locked the door.

Chapter Nine

The time was after ten o'clock when Professor Sykes returned to the conference room. Professors Angle, Marlow and Lytle were waiting for him.

He opened the door slowly and entered. His expression was one of sadness.

The professors noticed his demeanor. They waited for him to remove his coat and sit in one of the chairs before they approached him. Professor Marlow offered him a cup of coffee but he refused.

"What happened?" Professor Marlow asked. "Did he say something that we can use against him?"

"Strange," Professor Sykes answered. "I was expecting some type of wild man. I was expecting someone who was completely out of touch with reality."

"What did he say?" Professor Angle asked.

Professor Sykes was sitting and he looked upward. "Have you talked to him? Not ask him questions but talked to him."

"No," Professor Lytle answered. "We ask him questions and he answers them. Should we talk to him?"

"I am not sure," Professor Sykes answered.

"Strange answer," Professor Angle said. "Why should we not talk to him?"

Professor Sykes was sitting and he stood. He walked to the window and looked outward. There was only one window in the room and the view was of the left side of the hospital. It was dark and there was nothing to see. "He sat and said nothing for almost one hour."

He turned. "He began asking me questions. His French is excellent. I do not think he is self-learned. He has been speaking French for many years."

He stepped forward. "He asked me my name. I recalled the story of Napoleon visiting the Parisian suburb of Bercy. I have been there and I know the general area. Louis Gallois and Emmanuel Courvoisier were partners in the winery. I told him I was from Bercy and my name is Rober Gallois."

"He asked me if I was a kinsman of Louis Gallois. I told him I had heard the name but I am not familiar with the man. I am not a kinsman."

"Louis Gallois was an associate of Emmanuel Courvoisier," Professor Angle said.

"Yes," Professor Sykes said. "He knew that. He also knew of their warehouse. He spoke of several wines he sampled and he motioned toward the food preparation area. He said the cognac has a similar taste to one he had sampled."

"Interesting," Professor Marlow said. "You told him your name was the same as the man's name. Did he show any reaction when the name Rober was spoken?"

"None," Professor Sykes answered. "He showed no reaction."

"Interesting," Professor Marlow said. "What else?"

"Small talk mostly," Professor Sykes answered. "He asked the time of day and the day of the month. I told him."

Professor Sykes sat in the chair. "He said he wanted a bath and asked me to prepare it. I prepared his bath and he bathed. After his bath, I placed sleeping powder in his wine and he went to sleep."

"Doesn't sound like much," Professor Marlow said. "Anything else?"

"Yes," Professor Sykes answered. "While he was bathing he said he forgave me for helping his jailers. He understood my situation as it is similar to his own. When he is free, he will provide for me and my family."

"We have one more day," Professor Marlow said. "Try and get as much as you can out of him. Mention some books and ask him the names of prominent French history professors. Watch his face to determine if there is recognition."

Professor Sykes nodded his head.

Professor Angle moved forward. “You suggested we should not talk to him. Why?”

“It is his voice,” Professor Sykes answered. “I have never heard anyone speak like him. His words are carefully measured and his voice is mesmerizing. He does not act or speak like a person who is insane.”

The man lay in his bed pretending to be asleep. When the man who claimed to be his servant left the room, he stood and removed the wine soaked cloth from underneath his dressing gown. He smelled the sleeping powder in his wine before he drank it. He was of the belief the wine was poisoned and he turned from his servant and poured it onto the cloth.

He carefully measured his steps to the bath and placed the wine soaked cloth inside the large wet cloth on the floor. He walked to the food preparation area and reached for the wine carafe. Before he poured himself a small portion, he smelled the wine.

The man walked to his settee and sat. “Louis Gallois is well known in the city of Bercy,” he said to himself in Corsican. “Louis Gallois is the mayor.”

He raised the glass of wine to his lips when he stopped. “Never interrupt your enemy when he is making a mistake,” he said as he drank the wine.

Chapter Ten

Bam! Bam! Bam!

"Help me to escape and your reward will be great!" the man yelled in Corsican, as he beat upon the inside of the locked door.

Professor Sykes was frightened at first but his fear left as he realized the man was not violent. He began yelling in a language he did not understand when he served him his morning meal.

The man went to the door and beat upon it with his two fists. Then, he began to yell. Professor Sykes did not understand what he said. He spoke to him in French, in an attempt to calm him, but the man responded in the language he did not understand.

The man did not appear to be acting in a bizarre manner. His words were deliberate... they were not ramblings but precise and measured. The man did not appear to be frightened or in some form of duress.

It appeared the man was attempting to attract someone's attention.

He beat upon the door and yelled for almost one full hour. His actions of beating on the door and yelling tired him and he stopped. Both of the man's hands were bruised from beating upon the door. Professor Sykes spoke to him gently and requested to soak his hands in warm water.

He agreed.

As Professor Sykes prepared water to soak his hands, the man appeared sad. He sat on his settee and looked toward the area of the window. The window had been boarded shut. Wood boards covered the inside and the outside of the window. Captain Lawrence ordered the window closed. Why he ordered this he did not know. The man had demonstrated no violence. He was blind! *How could he escape?*

The man's actions did not appear to be the actions of a person insane. He moved about the room touching the walls and objects. The man appeared to be measuring and remembering the size of the room and the placement of every object in the room. He performed the same actions the previous day but Professor Sykes did not notice it. The man continued to move about the room, touching. He stopped at the eating table.

"I request to dine with my jailers," the man said in French. "This table is too small to seat six. I need a longer table."

Professor Sykes looked puzzled. There were only three people he called his jailers. He called professors Lytle, Marlow and Angle his jailers. "There are only three," he said in French.

"Six," the man said in French, "three inquisitors, two military officers and the man who guards the door. There are six."

The dinner was excellent!

The dinner was composed of a roasted section of pork, boiled potatoes, a wheat bread and wine. A larger table was placed in his room and seven chairs were arranged. Captain Lawrence and Lieutenant Simpson were placed nearest to him. The orderly named Jimmy was placed towards the end. A large chair, from the hospital director's office, was placed at one end. The man sat in the large oversized chair. The seat, arms and back were covered with brown colored leather.

The eating utensils, plates and bowls, were a hodgepodge. Nothing matched. The items were selected because of size and texture. The man could not see but he could feel. The wine goblets were actually small glass flower vases. The dining plates were metal serving platters. The dining utensils were metal forks and metal spoons. There were no knives on the table.

Professor Sykes served everyone. He carved the roast pork into small sections. It was not necessary to use a knife. Several candles, in holders, were placed on the table and lit.

The man acted strange during the meal. He never once, referred to anyone as his jailer. He never once, stated he was a prisoner. He laughed and told jokes in French. The orderly named Jimmy was seated beside Professor Angle and Professor Angle translated French into English.

He entertained his guests with stories. One story he told was of the Battle of the Pyramids July 21, 1798. Only twenty-nine French soldiers were killed and more than two thousand enemies were killed. He repeated dates and times exactly.

Professor Lytle asked him if he had seen the strange stone discovered near the pyramids.

He knew of the stone but he stated he had not seen it. He was told it was a green color and the stone was carved with different writings.

More than thirty minutes were spent discussing the stone and the origin of the man-like lion stone structure named the Sphinx. He told the story of how bored soldiers, fired their guns at the Sphinx, damaging the nose.

Professor Angle attempted to anger him. He was asked of the French defeat in the Battle of the Nile. British commander Horatio Nelson defeated the French fleet.

The man showed no emotion when asked. He stood and offered a wine salute. "Horatio Nelson, a man of great courage and his military success," he said in French.

Professor Angle translated the words and the orderly was puzzled by his toast. He leaned toward Professor Angle and asked him a question. Professor Angle was also puzzled by his toast and he asked Jimmy's question. "Why do you honor this man when you should hate him?" he asked in French.

The man's response was in French and startling. "A real man hates no one. I dislike what he did but I honor his courage and his military success. To hate this man and ignore Horatio Nelson's accomplishment in a fierce battle is the ramblings of a mad man."

Everyone in the room, including Jimmy, was impressed by his answer.

It was late when Professor Sykes returned to the conference room. He cleaned the food from the dining table and prepared his bath. After his bath, he placed sleeping powder in his wine. When he was asleep, he left the room.

Professors Angle, Marlow and Lytle were waiting for him. Captain Lawrence was also waiting. Everyone was puzzled. The man made no error in dates or times. His French was excellent! There was no mixing of the language from different time eras.

Names and titles of books were mentioned. The man showed no emotion and appeared unaware of the names mentioned or of the book titles.

The man was charming and entertaining. His words were carefully measured and delivered with certainty and his manner of speech was mesmerizing. It was as if they had been transported backward into time and dined with the Emperor of 1814 France, Napoleon Bonaparte.

The man showed no sign of a mental illness. He performed no actions or speech during the meal to appear to be insane. The only thing insane was his belief he was Napoleone Bounaparte.

"I am sorry your time was wasted," Professor Lytle said. "Tomorrow you return to the university with an unsolved mystery."

Professor Sykes looked thoughtful. "I do not want to leave just yet. I can request several days of leave. Professor Hargrove can teach my classes. He is well versed in the Napoleonic wars and the students will get their parent's monies worth. I am as puzzled as everyone and this is one mystery I want to solve."

Captain Lawrence smiled. "If you write a letter, I will personally deliver it. You can not write anything about this man or where we are."

Professor Sykes nodded. He took a sheet of blank paper from the table and he wrote a short letter. He placed the letter in an envelope and he addressed the envelope to Professor Marlin Akers, Chairman of the French History Department.

Captain Lawrence took the envelope. "I will leave tonight. I should return by tomorrow night. Thank you for your service."

He left the room as the professors sat together and discussed their dining experience.

Captain Lawrence left the hospital and entered the car. He drove the automobile to the front entrance and turned right, headed away from the city.

He drove the car more than three miles when he stopped the car. He exited the car and tore the letter from Professor Sykes into small pieces. He dug a hole in the ground with a knife from his belt and he placed the torn pieces of the letter into the hole. After covering the hole with dirt he drove the car to a small home nearby. He parked the car in front of the home. Two soldiers were on guard duty standing beside the front door and saluted him as one soldier opened the door and allowed entrance.

General Tate was waiting for him inside the home near the door. He heard the sound of his car and he motioned for Captain Lawrence to follow him into a private room.

"We have received disturbing news," the general said. He held upward a telegram. "Someone at the hospital has been talking and word has reached the French section of New Orleans. As we speak, there are rumors of an attempt to rescue him!"

"Rescue who?" Captain Lawrence asked surprised.

"Napoleon," General Tate answered.

Captain Lawrence burst into laughter. "Why would someone believe his story?"

General Tate frowned. "The French people in New Orleans are backward and superstitious. They believe in ghosts, voodoo, zombies, werewolves, vampires, demonic possession and reincarnation."

"Reincarnation?" Captain Lawrence asked surprised. "These people believe Napoleon Bonaparte has been reincarnated?"

"If you believe the telegram it appears so," General Tate answered. "They believe the spirit of Napoleon has possessed this man's body or Napoleon has been reincarnated. I thought they were the same thing but there appears to be a difference."

"Believe?" Captain Lawrence asked. "You do not believe the telegram?"

"It is not what I believe but what they believe," General Tate answered. "I do not think, I know, the man is a French spy. I think this story of reincarnation is a cover up for someone to attempt a rescue. I think the plan is to release him and take him to his commander in New Orleans. The story of reincarnation is a cover."

"I see," Captain Lawrence said. "Someone is exciting people in New Orleans with this false story. The people are superstitious and may believe it. When these people attempt to rescue him, the real people will use these people as a cover. Brilliant plan! The United States Government would never order soldiers to open fire on civilians."

"Exactly," General Tate said. "The puzzling thing is why was he sent here, to New York? There is nothing for him to report. The French are allies."

"It is possible he is not French," Captain Lawrence said.

"Explain?" General Tate asked.

"It is possible the man was taught French to appear French," Captain Lawrence answered. "The French government knows nothing about him. There are rumblings in Europe and it is possible another country sent him. Perhaps they want to know about our military capability. We have no idea where he has been or what he has been told." He shrugged his shoulders. "Who would suspect a blind man?"

"Interesting observation and most worthy of our serious consideration," General Tate said.

"What are your orders?" Captain Lawrence asked.

"The decision has been made to move him from the hospital," General Tate answered. "We are going to play his game for now. Preparations are being made to convert several rooms in the Binghamton Inebriate Asylum. This is a more secure location and it will allow us to prevent any attempt to rescue him. I am certain he will slip up. Once we can prove, without a doubt, which he is, he will tell us everything…names, dates and reasons."

It was late the next night when Professor Sykes entered the conference room. He was surprised to see Captain Lawrence sitting in the room.

"That was a quick journey," Professor Sykes said.

"I drove all night and I drove all day," Captain Lawrence said. "It was a tiring experience. I was told that you can take as much time as you need. Professor Akers said Professor Hargrove will take care of things. The Army will reimburse you for any lost wages."

Professor Sykes nodded his head.

"Did he make any mistakes?" Professor Lytle asked excited.

"Amazing," Professor Sykes answered. "He described the Battle of the Pyramids exactly. He described the gun placements, the troop's placements and the main attack by the Mamluks' cavalry."

The professors seemed excited.

"Excuse me," Captain Lawrence said as he stood. "You four experts were brought here, at government expense, to prove this man is insane. Each one of you is a college professor who teaches French history. Who is teaching who?"

Professor Lytle frowned. "We are attempting to prove this man is insane! He has answered every question correctly and he appears to have knowledge that is not in history books."

"You are saying this man is not insane?" Captain Lawrence asked.

"Of course not," Professor Lytle answered. "It is obvious this man is insane. Napoleon Bonaparte died in 1821. The man in that locked room is not Napoleone Bounaparte. You asked us to discover where he has obtained his knowledge and speech. We are attempting to do just that. We need more time."

"What is this second language he is speaking?" Captain Lawrence asked. "Is it a code?"

"No, it is a language but none I have ever heard," Professor Sykes answered. "He has used it on several occasions but I do not know what it is."

"Corsican?" Professor Angle asked. "Napoleon was born on the island of Corsica and he spoke two languages. It is possible the unidentified language is Corsican."

"What is Corsican?" Captain Lawrence asked.

"An obscure language," Professor Angle answered. "It is a form of Italian but different, much different. People who speak Corsican can not understand Italian and people who speak Italian can not understand Corsican."

"Where is Corsica?" Captain Lawrence asked.

"A small island off the western coast of Italy," Professor Angle answered. "Napoleon was born there when the island was under French rule."

"The Italian government transferred the island to the French in 1768," Professor Sykes said. "Napoleon was born one year later on August 15, 1769. His original name was Napoleone di Bounaparte. He later changed his name to appear French. He dropped the e after Napoleon and he also dropped the u in Bonaparte."

Captain Lawrence frowned. "Is that not the name and spelling of the person he claims he is?"

"Yes," Professor Marlow answered. "When he is asked his real name he says he is Napoleone Bounaparte. The name he dictated to us in French has the extra e and the extra u."

Captain Lawrence was sitting but he stood. "How can an illiterate blind man know the real name of Napoleon Bonaparte?"

"That is the most puzzling of this puzzle," Professor Lytle answered. "Very few people know Napoleon changed the spelling of his last name. Only one or two people know he changed the spelling of his first name."

"If you believe in numerology," Professor Angle said. "The original spelling of his name changed from the number of one, standing for power and victory, to four – the number of defeat."

"It is a paradox!" Professor Marlow said.

"Para who?" Captain Lawrence asked.

Professor Marlow laughed. "A paradox is a statement that is contrary to common sense but is perhaps true," he answered. "By reverting to the spelling of his original name, Napoleon Bonaparte may have reversed his destiny. According to numerology, he now has the number of one – power and victory! The Army under his command can never be defeated. As long as he is in command of an Army, that Army can never be defeated. The man in the locked room says he is Napoleone Bounaparte. He has returned the e in his first name and the u in his last name."

Professor Lytle shrugged his shoulders. "That is the only reason we can determine, at this time, he uses the historically correct name of Napoleone Bounaparte to replace the historically accepted name of Napoleon Bonaparte."

Captain Lawrence laughed. "I thought you were men of history and science…not witchcraft."

"A story often repeated concerning Napoleon," Professor Sykes said. "The story is related to the spelling of the first and last name. It is just a story."

"What about the di?" Captain Lawrence asked. "What does di mean? He does not use the word di."

"Of," Professor Sykes answered. "Translated the original name is Napoleone of the Bounapartes. It is a common practice to drop the di or of. In that time period, your name would be Russell of the Lawrence. I would be Abner of the Sykes. Professor Lytle would be Nathan of the Lytle. It is a common usage in speech to drop the di or the of. That is not an error."

Captain Lawrence nodded his head. "I have been ordered to give you as much time as possible. However, I have also been ordered to move him."

"Where?" Professor Marlow asked puzzled. "He is fine here. He has done nothing wrong." He shrugged his shoulders. "He yells on occasion. Why are you moving him?"

"I can not discuss the reason," Captain Lawrence answered. "He has become too visible and the patients and the hospital staff are talking about him. It is in his best interest to move him where no one will pay any attention to his mannerisms."

"Binghamton?" Professor Lytle asked.

Captain Lawrence nodded his head. "We are going to play his game for now. A special room is being prepared just for him. There will be additional rooms for everyone here."

"When do you move him?" Professor Sykes asked.

"When his room is prepared," Captain Lawrence answered. "However, before he is moved we are changing his clothing and returning him to a different patient's room. We have requested his parents come to the hospital for an interview and we will allow them to meet him. It is believed that his parents will force him to make mistakes."

Professor Lytle burst into laughter. "You are bringing Carlo and Letizia Bounaparte to the hospital?"

The professors laughed.

"Who are they?" Captain Lawrence asked. "His parents are Francis and Carolina Montpere. His name is Rober Maurice Montpere."

"That is one of the mysteries we are yet to solve," Professor Marlow answered. "The man correctly answered Napoleon's parents were Carlo and Letizia Bounaparte. He correctly gave the name of Napoleon's mother's maiden name, Ramolino."

"You will not find that in a French history book," Professor Sykes remarked.

"If this second language is a language and it is Corsican, where would you locate someone who knows the language?" Captain Lawrence asked.

"The only place you could possibly locate someone who knows the language is the Italian section of the city," Professor Lytle answered. "It is an obscure language."

Chapter Eleven

"When and where was your son born?"

"June 14, 1880 in New York," the man's mother answered.

Captain Lawrence and Lieutenant Simpson sat with professors Sykes, Lytle, Angle and Marlow. Captain Lawrence requested the parents of the man in the hospital to come to the hospital for questioning. The man's mother and father and paternal grandmother were brought to the hospital in a military vehicle.

"When and where were you born?" Captain Lawrence asked her.

"November 12, 1862 in Virginia," she answered.

"When and where was your father born?" Captain Lawrence asked her.

"January 22, 1836 in France," she answered.

"When and where was your grandfather born?" Captain Lawrence asked her.

"October 19, 1814 in France," she answered.

Captain Lawrence shuffled several papers and nodded toward Professor Sykes.

"How long has your son been blind?" Professor Sykes asked the man's mother.

"He was born blind," she answered.

"Where did your son attend school?" Professor Sykes asked the man's mother.

"He did not attend school," she answered. "He is blind and he can not read or write."

"If he can not read or write, what does he do?" Professor Lytle asked.

"Sell apples," she answered. "He sits in front of our building and sells apples."

The man's father leaned forward. "Our son can not read or write but he knows money. He can tell you the amount. He feels the size and the weight."

"Does your son speak any language other than French?" Professor Sykes asked the man's mother.

"He does not speak French," the man's father answered. "He speaks English."

Professor Lytle narrowed his eyes. "The man who you claim is your son does not speak English. He only speaks French." He paused. "There is another language he speaks but we have not been able to identify what it is. That young man only speaks French."

"He did not speak French until his fever," the man's father said. "He has never spoken French until his fever."

Professor Angle chuckled lightly. "Never? What language does your mother speak?"

"French and English," the man's father answered. "She speaks French but not in our home. My son has heard her speak French but he does not speak French. He speaks English."

"A waste of my time," Professor Marlow said. He stood. "It is obvious that the young man heard French spoken in the home as a young boy. For what ever reason, he is playing a game with us." He turned and left the room.

Lieutenant Simpson shrugged his shoulders. He shuffled several stacks of paper in front of him and smiled slightly. "When did your son's fever start?" he asked the man's mother.

"Three months ago," she answered. "He became ill and he would not eat. His fever began to get worse. He was very hot to the touch. We cooled him with water but his fever would not go down."

The man's father leaned forward. "He had been ill for several days when he began having the dreams. He was delirious and would scream and yell."

"What language did he scream and yell in?" Professor Sykes asked. "French?"

"English," his mother answered. "All of his dreams were in English. My son does not speak French."

Captain Lawrence smiled slightly. "Do you remember any of his dreams?"

"Oh yes," the man's father answered. "They were strange. He thought he was in a war and he would shout commands."

"When did you take him to the hospital?" Lieutenant Simpson asked the man's father.

The man's father started to answer the question when Captain Lawrence raised his hand to stop him. This whole affair had been boring to Captain Lawrence. He did not want to interview the man's parents but it was procedure. What the man's father said pique his interest.

"Excuse me," he interrupted. "Before you answer Lieutenant Simpson's question, what kind of commands?"

"Military commands," the man's father answered. "He thought he was in a battle and he was ordering his soldiers."

Captain Lawrence was intrigued. "What type of orders?"

The man's father shrugged his shoulders. "Move to the left. Move to the right," he answered. "Change the trajectory of the cannons. Advance. Retreat. Advance."

"Curious," Captain Lawrence said. He leaned forward. "Is that all?"

"He planned a battle," the man's mother answered. "He had one dream that kept repeating. He acted like he was speaking to different men. They were planning a battle and he was explaining where the men and cannons were to be placed."

Captain Lawrence smiled. "Did he ever say what battle?"

"Brienne," the man's father answered. "He and many men were planning the battle of Brienne."

Professor Sykes interrupted. He nodded his head toward Captain Lawrence. "One of Napoleon's greatest victories was the January 29, 1814 victory of Brienne. One month later, he scored victories at Champaubert, Montmirail and Montereau."

"We are related to Napoleon," the man's father said proudly.

Professor Angle burst into laughter. The three people sitting in front of him were obviously poor. There is no way they were remotely related to Napoleon Bonaparte.

"How?" Professor Angle asked in a snicker.

"He is our son's great-great grandfather," the man's father answered.

Captain Lawrence was not amused at the man's answer. "How can your son be related to Napoleon?"

"Before the battle of Brienne, he was introduced to a young farm girl," the man's father answered. "Napoleon liked her and he ordered her to his headquarters many times. Nine months later, she delivered an illegitimate male child. She claimed the boy was the son of Napoleon. He was given the name of Rober."

Professor Sykes smiled slightly. "Can you prove this?"

"No," the man's father answered. "It is a family rumor."

"When and where did you say your grandfather was born?" Captain Lawrence asked the man's mother.

"October 19, 1814 in France," she answered. "Rober was born near the town of Brienne."

Professor Sykes' curiosity was aroused. "You said your father was born in France in 1836. Where?"

"Paris," the man's mother answered. "Rober was twenty-two years old when my father was born. Shortly before I was born, my mother and my father came to America. My grandfather was fifty-two years old when he died."

"Where did your grandfather die?" Professor Sykes asked.

"I do not know," the man's mother answered. "I was told he died in Paris but no one knows."

"Where did your grandmother die?" Professor Sykes asked.

"I do not know," the man's mother answered. "Nothing is known about her after Rober's birth."

"If your maiden name was Montpere, why is your son named Rober Montpere?" Professor Lytle asked.

Rober's father started to answer the question when Rober's mother placed her hand on his arm. "We were not married when Rober was born." She lowered her head. "To hide our shame, Francis changed his name from Boutin to Montpere."

"That is correct," Rober's father said. "I changed my name. I was working on a merchant boat when I met Carolina. I was at sea when Rober was born. He was eight months old when I first saw him." He looked at Carolina lovingly and held her hand. "We have told no one the truth. I changed my name to protect the two people I love."

Captain Lawrence looked puzzled. He stood and walked toward the door and turned. "Has your son heard the story about his being related to Napoleon?"

"Yes, many times," the man's father answered. He shrugged his shoulders. "It is a family rumor."

"Has your son visited France," Professor Sykes asked. "Specifically, has he ever visited the Palace of Versailles?"

The man's mother and father shrugged their shoulders. "He has never been outside the city of New York," his father answered. "I have no idea the palace name you said."

"Your son has never visited the Palace of Versailles?" Captain Lawrence asked.

"No," the man's mother answered. "I have never heard of it."

"Can we see our son?" the man's father asked.

"I think we have enough," Captain Lawrence said. He looked at the people sitting. "If there are no further questions, we will adjourn."

Professor Sykes raised his hand. "I have one further question. "When did your son stop speaking English?"

"When he recovered from the fever," the man's mother answered.

"That is correct," the man's father added. "When he recovered from the fever, he began speaking in a language we did not understand. It was not French because my mother knows French. It was a language she had never heard."

"Where was he?" Professor Sykes asked.

"In this hospital," the man's father answered. "We thought he would die from the fever and we brought him to the hospital. He did not die. When he recovered, he was speaking in a language no one understood."

"We came to see him the day he recovered," the man's mother said. "We were in his room attempting to speak to him when the doctor ordered us away." She looked puzzled. "The doctor forbids us to see him."

Captain Lawrence looked at Professor Sykes. "If there are no further questions, we will adjourn."

"Are we allowed to ask questions?" the man's father asked.

"Of course," Captain Lawrence answered. He walked from the door and returned to his seat.

The man's father stood. "What interest does the American Army have with my son?"

Captain Lawrence looked uneasy. "Fair question," he answered. "Unfortunately, I can't answer it."

"You can tell me something," the man's father said. His voice appeared to shake and his question was a pleading.

"He is our son," the man's mother said. "He has done nothing wrong. He was ill and now he has recovered. Why is the American Army interested in our son?"

Captain Lawrence frowned slightly. "You must understand what has happened. A young man is brought to the hospital very ill. When he recovers, he speaks French. The man is of military age and it is an unusual situation. It was believed his lack of vision was a war injury. I can not disclose certain information we have concerning tensions in Europe but I want to assure you that no harm has come to your son. He is being treated very well."

The man's father and mother nodded.

"I will take you to your son," Captain Lawrence said. "If you will please follow me, I will take you to him."

They stood and walked from the room.

Chapter Twelve

When they left the room, Professor Sykes was sitting and he stood. "This is a waste of time. I think the man's language can be explained in that he has been exposed to French from his grandmother."

"It is obvious he is not a French combatant," Professor Lytle said. "We have not uncovered any evidence he ever left New York. The parents confirmed his lack of vision. Dr. Chambers stated his lack of sight was a physical deformity that often occurs in different generations."

"Curious," Professor Angle said. "The parents claim there is a direct blood relationship to Napoleon."

"They also claim their son has never been to France," Professor Lytle said. "There is no way he could describe Versailles."

"The stories of him being related to Napoleon may have affected him," Professor Sykes said. He looked thoughtful. "The imagination can be very powerful. The man has probably imagined he was Napoleon when he was a young boy and played battles."

Lieutenant Simpson stood. "Do you think Professor Marlow is out?"

Professor Lytle laughed. "Professor Marlow is a strange bird. He is brilliant in French history. Professor Marlow probably knows more about Napoleon than any one of us. If he is interested, he will take it to the end. If he loses interest, he drops it. He is probably in his room packing. I can't think of anything that would make him change his mind. He's out!"

The men left the room.

Chapter Thirteen

Captain Lawrence led the man's parents and his paternal grandmother to a different section of the hospital. This section of the hospital seemed strangely deserted. They did not see any nurses or orderlies.

They continued to walk down the long hallway. They turned a corner where an orderly was sitting in a chair outside a patient's room. The orderly was older, in his late fifties and he was wearing white trousers and a white shirt. As they approached the room, the orderly stood.

"How is he?" Captain Lawrence asked.

"Quiet," the orderly answered.

"These are his parents and his grandmother," Captain Lawrence said.

"Ladies, Sir," the orderly said. He turned to the door and lightly knocked. A man's voice answered the knock but the language spoken was not French, it was Corsican.

"That is not French," the man's father said. His wife nodded her head.

"He has been using that language most of the day," the orderly said. "He was speaking French this morning. Professor Marlow visited him and he must have said something that upset him because he started using that language.

"Have you ever heard that language?" Captain Lawrence asked the man's mother and father. "We can not identify it."

"No," the man's father answered. "I have never heard anything like it. It sounded like nonsense. Are you sure it is a language?"

"Yes," Captain Lawrence answered. "Many words are repeated and there is a flow. It is a language but a language we have not yet identified."

He nodded his head toward the orderly and the orderly unlocked and opened the door. "You have visitors."

The room was a standard patient's room. It was small. There was a single bed, a cabinet for personal items and a chamber pot beside the bed. The only thing unusual about the room was the number of chairs. There were six chairs in the room.

There was one window and their son was sitting in one of the chairs facing the window. He was wearing the clothes he wore when he was taken to the hospital. He was wearing black trousers with a blue shirt. He was not wearing his shoes. He wore a pair of brown shoes to the hospital and his shoes were placed near the edge of the bed. His feet were covered with a pair of black socks.

The only thing unusual was his head. The top of his head was bandaged, to cover his eyes. He appeared to be in deep thought and he did not hear the orderly's voice or the sound of the door opening and closing. The young man lightly licked his lips as he faced the window.

"Rober!" his mother said excited. She walked to him and hugged him. When she placed her arms around him, he was startled and stood. He pushed his mother's arms from him and he shouted something she could not understand.

"Rober!" his father said angered. "You will not act in such a manner!"

"You understood him?" Captain Lawrence asked excited.

"No," Rober's father answered angered. "I did not understand one word but it was how he said it and his manner."

"Rober!" his mother pleaded. She attempted to place her arms around him again and he pushed her back. He pointed his right index finger toward her and he unleashed a barrage of words that were frightening. He appeared to be threatening her.

The orderly heard his outburst and slowly opened the door. "He will not harm you," the orderly said. "He yells like that a lot." The orderly smiled and closed the door.

Rober's mother began to weep as her son continued to yell at her in a threatening manner, in a language they did not understand.

Rober's father held to his wife. "We will leave now," he said quietly.

Captain Lawrence nodded. He walked to the door and opened it. They walked into the hallway and Rober's father stopped. "I do not know what to think. That young man looks like our son and his voice sounds like our son." He paused as he looked to the opened door. He could see his son standing by the window. His right arm was outstretched and he was pointing his index finger toward the opened door and yelling in a language he never heard.

He held to Carolina as she wept. "I do not know who that man is in that room." He began to weep as he held to his wife. "Whoever he is, he is not our son."

Chapter Fourteen

"Do you speak Corsican?"

The man who was asked the question peered curiously from inside the partially opened door. The man who asked the question was dressed as a military soldier. There were two soldiers and both soldiers wore gun belts.

"No," the man answered.

"Do you know anyone who speaks Corsican?" the soldier asked.

"No," the man answered.

The soldier handed the man a card. "Please ask your friends and your neighbors. If they know of anyone who speaks Corsican, have them contact this person."

"Why?" the man asked.

"We need someone who knows Corsican to interpret," the soldier answered. "We will pay them well."

The man nodded his head and slowly closed the door.

Captain Lawrence and Lieutenant Simpson stood on the stoop of a section of rundown buildings in the Italian section of New York City. They began their search on Twelfth Street and they had knocked on more than seventy doors.

They turned to walk down the steps to the street when they noticed a small crowd of people were following them. They nodded to the people in the crowd and smiled. As they were walking up the steps to knock on another door, a young boy approached them.

"I know someone who speaks Corsican," the boy said.

Captain Lawrence turned and smiled. "Who?"

"Her name is Mama Leon," the boy answered. "She is very old and from Corsica and she knows the language."

"Will you take us to her?" Lieutenant Simpson asked. He reached into his right trouser pocket and handed the boy a silver dollar.

The boy's eyes widened when he received the silver dollar. He looked puzzled and pointed toward his left. "Mama Leon lives there," he said.

"We have already been there," Lieutenant Simpson said.

"Mama Leon lives there," the boy repeated.

They followed the young boy toward the end of the street. He walked up the steps and into the building. They followed the boy up a section of stairs where he stopped before a door. "Mama Leon lives there," he said.

Captain Lawrence knocked on the door. They waited a few minutes and an older man opened the door. They recognized the man because they had spoken to him earlier.

"Is Mama Leon home?" Captain Lawrence asked.

The man frowned. "No," he answered.

The young boy spoke in Italian and held his hand outward. In his hand was the silver dollar. He nodded toward one of the soldiers and smiled.

"What do you want?" the man asked.

"We need her help," Captain Lawrence answered. "There is a man who has been injured. We do not understand what he is saying and we were told the language is Corsican. If Mama Leon can speak Corsican, we need her to interpret what he says." He paused. "We will pay her."

The man looked at the two soldiers and the young boy. "How much?"

"Ten dollars," Lieutenant Simpson answered. He reached into his trouser pocket and he removed a large fold of money. He counted two five dollar bills and handed them to the man. "We need Mama Leon's help. Can we speak to her?"

The man's eyes widened. He had never seen ten dollars at one time. "I am her son Victor. She does not speak

English and I will need to interpret for her. How much will you pay me?"

Lieutenant Simpson removed two ten dollar bills from the money fold and handed the money to the man. "We need Mama Leon's help. Can we speak to her?"

The man and boy's eyes widened. They had never seen so much money at one time.

"Come in!"

They entered the apartment to see it sparsely furnished. There were several chairs near the walls and a bed near the corner. A woman was standing in a doorway. She looked young, under the age of thirty, and in her arms she held an infant girl.

The room was filled with the smell of food cooking.

Victor spoke to the woman in Italian and he showed her the money. Her eyes widened and she walked through the doorway.

Victor motioned for the two soldiers to sit in the chairs. They sat and waited as an old woman walked through the doorway. She appeared to be over the age of seventy and her hair was completely white. She was wearing a print dress. The dress was old but clean. Victor motioned for her to sit and she sat in a chair in the farthest corner of the room. Victor kneeled at her feet and spoke quietly in Italian. She leaned forward and whispered in his ear. He showed her the money and nodded.

"Who is this man?" Victor asked.

"We don't know," Captain Lawrence answered. "We need someone who speaks and understand Corsican to ask him."

"Where is he?" Victor asked.

"He is currently in a hospital," Captain Lawrence answered.

"How old is he?" Victor asked.

"Twenty-nine," Captain Lawrence answered.

Victor turned to Mama Leon and spoke quietly in Italian. She listened intently. She shrugged her shoulders and leaned forward and whispered in his ear.

"My mother can not help you," Victor said. "She speaks Corsican but there are many dialects. If the man is young, she may not know the dialect." He stood and handed the money to Lieutenant Simpson.

Lieutenant Simpson did not accept the money. "We need Mama Leon's help. If she can recognize the language, we will know the man is speaking Corsican." He reached into his trouser pocket and removed the fold of money. He counted two ten dollar bills and handed the money to Victor. "Will she help us?"

Victor looked puzzled as he accepted the additional money. He turned to Mama Leon and kneeled before her and he spoke quietly in Italian.

Mama Leon listened to Victor and she looked puzzled. She leaned toward her son and whispered into his ear.

Victor turned. "She will help. How long will this take? Sophia is preparing dinner and it will be ready to eat in three hours."

"I do not know," Captain Lawrence answered. "If the man is speaking Corsican and Mama Leon understands him, we will need her to ask him questions and give us his response."

"Pack clothing and personal items for several days," Lieutenant Simpson said. "All of your needs will be taken care of."

"Where are we going?" Victor asked.

"The hospital," Captain Lawrence answered. "The man is at a hospital. If Mama Leon understands him, you will need to stay at the hospital for several days."

"Who is this man?" Victor asked.

"We do not know," Lieutenant Simpson answered.

"When do we leave for the hospital?" Victor asked.

"Now!"

The young woman they had seen earlier packed several items. There was only one suitcase. It was old and battered and the items were tightly packed inside. They left the building and followed the two soldiers to a parked car.

The car was surrounded by men and boys. They were looking at the car. As the two soldiers approached, the small crowd parted.

The car was a Badger!

The Badger Four Wheel Drive Auto Company was founded in 1908. It was the first four wheel drive car ever made. Very few cars were manufactured but almost every car manufactured was purchased by the United States Army.

The car was a touring car, with only a roof. The words U.S. Army was painted on the side and the name, General Tate with two stars, was painted in small letters underneath the U.S. Army insignia.

The crowd of men and boys, who had parted, rejoined when they saw Mama Leon and Victor following the two soldiers. Victor was carrying a suitcase and the two soldiers were armed.

One soldier wore the green uniform and one soldier wore the light brown uniform. They were both armed with Colt 1909 .45 caliber revolvers. The guns were in leather Webley holsters and the lanyard was attached to their belt.

Captain Lawrence and Lieutenant Simpson stopped.

Victor approached the small crowd. He spoke to the men in Italian and showed them the money. The young boy held out his hand and proudly displayed the silver dollar. The men nodded and smiled as they moved away from the car.

They entered the car and Lieutenant Simpson drove the Badger slowly down the street. The men and boys followed the car for several blocks.

The car's ride was smooth. The month was April and the weather was warm. The car was driven away from the city. Victor looked perplexed. They were to go to the hospital but they passed the road to the hospital. They were driven away from the hospital. They traveled for almost one hour when Victor saw where they were going – Binghamton Asylum for the chronic insane.

I am Napoleone Bounaparte

The Castle of the Hill it was called because it looked like a medieval castle. It was built on a hill that overlooked the Susquehanna River Valley. It was very large and made of stone. As they passed the gate to the main entrance, a soldier stood to attention.

Captain Lawrence saluted as the car was driven to the main entrance. There was one car parked in the front, a Cadillac with the words U.S. Army painted on the side.

They exited the car and walked through the massive front doors.

The asylum was very clean. Nurses, orderlies and doctors walked in the hallways, going in and out of rooms. The only thing Victor noticed unusual was the soldiers. As Victor walked down the corridor, he noticed soldiers. Each soldier was armed with a rifle and each soldier wore a gun belt.

They walked down the main corridor and turned left. This whole section of the asylum was guarded. Two soldiers stood at the entrance to this section of the hallway. They held their rifles and they were placed in a position to prevent anyone from entering.

When the two soldiers noticed Captain Lawrence and Lieutenant Simpson, they stood to attention and moved backwards to allow entrance. Lieutenant Simpson motioned for one of the soldiers to take the suitcase.

Victor and his mother walked down the hallway. Toward the end, there were many men standing and sitting. Benches were placed in the hallway and two men were sitting at the end, looking at documents. They were arguing with each other.

As they neared the end of the hallway, one of the soldiers approached them. "Who are these people?" General Tate demanded.

Captain Lawrence and Lieutenant Simpson stopped walking and saluted. "Victor Leon and his mother Angelina," Captain Lawrence answered.

General Tate's eyes widened and he smiled. "Who speaks Corsican?"

"Victor's mother speaks Corsican," Captain Lawrence answered. "She was born in Corsica and she knows many dialects. She is affectionately called Mama Leon."

General Tate's eyes narrowed and his face angered. He pointed toward Victor. "Why is he here?" he snarled.

"Mama Leon does not speak English," Captain Lawrence answered. "We brought him with us to interpret."

The general's eyes brightened. "Thank you for helping us," he said as he shook the hand of Victor and Mama Leon. "All of your expenses will be taken care of and we will pay you well. On behalf of President William Taft, I thank you!"

Their conversation was interrupted as loud screams and rants came from the room at the end of the hallway. The noise startled Victor and Mama Leon. The two men sitting on the benches arguing stood and began writing on paper.

"That's not Corsican!" Victor said. "That's French!"

As quickly as the loud screams and ranting started, they stopped.

"That is French," Victor said. "Mama Leon does not speak French."

"Do you speak French?" Captain Lawrence asked.

"No," Victor answered. "I don't speak French but I know French when I hear it. That language is French."

"He speaks two languages," Lieutenant Simpson said. "We believe one language is Corsican."

"What do you want Mama Leon to do?" Victor asked.

"Obvious," Captain Lawrence answered. "Ask her to walk to the door and ask the man, in Corsican, who he is."

Victor leaned toward Mama Leon and whispered in her ear. She nodded and walked to the door. As she walked to the door, the men standing near the door moved backward to clear the hallway. She walked to the door and stopped.

There were no sounds coming from the room. She tapped lightly on the door and said something.

There was a pause and then a loud laughter came from inside the room. Someone inside the room responded.

Mama Leon laughed and she said something.

A soft voice responded and Mama Leon laughed. She looked angry and shook her right finger toward the door. She wasn't angry as she laughed and said something.

A voice came from the room. The words were soft and gentle.

Mama Leon had a very large smile on her face. She attempted to turn the door knob and enter the room but the door was locked. She had an angry look on her face as she attempted to open the door. She turned to Victor and said something.

Victor reached toward her and pulled her away from the door. She attempted to reach for the door knob and spoke angered as he pulled her away.

Victor pulled her away from the door and pushed her further down the hallway.

"Who is in there?" Victor demanded.

Several of the men who stood in the hallway rushed toward them.

"Is the language Corsican?"

"Who is he?"

"What did he say?"

Mama Leon spit at the men and she said something angered. Captain Lawrence tapped on Victor's shoulder and he motioned for Victor to bring her into an opened door. The men attempted to follow them but Captain Lawrence motioned to two soldiers. The two soldiers rushed to the door and stood guard.

The room they entered was an empty patient's room. There was one single bed with two chairs and a small table in the room. It looked like it had not been occupied for several weeks.

Mama Leon sat in one of the chairs and fumed. She was visibly upset.

"Is the language he spoke Corsican?" Captain Lawrence asked.

"Yes," Victor answered. "Mama Leon spoke to him in Corsican and he answered. The man in the room can speak and understand Corsican."

"What did he say?" Captain Lawrence asked.

Victor spoke softly to his mother in Italian. She shrugged her shoulders and whispered in his ear.

"He is difficult to understand," Victor answered. "The dialect he spoke has not been used in many years. She recognized it from a dialect spoken when she was a child. The dialect was used in the area of Ajaccio."

"Where is that?" Captain Lawrence asked puzzled. "I have never heard of Ajaccio."

Victor shrugged his shoulders. "That is where Napoleon was born. He lived there as a child before he went to military school."

"You know about Napoleon?" Captain Lawrence asked surprised.

"A little," Victor answered. "Mama Leon knows more than I do. As a child, she visited Ajaccio many times. She has visited the home where he was born."

Captain Lawrence looked puzzled. "Where who was born?"

"Napoleon," Victor answered. "Mama Leon has visited the home where Napoleon was born many times."

Captain Lawrence became very excited. "Can she describe the home?"

Victor leaned toward Mama Leon and whispered in her ear. She nodded and spoke into his ear.

"Yes," Victor answered. "She has been there many times and she can describe the home." He paused. "She visited the home before it was repaired and changed. She can not describe the new home but she can describe the old one."

Captain Lawrence clapped his hands and laughed. "We got him!"

He rushed from the room into the hallway. "We got him!" he shouted.

The men in the hallway laughed and patted each other on their backs.

General Tate approached Captain Lawrence. "What do you have?"

Captain Lawrence saluted. "Mama Leon says the language is Corsican. It is from the area where Napoleon was born and she has visited the home. She can describe the house where Napoleon was born."

General Tate became excited. "Who has his description of his childhood home?" he yelled.

A man raised his hand and he held upward several sheets of paper.

"I want this done right!" the general yelled. "Go over every detail. I want a listing of every board and every window. I want to know exactly how many nails and how many panes of glass."

"Good job!" General Tate said to Captain Lawrence. "Have them rest because tomorrow is going to be a long day. How much did you pay them?"

"Fifty dollars," Captain Lawrence answered.

"Double it tomorrow!" General Tate ordered.

Victor sat in the empty patient's room with his mother. She was visibly upset and Victor did not like how the soldier shouted and left the room. He did not know why there were soldiers in an asylum. The man in the room must be very important.

"What did the man say?" Victor asked his mother in Italian.

She calmed herself down and smiled. Mama Leon answered his question in Italian. "I asked who he was and he answered he must be dead because he hears the voice of an angel. He has never heard such a beautiful voice and he asked the angel's name. I told him I was Angelina Leon and he asked me if I was married."

"I laughed at his joke and I told him he was a mischievous boy. He laughed and said it was my beautiful voice that made him so. Then he asked me to come into the room that he may meet me."

Mama Leon frowned. "I attempted to open the door and it was locked. As I pulled on the door he spoke again in Corsican. I attempted to open the door but you pulled me away from it."

Victor looked perplexed. "What else did he say?"

Mama Leon placed her hands to her face and she began to weep. "Help me!" she answered in Italian.

Chapter Fifteen

Their first night's stay in the asylum was a terrible one. There were long periods of silence broken by short bursts of ranting and raving. The language spoken was French. It was near dawn when the man in the locked room shouted in Corsican. Mama Leon was not asleep. The loud screams in French unnerved her and she could not sleep. When she heard the man scream in Corsican, she opened the door to her room and peered down the hallway.

Many armed soldiers were in the hallway and they were unfazed by the screams. She listened carefully as the man screamed again. He screamed in French and she did not know what he said.

Chapter Sixteen

For three days, Mama Leon was interviewed by two men, professors Lytle and Angle. They asked questions about the town of Ajaccio and the home where Napoleon was born. They asked the same questions: How many steps to the front door? Are the steps wood or stone? How many windows are located on the front of the house? How many rooms are located on the first floor? Where is the well located? Where are the stables located?

Many of the questions were rephrased to trick her. She answered the questions the same. The interview would last for one hour and then stop. There were many long breaks and the interviews began again.

Her room was moved to a different floor. She was far from the man in the locked room and she could not hear his screams at night.

On the third day she was told why she had been asked the same questions many times. Mama Leon was to meet the man in the locked room and ask him the same questions she was asked…in Corsican. She was to compare his answers with her answers.

Captain Lawrence assured Victor that his mother was safe. The man in the locked room was not dangerous. He yelled many times but he had not attempted to harm anyone. The armed soldiers were a precaution.

The morning of the fourth day, Mama Leon was interviewed again. The two men went over the questions she was to ask. After a long break, Victor and Mama Leon were taken to the man in the locked room. Captain Lawrence knocked on the door several times and identified himself. She could hear the sound of several locks turning. One sound was of a chain being moved. The door slowly opened and an armed soldier allowed them entrance.

The room was magnificent!

It was a patient's room that had been enlarged. It looked like four or five patient's rooms had been combined. The room was only one room but it was very large. There was a section for the bedroom, a sitting room, an indoor toilet and a large area for cooking and eating. The eating table looked like it was thirty feet long with twenty chairs. A large, ornate chair, like a throne, was at the end. The table was decorated with a large candelabrum.

There were no electric lights and the room was lit with candles.

The room was arranged so everything could be seen from any area of the room. There was no place to hide and the furniture was arranged to prevent anyone from hiding behind it. The room had four corners and one armed soldier was in each corner.

Four chairs had been arranged to face an ornate settee. The chairs were ornate, covered in a velvet fabric. Mama Leon and Victor were led to the chairs and they sat.

When they entered the room, a man was standing near the eating table. His back was turned to them as they entered. The man was wearing a type of dressing gown that was very ornate. It looked like crimson red velvet. The dressing gown went to the floor and flowed outward. The end was trimmed in white. When the man turned toward them, Mama Leon gasped.

The man appeared to be French and thirty years of age. He was not tall but not short. His hair was black and cut short. He was neither handsome nor ugly. It was not his looks that made her gasp. It was his eyes!

The man's eyes looked like he was dead. There were no pupils and his eyes looked sunken into his head. They were a dull, grayish white in color.

The man smiled slightly. His teeth were even and a white color. He was clean shaven and he motioned for them to sit.

They were already sitting but he could not see them. The man was blind!

He walked toward the settee. The man was blind but every step was measured. He knew where everything in the room was located. He walked toward the settee with an assurance; a walk reserved only for kings and queens. As he walked, his right hand reached downward to pull the long end of the dressing gown. He walked to the settee and casually sat. His head moved to the left and right. It appeared he was listening for sounds, any sound. He lifted his head, sniffing the air. He paused slightly. He noticed the smell of Mama Leon's perfume. She rarely wore perfume but Lieutenant Simpson had given her a bottle of perfume. The perfume was very old and very valuable. It was French perfume and named Midnight Rosée. The English name was Midnight Dew. It was alleged to be the favorite perfume of Napoleon's second wife. There were few bottles in existence and it had a slight citrus scent. She was requested to wear the perfume when she met the man in the locked room.

The man sniffed the air and smiled. "Midnight Rosée" he said in French. "My angel?" he asked in Corsican.

Professor Angle looked puzzled when the man recognized the scent. The perfume had not been manufactured in over one hundred years. The man knew and recognized the scent. He knew the name of the perfume.

Captain Lawrence had ordered no one but Mama Leon to speak during the meeting. He nodded for her to speak to the man in Corsican.

"Yes," she answered. "How is your health?"

"Tired," he answered. He moved his right hand outward.

When they entered the room, they did not notice a man sitting in the food preparation area. The man was dressed strangely. He wore a type of servants clothing and spoke in French, "White or red?"

"Red for me," the man answered in French, "white for my angel."

The man, dressed as a servant, poured two glasses of wine. He placed the glass with the red wine in the man's hand and handed the glass with the white wine to Mama Leon. He bowed toward her and moved backward to the food preparation area.

"Thank you," she said in Corsican. "Why do you call me your angel?" she asked as she sipped the wine.

"Your voice," the man answered. "It is very beautiful and soothing."

"What year is it?" Mama Leon asked.

The man paused and sipped his wine. "1814," he answered.

"What month is it?" Mama Leon asked.

"That is a difficult question to answer," the man answered. "I think it is February or March." He reached upward to his eyes with his left hand and rubbed them. "Since my injury I am unable to tell night from day."

"How were you injured," Mama Leon asked as she sipped her wine.

"I do not know," he answered. "I awoke and I could not see."

"Where are you?" Mama Leon asked.

"I do not know," the man answered. "I am told I am in America."

Mama Leon paused. She placed the glass of wine on the floor. When she looked downward to place the glass, she noticed the rug. It was very ornate in multiple colors.

"I am from the area of Ajaccio," she said. "It has been a long time since I visited the area. Do you know the place?"

The man laughed. "I was born there August 15, 1769," he answered. "My home is still there. Have you ever visited my home?"

"Many times," Mama Leon answered. "I fell once on the wooden steps leading to the door."

The man cocked his head slightly. "The steps are made of stone not wood."

Mama Leon laughed. "There are four wooden steps and I fell on the third step and injured my leg."

The man looked puzzled. “There are three stone steps, not four.”

Mama Leon laughed. “No, there are four wooden steps. From the steps you can see the well to the left of the house.”

The man frowned. “When were the stables removed?”

“The stables have not been removed,” Mama Leon answered.

The man paused, thinking. “You can not see the well from the front steps because it is located behind the stables. My mother did not like where the stables were placed because it was a distance to the well.”

Mama Leon looked to Victor and nodded her head.

“I am sure it was your house,” Mama Leon said. “There are four rooms downstairs and three rooms upstairs.”

“You forgot to count the food preparation area,” the man said. “There are five rooms downstairs and three rooms upstairs. I was born in the upstairs room in the front. That was the room I shared with my brother Joseph. We would climb out the window at night to the tree and play.”

Mama Leon laughed nervously. She did not know who the man was but his voice, his manner of speaking, was mesmerizing. She began to become afraid of him. There was something about him, the way he spoke, the way every word was carefully measured that terrified her. Mama Leon wanted to leave.

Captain Lawrence could see fear in her face. She began to stand when Captain Lawrence motioned toward her. There was one question she was told to ask, in Corsican, before they left the man in the locked room.

She calmed herself and smiled. “I am afraid we have not been formally introduced. I told you my name but you have not told me yours.”

The man placed his glass of wine on the floor and stood. “My injuries have made me forget my manners and I do not look like I once did. I am of the certainty you did not recognize me when you entered and I forgive you.”

"I am Napoleone Bounaparte."

Mama Leon frowned and she looked puzzled.

Captain Lawrence motioned for them to leave.

"I must leave," Mama Leon said. "I would like to visit you again."

"Yes," the man said. "I would like to have you visit again and enjoy dinner. I will arrange a date and time and I will have my servant contact you." He held his right hand outward for her to kiss.

Captain Lawrence motioned for Mama Leon to approach him and kiss his hand.

She stood and approached the man. As she walked toward him, fear began to grip her. It was like a dream; a nightmare.

She kneeled and looked at his right hand. It was bruised and battered. His hand looked like he had battered it against a stone wall. A very ornate gold ring was on his second finger and the ring, also, was damaged. She closed her eyes and in disgust kissed his right hand.

"Why did you ask me to help you?" she whispered in Corsican.

He leaned forward. "I am being held a political prisoner," he whispered in Corsican. "If you help me to escape, I will reward you."

"Goodbye," Mama Leon said in a frightened voice as she stood. The people sitting in the chairs stood and followed her to the door. As she neared the door she noticed multiple locks. The armed soldier opened the door and they exited. When they exited, she could hear the sounds of many locks.

She leaned toward Victor and whispered in his ear. He turned toward Captain Lawrence. "He answered every question correctly."

Chapter Seventeen

"Professor Marlow is back!"

Lieutenant Simpson had opened the door. He nodded his head, gave the message, and closed the door.

Professors Lytle and Angle were sitting in a patient's room that had been converted into a conference and reference room. The bed and cabinet had been removed and replaced with a table from the dining area. The table was littered with papers and stacks of papers and books covered the floor. They were comparing notes and looked upward when Lieutenant Simpson opened and closed the door.

"Where's Professor Sykes?" Professor Lytle asked Professor Angle.

"Servant duty," Professor Angle answered. "He doesn't drug his wine until ten. I wonder why Professor Marlow came back. Do you think he found something?"

"Nothing to find," Professor Lytle answered. "We have covered almost everything. Every question has been answered correctly." He leaned backward and exhaled. "We are missing something! There has got to be a logical explanation why he knows these things. Somewhere, somehow, I think someone is giving him the answers."

"Professor Sykes?"

"No," Professor Lytle answered. "He is as puzzled as we are."

"Professor Marlow?"

Professor Lytle did not answer. He raised his eyebrows.

"That thought crossed my mind also," Professor Angle said. "He is a strange bird. He was acting strange before he left."

Professor Lytle looked thoughtful. "If Professor Marlow is giving him the answers, why would he do it? There is nothing for him to gain. The young man has nothing to gain. There is nothing here that would interest anyone outside of academia and who cares about an insane man who believes he is Napoleone?"

"I wonder why he returned," Professor Angle said. "When he left he said he had washed his hands of the whole affair. Perhaps he thought we were on to him and he wanted to leave before we challenged him."

"We have no proof," Professor Lytle said. "The one person who has the most contact is Professor Sykes. Everyone knows what everyone knows."

The door opened and Lieutenant Simpson stepped inside. "Professor Marlow has returned and he has requested you join him in his room."

The three men walked down the corridor of the asylum to a section that had been separated. This section was patient's rooms that had been assigned to people working on the case. They walked to the room that had been assigned to Professor Marlow. The room had been abandoned for several days. He left but then returned.

The door was open and six chairs had been placed near Professor Marlow's bed. The bed was littered with papers and Professor Marlow's unopened suitcase was placed by the bed. He was sitting on the bed with a very large smile on his face.

"Come in and sit," he said laughing. "I have partially solved the mystery!"

Professors Lytle and Angle entered the room. Professor Marlow raised his hand to stop Lieutenant Simpson from entering the room. "Private meeting! We need to discus some issues and come to an agreement. You will be fully informed at our conclusion."

Lieutenant Simpson shrugged his shoulders. He nodded as he closed the door.

"Have you found something?" Professor Lytle asked excited as he sat in one of the chairs.

"Depends upon your interpretation," Professor Marlow answered.

Professor Angle did not appear excited. He was unsure of why Professor Marlow had returned. He sat in one of the chairs and frowned. "Why are you back?"

"I found something that interested me and I want to continue," Professor Marlow answered.

Professor Angle shrugged his shoulders. "You have appeared to be negative from the very beginning. Everyone kept an open mind but you. You said you were out. What do you have to tell me that would make me want to trust you?"

Professor Marlow laughed. "You do not trust me?"

Professor Angle stood. "You left!" he yelled. "You said you were out! We needed you and when you backed out of the project you left us in a bind."

Professor Marlow snarled and stood. He did not like what Professor Angle was saying. "There are three of you!"

"Two," Professor Angle said. "Abner Sykes does not count! He is on constant servant duty. The only time we can meet is when he drugs his wine!"

He sat in his chair and huffed. "I am very busy and I do not have the time to listen to nonsense. If you have something to say, say it!"

Professor Marlow sat on the edge of his bed and smiled. "I have partially solved the puzzle!"

"This had better be good," Professor Angle said.

Professor Marlow smiled. "He has answered every question correctly. I have been searching for evidence that this man has somehow been given answers to our questions before we asked them."

He looked at Professor Angle.

"When the man's parents said he had been exposed to the French language, I was convinced that the issue of his language was solved."

"Why are you looking at me?" Professor Angle asked. "Why would I give him answers?"

Professor Marlow stood. "Because no one could answer those questions correctly unless someone gave him the answers."

Professor Lytle stood and he looked at Professor Angle shocked. "Are you accusing Professor Angle of giving him answers?"

Professor Angle stood. "Are you accusing me?"

Professor Marlow smiled. "I am not accusing either one of you."

"Professor Sykes?" Professor Angle asked surprised.

"Heavens no!" Professor Marlow answered.

Professors Angle and Lytle sat in their chairs. "What are you talking about?" Professor Angle asked bored. "My time is valuable. If you have a point to make, make it!"

Professor Marlow laughed. "Every one of us has been thinking the same thing but we are afraid to mention it. It was not me! When I left I was convinced one or more persons were giving the man answers. I thought this whole affair was a charade and I wanted no part of it."

"What is your point?" Professor Angle asked bored.

"I have eliminated that possibility," Professor Marlow answered.

Professor Angle seemed interested. "What are you talking about?"

Professor Marlow laughed. "The man answered a question correctly that we did not know the correct answer to. We thought we knew the correct answer but we didn't."

"What question and what answer?" Professor Angle asked puzzled.

"His description of the Palace of Versailles," Professor Marlow answered.

"He answered every question correctly," Professor Angle said. "What did he know that you claim we did not know?"

"The secret room located in the Palace of Versailles," Professor Marlow answered.

"We discussed that question and that answer," Professor Angle said. "There is a secret passage from the king's bedroom to the queen's bedroom. That passage was used by Marie Antoinette when the women attacked the palace. The Bread March of Women occurred October 5, 1789." He looked at Professor Lytle. "That is information anyone who has visited the palace would know. The only thing we can not discover is who told him."

"Yes," Professor Marlow said. "I am not referring to that secret passage."

"If you are referring to the secret passage located in the hallway of the third floor, that passage was discovered thirty years ago," Professor Angle said. "A cleaning person accidentally pressed a molding on the wall and a panel opened."

He shrugged his shoulders. "That information is also easily obtained by anyone who has visited the palace."

He stood. "If you are finished?"

"Not yet," Professor Marlow said laughing. "Do you recall his description of the secret room in the hallway on the third floor?"

Professor Angle sat and he looked bored. "He was asked more than ten times." He shrugged his shoulders. "There is a secret hiding room located on the right side of the hallway on the third floor. Admittance is accessed by pressing a wood molding and sliding the panel."

Professor Marlow giggled. "Where does it lead?"

Professor Angle shrugged his shoulders. "The passage leads to another section. The stairs go to the ground floor and exit near a rear door." He stood. "We have gone over this more than one hundred times. There are multiple secret passages in the palace. If you are finished?"

Professor Marlow laughed. "Give me five minutes and you can leave. I'm staying!"

Professor Angle frowned and he sat. "I do not think that whether the panel on the wall is located on the bottom or the top indicates some secret knowledge that no one but Napoleon would know. What difference does it make if you push one panel or two? There is a secret passage on the third floor of Versailles that is not a secret."

Professor Marlow giggled. He held his hands outward and walked to the end of his bed. He held his right arm upward. "He correctly answered the question that Napoleon never lived in the Palace of Versailles. Most people, including the French, incorrectly think Napoleon and Josephine lived in the palace. It was in ruin after the French Revolution. Napoleon took pity on the palace and he ordered it restored."

He held his right arm upward as he walked to the end of his room to face the wall. "There is a secret hiding room located on the right side of the hallway on the third floor. Admittance is accessed by pressing a wood molding and sliding the panel."

Professor Marlow bent downward and he acted like he was pressing a panel and then he touched the wall and he acted like he was sliding the wall.

Professor Lytle frowned. "I agree with Professor Angle. What difference does it make whether the panel on the wall is located on the bottom or the top? What difference does it make if you push one panel or two?"

Professor Marlow giggled. He turned a complete one hundred eighty degrees and held both of his arms outward. "There is a secret hiding room located on the right side of the hallway on the third floor. Admittance is accessed by pressing a wood molding and sliding the panel."

He walked to the end of his bed and bent downward. He acted like he was pressing a panel and then he reached upward, to empty air, and he acted like he was sliding an imaginary wall.

Professors Angle and Lytle both stood.

"There are two secret passages on the third floor?" they both asked.

Professor Marlow was excited. He walked to his closed suitcase and placed it on the bed and he opened it. There were no clothes or personal items inside, it was filled with papers. He removed a telegram and he held it upward. "It was discovered three weeks ago!"

Professors Angle and Lytle rushed toward the bed. Professor Angle grabbed the telegram as Professor Marlow laughed.

"How? How?" Professor Angle asked excited.

"He answered the question correctly but we misinterpreted our question and his answer," Professor Marlow answered.

"What question?" Professor Lytle asked.

Professor Marlow laughed. "He was asked if there was a secret room in the palace not a secret passage."

Professor Angle stared at the telegram. "This is a room?"

"Yes," Professor Marlow answered excited. "It is large enough to hold ten to twenty people. The entrance is accessed by pressing a section of the molding. Pressing the section of molding only releases a catch on the panel. You must hold the molding and then slide the panel. You do not open the panel, you slide it."

"What is its purpose?" Professor Angle asked.

"A temporary hiding place is my guess," Professor Marlow answered. "The wall panel is too thick to be penetrated by a musket shot." He laughed loudly. "There is no possible way someone could have given him the answer to a question we did not know the correct answer to."

Professor Lytle looked thoughtful. "Does this not sound too convenient? Who is the person who claims to have discovered this?"

Professor Marlow frowned. "A friend of mine. I sent him the description of the hidden room and I asked him to verify it. He knows several people who are in charge of the palace and they allowed him to search."

"And he found it?" Professor Lytle asked with a smirk.

"He was not alone when he found it," Professor Marlow answered. "Staff of the palace is sending photographs, drawings and dimensions by post. If you read the telegram, that room does not appear to have been opened in more than one hundred years. It is their guess it was built but never actually used."

Professor Angle looked thoughtful. "It is additional evidence."

"Additional?" Professor Marlow asked angered. "It is the only piece of evidence we have that is tangible. This is not a sentence in a book or a report from a fifth generation. You can see it! You can feel it!"

Professor Angle nodded his head. "This does partially solve the puzzle. We know no one is giving him the answers. The question that remains is how does he know those answers?"

Professor Lytle frowned. "There has got to be a logical explanation. How can a twenty-nine year-old illiterate blind man know everything about Napoleon?"

Chapter Eighteen

"Lightly cover my potatoes with the salt seasoning," he said in Corsican.

Mama Leon reached for the bowl of salt and used the spoon to lightly dust his potatoes. She was terrified of him!

She sat to his immediate left and Captain Lawrence sat across from her at the dining table. He sat at the end, to her immediate right. Victor sat to her left, to interpret, and Professor Angle sat to his immediate left.

Professor Marlow sat the opposite of Professor Angle and Professor Lytle sat at the end. Professor Sykes served their meal.

The meal was composed of roast chicken with a bread stuffing. He likes to eat boiled potatoes and the potatoes were served with bread. The bread was hard and Mama Leon did not like the bread. She ate slowly.

Captain Lawrence noticed her fear and he frequently smiled. He nodded in approval when she placed salt on his food. He did not understand Corsican but what occurred seemed natural, he said something in Corsican and she responded by placing salt on his food.

What he said next would have chilled Captain Lawrence and placed fear in the minds of the four professors, if they understood the language. "I do not trust anyone in this room but you," he said in Corsican.

Mama Leon's face whitened.

His speech throughout the dinner had been interspersed with French and Corsican. He frequently shifted dialects in Corsican. It seemed he suspected someone, perhaps Victor, knew the dialect. To confuse Victor, he shifted dialects.

Mama Leon was too afraid to speak to Victor of what he had said. His manner of speaking was gentle and kind. His words were carefully measured and mesmerizing. It was what he said earlier that frightened her. "I can be your benefactor or a displeasing enemy."

What followed next was even more frightening. She felt his left hand on her right knee as he placed an envelope on the right knee above her dress. The envelope was small but thick. When she placed her right hand on it, it felt like multiple sheets of paper.

He casually ate a small portion of chicken. "You will place the envelope outside the stone wall of my prison," he said in Corsican as he wiped his mouth.

Mama Leon did not nod her head or agree. She looked to the others. Captain Lawrence was involved in a conversation with Professor Marlow. Professor Lytle was eating and no one was paying attention.

"Turn to the right outside the stone wall entrance and walk to the end," he said in Corsican. "Drop the envelope to the ground and return."

She was unsure who the man was she was sitting beside. He said his name was Napoleone Bounaparte. She knew this was false because Napoleon died almost ninety years ago. This man was young, almost thirty.

He told her he was a political prisoner. This story made sense to her. He appeared to be of royal blood. His mannerisms were not those of a common person. She was unsure of why he was being held a prisoner and why he pretended to be Napoleon. None of this information made sense to her. For some reason, the American Army was keeping him prisoner in a hospital for people who were insane.

The man gave no indication he was insane. He acted normally. He did not dress normally but kings and queens wear gowns and robes. It was not unusual for a king to wear a robe.

He spoke Corsican and she was paid to interpret.

She and Victor were paid one hundred American dollars a day to interpret. They had been here two weeks. In fourteen days they had earned one thousand four hundred American dollars. In the year 1910, it was a small fortune.

She agreed to help him. She agreed because she was afraid of him.

The dinner proceeded. He told stories in French. Professor Angle interpreted for Victor. Victor interpreted for her. She would nod and frequently laugh but her laugh was tense and forced.

As they spoke, she carefully placed the envelope under her dress. She wore a long undergarment and she placed the envelope within its folds. Before the dinner was complete, Professor Marlow nodded to her. There was a question she was to ask in Corsican.

He stood and nodded that the dinner was over. He smiled to his left at Mama Leon. "It was a most enjoyable evening," he said in French. "I enjoyed your company."

Professor Angle interpreted for Victor and Victor whispered into his mother's ear.

"When did you last see Maria?" she asked in Corsican.

He smiled slightly. "It has been many months since I was in the company of Marie," he answered in Corsican. "I miss her dearly and my adopted son Eugene."

"I asked about Maria not Marie Louise," she said in Corsican.

He paused and frowned slightly. "It is not wise to pass rumors," he said in Corsican. His voice was tense and he appeared to be controlling his temper. "A lady does not ask and a gentleman does not answer."

Mama Leon smiled and she laughed slightly. "You're Imperial Majesty," she said in Corsican. "It was not my intent to anger or to inquire of personal matters. My question was when you met her last. It is a question I believed I could ask."

He smiled. "If your question is of the farm girl named Maria Colette Montpere," he said in Corsican. "I have not seen her in many months. I had the pleasure of her counsel in January."

Professors Angle, Lytle and Marlow looked puzzled. They looked to Professor Sykes who also looked puzzled. They did not understand Corsican but the name Montpere was easily recognized. It was the last name of his great grandfather Rober Montpere.

Maria Colette Montpere is the name of the French farm girl who claimed her son was fathered by Napoleon Bonaparte.

Mama Leon smiled. Her smile was nervous. "I will place your letter as you requested," she said in Corsican.

He smiled and held his left hand toward her. "Your reward will be great and my generosity immense," he said in Corsican.

She kissed his hand and turned to leave the room. She stopped and looked back. "I do not seek reward, only forgiveness if I have offended you," she said in Corsican.

"Angels cannot offend, angels can only bless," he said in Corsican.

Professors Angle, Lytle and Marlow approached him and kissed his hand. Victor and Captain Lawrence also kissed his hand. They left the room as the soldier locked the door from the inside.

Victor listened to Mama Leon as she whispered into his ear. He began to speak to Professor Marlow but Professor Marlow was excited. "We know what he said," Professor Marlow said in English. "It is not necessary to interpret. He knows the name of his distant relative!"

He turned to professors Angle and Lytle. They began whispering to each other as they walked from the locked door.

"Thank you," Captain Lawrence said to Victor. "You have been much help. Unless there is more they want asked, I think you can leave tomorrow."

Victor whispered to his mother. She frowned and whispered in his ear.

"Can we stay a few more days?" he asked in English. "My mother thinks she may be of additional help. You do not have to pay us."

Captain Lawrence smiled. "I will ask the general. We may need her again to interpret and we will continue to pay you." He smiled and walked away from the locked door.

Victor whispered to his mother and Mama Leon nodded her head. She and Victor began walking away from the door behind Captain Lawrence.

"Let me out!" he yelled in French.

He had walked to the locked door behind them and he screamed in French. He beat his hands against the door. "Let me out!"

As quickly as his outburst began, it stopped.

Professors Marlow, Angle and Lytle were shocked by his outburst. They hurriedly returned to the locked door to listen. There were no other sounds.

Chapter Twenty

Mama Leon did not sleep that night. She was concerned for her and her son's safety. She did not tell her son of the letter or of his mixed words. She lay awake in her bed waiting for morning.

She awoke Victor early and told him she wanted to walk. She wanted to walk to the front wall of the asylum and walk to the end of the wall. The season was spring and she wanted to see the valley.

He agreed. They ate a light breakfast of flour cakes and began their walk.

The walk to the front of the asylum was not tiring. Mama Leon was old but she walked very well. They spoke in Italian of who the man was and why he was guarded. Victor did not know.

They walked to the main entrance where a soldier stood as a sentry. He nodded to them as they walked past him to the right. This walk was tiring. The combination made Mama Leon breathe heavily. When they approached the far wall, she requested to sit and rest.

They sat at the edge of the two stone walls. One wall led south. The end of this wall was too far to see clearly. She sat in the grass and looked at the wooded area. The woods were very thick and she could not see beyond twenty to thirty trees. The trees were a mixture of birch and pine.

Colors of light and dark brown, black and bright green dotted the landscape. As far as she could see were small mountains. Large sections of the valley were green where the leaves of the trees budded.

The underbrush was thick. Leaves from the fall season and broken tree branches covered the ground. This area of the woods appeared to be difficult to walk through.

She sat and spoke to Victor. She told him stories of her youth and how she would walk through the woods on the island of Corsica. The trees were different in Corsica. The trees were smaller.

As she spoke, she adjusted her dress many times, slowly removing the envelope. She moved it towards her back to the stone wall. As she stood, she placed her right foot in front of the envelope to conceal it from Victor.

Motioning for Victor to lead, she followed. Mama Leon did not look back.

They walked to the front entrance and smiled pleasantly as they passed the sentry. Mama Leon breathed a slight sigh of relief. She followed his orders and she left the envelope where she was ordered to place it.

The envelope lay against the stone wall. It was more than one hour when a section of the underbrush at the edge of the woods moved. The man crawled from his hiding place to the edge of the woods. He crawled along the ground until he reached the envelope. Carefully placing it under his grayish shirt, he crawled to the woods and reentered his hiding place.

The edge of the woods remained motionless.

It was more than one hour before two sections of the underbrush moved. The man who retrieved the envelope crawled from his hiding place and joined another man, who crawled from his. They crawled into the woods. When the two men crawled a distance of fifty American yards, they stood and ran south.

The edge of the woods remained motionless.

It was more than one hour before two additional sections of the underbrush moved. Two men crawled from their hiding place and crawled toward the woods. The two men crawled a distance of fifty American yards, stood, and ran south.

The first two men ran a distance of five American miles and waited for the additional two men. The two men joined them and the four waited. Two hours later, two additional men joined them. The six men walked a short distance, mounted horses, and rode south.

Chapter Twenty - One

"Astrid, I have been waiting for you!"

Astrid walked to the table at the Cherbourg French café and she quickly sat in the empty chair.

"Where have you been?" Amaury asked in English. "We were to meet almost three weeks ago. I was concerned!"

"I think I am being followed," she said in English.

"More secrets?" Amaury asked in English. He motioned for the waiter. The waiter came to the table and he poured two glasses of wine. The waiter presented the glass of wine to Astrid but she waved it away. The waiter placed the glass of wine on the table, bowed, and walked away.

Amaury noticed her uneasiness. She looked to her right and her left. Several times, she moved in her seat. Astrid was usually a beauty. She was young, thin and full of spirit. She looked disheveled, her hair was not combed and she looked like she had not slept.

"What is wrong?" Amaury asked in English.

"This whole affair has somehow become insane," she answered in English. "I have been dismissed and Captain Lawrence paid me one hundred dollars. He demanded I speak to no one of the man who says he is Napoleon."

"The man is insane," Amaury said. "The Army officer looks the fool."

"I think I have been followed," Astrid said. She leaned forward. "Is this professor named Abner Sykes important?" she asked in English.

"Yes," Amaury answered in English. "Abner Sykes is the world's foremost authority on Napoleon. He is currently teaching at Harvard University. I met him six months ago at a luncheon. He spoke on Napoleonic code."

Astrid looked to her left. "Where is Harvard University located?" she asked in English.

"A suburb of Boston in the state of Massachusetts," Amaury answered in English. "Abner Sykes is in Boston."

"Not anymore," Astrid whispered in English. "He is here in New York. He was at the city hospital three weeks ago."

Amaury laughed. "Perhaps there are two insane people at the hospital," he said in English. "One person thinks they are Napoleon and one person thinks they are a college professor." He took a large drink from his wine glass. "Napoleon is in France and Abner Sykes is in Boston."

Astrid smiled slightly. She seemed to relax and she sipped from her wine glass. She laughed at his joke but her laugh was nervous. It seemed like a frightened laugh.

"They are both in New York," Astrid said in English. "Captain Lawrence convinced Professor Sykes to come to New York."

"I do not think so," Amaury said in English. "I can not think of one reason why Abner Sykes would come to New York and interview an insane man."

"They do not think he is insane," Astrid said in English. "He has answered every question correctly."

Amaury shrugged his shoulders. "I admit knowing the names of Napoleon's brothers and sisters are a difficult answer and one that I did not know," he said in English. "There is more to Napoleon than the immediate family." He sipped from his wine glass. "Have they asked him questions about the battles?"

"Yes," Astrid answered in English. "The three professors have asked him many questions about battles and he knows all the answers."

Amaury shrugged his shoulders. "The only questions and answers I have any interest in are the ones Abner Sykes would ask," he said in English. He leaned forward. "Do you recall any questions Professor Sykes asked?"

"No," Astrid answered. "He has just arrived and he is dressed as his servant. Captain Lawrence placed the professor in the man's room to pretend he is a servant." She shrugged her shoulders. "I saw him once. After he arrived, I was dismissed."

Amaury leaned backward in his chair. He reached for his wine glass and stopped. "What does this professor, this man, look like who claims to be Abner Sykes?" he asked in French.

"English!" Astrid said in English. "You are to speak in English. He is thin, not too tall, short untrimmed beard, long untrimmed hair, dirty clothes and he smells."

Amaury smiled. "That describes Abner Sykes," he said in English. "Why were you dismissed?"

"I was helping the three professors before Professor Sykes arrived," she answered in English. "One of the professors made the joke that the man was the reincarnation of Napoleon. We were discussing this possibility when Captain Lawrence entered the room. He appeared to be upset that the three men were confiding in me."

"Several days later, I was with the three professors and we were discussing several of the answers. Captain Lawrence pulled me to the side and he told me I was no longer needed. He gave me one hundred American dollars and I was to tell no one, of what has occurred."

"Curious," Amaury said in English. "I can not think why you were dismissed."

"I can not either," Astrid said in English. "I was compiling a listing of the questions and the answers. It was I who discovered something they had missed."

Amaury smiled. "What did they miss?"

Astrid looked to her right and her left. She sipped from her wine glass and leaned forward. "He can not answer any question after the date of January 1814," she whispered in English.

Amaury smiled. He mocked Astrid by looking to his left and his right. He sipped from his wine glass and leaned forward. "Why?" he whispered in English.

"This is not funny!" Astrid said in English. "For some reason, he knows everything about Napoleon up to January 1814. He knows nothing after that date. He does not know of the Battle of Waterloo or how Napoleon died."

"He has given incorrect answers?" Amaury asked in English.

"No," Astrid answered in English. "He gives no answers. He says he does not know."

"This is getting more curious," Amaury said in English. "If the man knows information as trivial as the names of Napoleon's siblings, he would know the date of Waterloo."

"That is the strange part," Astrid said in English. "He can tell them the date he married Josephine and he can describe her body." She paused and sipped her wine. "Did you know Josephine had a mole near her left armpit?"

Amaury smiled. "No," he answered in English. "I really did not know that information and it is information I will quickly forget."

Astrid smiled. "How could someone know that much detail and not know about Waterloo?" she asked in English. "That is when the discussion started about reincarnation."

"What do a woman's mole and its placement have to do with reincarnation?" Amaury asked in English amused.

"He thinks it is 1814," Astrid answered in English. She looked to her right and her left. "It is as if, the spirit of Napoleon from the year 1814 was suddenly placed in this man's body in 1910."

Amaury laughed. "Such a thing is impossible," he said in English.

"So it is," Astrid said in English. She leaned closer. "It is much more than that. This man is blind. He was born blind." She moved closer. "He can describe things that only a person who has had sight could describe."

Amaury smiled. "What things?" he asked in English.

Astrid shrugged her shoulders and moved closer. "Sunsets, sunrises, trees, flowers, horses, guns, uniforms, cannons," she whispered in French.

"That is not unusual," Amaury said in English. "Blind people can repeat what they have been told."

"No," Astrid said in French. "He describes things in a manner only a person who has seen these things can describe." She shrugged her shoulders and smiled slightly. "He described the Consul Seal of Napoleon."

Amaury narrowed his eyes.

She placed her hand on his right arm. "I think, at one time, he could see," she said in English.

Amaury smiled. "How can a blind man, blind from birth, see?" he asked in French.

"Close your eyes," Astrid said in French. "Close your eyes and describe to me how to saddle a horse."

"What type of horse?" Amaury asked laughing in English.

"A soldier's horse," Astrid answered in English. "Please close your eyes and describe to me how to saddle a soldier's horse."

"Can I sip my wine?" Amaury asked laughing. He closed his eyes, reached for his wine glass and sipped. "You get a horse and place the saddle on the horse's back." He opened his eyes and sipped from his wine.

"I am serious," Astrid said in French. "Close your eyes and describe to me how to saddle a horse."

Amaury smiled. "Only for you," he said in French. He closed his eyes. "You shake the blanket and place the blanket on the back of the horse. You place the saddle on the horse's back and move the stirrups, upward, on top of the saddle. You adjust the chest strap and replace the stirrups. You place the bit in the horse's mouth and move the reins to rest on the saddle horn." He opened his eyes and sipped his wine.

"You left out one step," Astrid said smiling in English. "What is the last thing you do before you mount the horse?"

Amaury smiled as he closed his eyes. "You place one of your hands underneath to feel the tension of the strap against the horse." He opened his eyes.

"Exactly," Astrid said. She squeezed his arm. "You said two things that only a person who has saddled a horse many times would know."

"Place the saddle on the horse?" Amaury asked laughing in French.

Astrid squeezed his arm again and Amaury smiled. "No," she answered in French as she removed her hand. "Shake the blanket and check the tension of the strap before you mount." She moved backward. "This man has never saddled a horse. This man has never seen a horse. He has never seen a horse that had a saddle. He can describe in detail how to saddle a horse. The only explanation is that he has saddled a horse, hundreds, perhaps thousands of times."

Amaury looked puzzled. He sipped his wine as Astrid sipped her wine. She was very beautiful but something was wrong. She carefully sipped her wine as she looked to her left and right.

"Why do you keep looking to your right and left?" Amaury asked in English.

"I think I am being followed," Astrid answered in English. "I am afraid they are going to kill me."

"Who?" Amaury asked in French. "The man who claims he is Napoleon? I thought he liked you."

Astrid did not notice Amaury spoke in French, again. "The American Army," she answered in English. "I think they are to kill me because of what I know and what they believe."

"And what is that?" Amaury asked in French.

Astrid looked frightened. "Napoleon Bonaparte has been reincarnated," she answered in English. "If he is ever released or rescued he will kill every one of them. He will raise an Army and conquer the United States."

Amaury laughed. "He will never be released," he said in English. "He will never be rescued because the story is too fantastic to be believed." He waved his right hand in the air. "It is just a story, nothing more, nothing less."

Astrid nodded her head no. She moved closer to Amaury. "There is something else," she whispered in English. "Before I was dismissed, I heard that this story has reached New Orleans. As we speak, an Army is being formed to rescue him."

Amaury moved backward into his chair. "How many?" he asked in English.

She looked to her left and her right and moved closer. "One to five thousand," she whispered in English.

"From where?" Amaury asked in English.

"Farmers, laborers, the unemployed," she answered in English.

"Any professional soldiers?" Amaury asked in English. He looked to his left and his right. "They can not succeed without the assistance of professional soldiers," he whispered.

"None that they are aware of," Astrid answered in English. "The United States Army would not fire on civilians."

Amaury laughed. He stood and he laughed. "You are the one insane if you believe the United States Army would not harm civilians." He hugged Astrid. "I love you for bringing me much humor." He sat in his chair and sipped his wine. "The only thing about this story that is truly insane is why the United States Army has not killed him." He laughed.

Astrid frowned. "Don't you know?" she asked in English.

Amaury smiled. "There are many things I do not know. One of those things is why the Army has not killed him. If they are afraid of him, the easiest solution is to kill him."

"They will not kill him because they need him," Astrid said in English. "The United States thinks there will be a war with Germany and they want to use him."

Amaury was startled!

He reached for his wine glass, missed, and it tipped over. Astrid move quickly to wipe the spill.

What Astrid said was classified information, only known by a few. He had been in many secret meetings where this possibility was discussed. Astrid would not know this information unless she had been included in a very specific, military strategy session.

Only a select few knew Germany had begun to increase their munitions of war. The one country most concerned was France.

As she righted his wine glass and refilled it from her glass, he became concerned, very concerned. Officials of the American Army believed this man was Napoleon and, according to her, they were keeping him to protect America from German aggression.

He needed to dissipate what she said and discount everything she had said.

Amaury smiled. "There is nothing to be concerned of," he said in French. He stood and held his hand outward for Astrid to stand. "This is a story that will be dismissed. Many people will realize it is just a story. Go home and do not worry."

"I know something else," Astrid said in English. "The American Army moved him from the hospital."

"To where?" Amaury asked in English. "Why would they move him?"

"Binghamton," Astrid answered in English. "They are afraid someone will rescue him. They moved him to Binghamton." She leaned closer. "The four professors went with him. Professor Sykes is at Binghamton posing as his servant," she whispered.

"There is no rescue," Amaury said in English. "It is a rumor. It is a story as false as this man's belief he is Napoleon."

He smiled but his smile was false. He was concerned. This whole affair seemed bizarre and out of place. "Do not be concerned. The Americans will not harm a woman, a beautiful, exciting French woman who will one day be his queen. Napoleone Bounaparte would not allow such a thing to occur!"

Astrid took his hand and stood. "Can we meet in three days?" she asked in French.

"Why wait?" Amaury asked in French. "Let us meet in two days."

Astrid laughed and she kissed Amaury on his cheek. "Two days," she said in French as she walked away.

He watched her as she walked away. Astrid was a very beautiful woman but something was wrong, very wrong. He sat at the table thinking.

"Is it possible, Napoleon Bonaparte has been reincarnated?" he said to himself in French. "The story of a rescue is false, why would they move him to Binghamton? How can a blind man know how to saddle a horse?" He sipped his wine, unsure of the answers to his own questions.

"Have you heard?"

Amaury was sitting in a chair at the outside Cherbourg French café. Four days had passed and he was expecting Astrid.

The man who spoke staggered to the table and he sat in the empty chair. "Astrid was found in the river yesterday," he said in French. He lowered his head. "A fisherman found her."

The man raised his head and leaned forward. "She did not have any money and we are asking people to donate for her expenses."

"Where is she?" Amaury asked in French. He was angered.

"City hospital," the man answered in French.

"Have you seen her? Have you been to the city hospital?" Amaury asked in French.

"Yes," the man answered in French. "I was there yesterday."

Amaury stood. He was six foot two inches tall and he weighed one hundred seventy-three pounds. His body was solid muscle and he tensed. "Have you heard of any rumors about that hospital?" he asked in French. His question was abrupt.

"Only Napoleon Bonaparte has been moved by the American Army," the man answered in French. "We were to get him out of the hospital but they moved him."

"Who are we?" Amaury asked surprised.

"Frenchmen," the man answered. "An Army of Frenchmen is being raised in New York to free Napoleon. The Army moved him where we can not find him. The Army heard about our plans and they moved him."

"Will you help?"

"Where did they move him?" Amaury asked.

"I do not know," the man answered. "Some Frenchmen went to the hospital yesterday to look at where he is. We were to plan an escape to free him but he was not there. No one knows where he is."

He leaned closer to Amaury. "You are a military soldier," he whispered. He nodded as he reached into his coat pocket and removed a small food preparation knife. It was not a weapon; the handle was made of wood and the blade was less than four inches in length. The single blade edge was dull.

The man looked to his left and his right as he slowly replaced the knife.

He smiled, nodded and winked. "We are looking for men, good men. Will you help us free Napoleon?"

"How many soldiers are in your *Grande Armée*?" Amaury asked in French, as he sipped the remainder of his wine.

"Forty-two," the man whispered in French. "We all have knives like this one and we planned an assault on the hospital to free him but they moved him."

"Will you help us?"

Amaury knew the man. His name was Andre and was a drunkard. The smell of wine was on his breath and he appeared to stagger when he approached the table. Andre was not a soldier, he was a drunkard! He was five foot three inches in height, sixty-two years of age and Amaury guessed his weight at one hundred eight-six pounds. Andre had no idea what he was doing and who he was up against. Forty-two men were armed with dull food preparation knives and the American soldiers were armed with fixed bayonet rifles and pistols.

He did not like the American soldier but he respected him. Amaury witnessed the American soldier in maneuvers. They were fearless and followed orders exactly. Four American soldiers could easily disperse forty-two untrained men with food preparation knives. The American soldier would not hesitate to open fire. Every man would be killed within thirty seconds of an assault.

Amaury placed his empty wine glass on the table. He removed a fountain pen from his coat pocket and he wrote on the cloth napkin that was placed on the table. He handed the napkin to Andre. "Take care of Astrid," he said in French. "She always liked roses."

He walked from the table. "I will not have you beg for money!" he said angered in French as he walked away. "Send the charges to that address."

As Amaury walked away from the table angered, he reached behind his waist into his coat. Amaury was wearing a short brown leather coat. He reached into the back waist band of his trousers, under his coat, and removed a Colt .45 caliber Army Automatic Model of 1910 pistol from its holster. As he walked, he removed the clip, checked it, and returned the pistol to the holster hidden under his coat.

He turned left, walking briskly in the direction of the city hospital. He walked past several restaurants. As he turned the corner, toward his left, he removed a French soldier's assault knife from its holder hidden under his left leather coat sleeve. The knife handle and blade were made of French carbonized steel. He removed the knife by inserting his hand on the handle, composed of a grip with four circles that protected his knuckles. The blade was nine inches long, double edged; ending in a needle point.

He felt the sharpness of the blade as he walked faster. He replaced the knife to its holder as he began to run.

Chapter Twenty-Two

"Do I get my money?"

The American soldier stood with his hand held outward. "It is just as I told you. The Army is holding a French soldier as a political prisoner."

"What do you know of this Frenchman?" Pierre Serge asked. The American soldier was standing in the office of one of the French delegates to New York City. Several men were standing in the room with them. There were a total of six men, including the American soldier.

"Only what I have heard and seen," the American soldier answered. "I guarded him inside the room twice. They are rotating guards. I was in his room twice and I have guarded the outside door." He turned to one of the five men. "I did as you asked. I read the French words as best as I could and he sent that envelope."

He pointed to the pages that were in the envelope. "That is proof I did as you asked. Do I get my money?"

"Of course," Pierre answered. "He walked to his desk and removed an envelope from one of the drawers. The envelope was thick and he handed it to the soldier. "What have you heard?"

The American soldier opened the envelope. His eyes widened; the stack of American money looked like one hundred dollars. "Most of what I have heard sounds loony. The man claims he is Napoleon. Four professors have been asking him questions. They come and go into his room and sometimes he yells and beats his hands against the door. It sounds like he is yelling for help but I do not understand French."

"Who are these four professors?" one of the five men asked.

"Professors Lytle, Marlow, Angle and Sykes," the American soldier answered. "Professor Sykes is pretending to be his servant."

"Who is the older woman?" the man asked.

“I do not know her name because she whispers,” the American soldier answered. “She speaks a language only he knows.”

“What is this language?” Pierre asked. He continued to look at the pages that were contained in the envelope.

“Some language from Italy,” the American soldier answered. “I do not know the language.” He turned to the man who asked him questions. “Only she knows the language. The four professors do not know it. She speaks to him in the language and he speaks to her. Her son named Victor interprets.”

“Good job!” Pierre said. He handed one of the men the pages from the envelope and he walked to the American soldier. “What is your name and rank?”

“Corporal Mark Benson,” the soldier answered. “I am not a traitor. It just doesn’t seem right to keep that blind man in that room.”

“Curious,” Pierre said. “Why would the Army keep a blind man locked in a room?”

“They believe he is Napoleon,” the corporal answered. “I told you it was loony. The general thinks Napoleon has been reincarnated in the body of a twenty-nine year-old blind man.”

The men in the room laughed.

He paused and took a deep breath. “There are rumors Germany is preparing for war and the general wants to use Napoleon Bonaparte to protect the United States.”

The men in the room stopped laughing.

“Do you believe this man is Napoleon?” one of the men in the room asked.

“No,” the corporal answered. “I have not seen pictures of Napoleon but the man in the locked room wears a robe and he asks like he is a king.”

“We have a continued need of your services,” Pierre said. “I want you to observe and if you see or hear of anything further, report. Of course, we will pay you well.”

The corporal nodded his head. “I just do not think it is right to keep a blind man in a locked room.” He saluted and exited the room.

“When do you want me to kill him?” one of the men asked in French.

Pierre waved his hand. “Not yet,” he answered in French. “We still need him.”

A man was waiting in an adjoining room. He was waiting for the American soldier to leave. A side door opened and he entered the room. In his hand he was holding one of the sheets of paper from the envelope and he carried a framed letter. He saluted.

Three of the men in the room returned the salute.

“Strange,” the man said in French. “The writing on the paper is uneven and several sentences cross but the signature looks the same.” He held upward a framed letter written and signed by Napoleon Bonaparte in the year 1812. “The signatures appear to match.”

Pierre looked puzzled. “Whoever is in that locked room thinks he is Napoleon,” he said in French. He held upward several pages from the envelope. “We have been ordered to setup a base camp in the valley. From there, he will launch an attack on Washington.”

One of the men in the room laughed. “He also wants us to help him escape from his prison,” he said in French.

The men in the room laughed.

Pierre laughed. His laugh was different from the others. His laugh was not one of ridicule but a laugh of circumstance.

“There is some reason the Americans want to keep this man hidden,” Pierre said in French. “Binghamton is an insane asylum. Only insane people are placed there.”

“If the man thinks he is Napoleon, he is insane,” one of the men said in French. He laughed slightly.

“If he is insane, why is he guarded?” one of the men asked in French. “What can a blind man do?”

Pierre held upward the pages from the envelope. "Order French soldiers to prepare to attack Washington," he answered in French.

"What do you want us to do?" one of the men asked.

Pierre walked to his desk and sat down. "This is very curious," he said in French. "I do not believe Napoleon has been reincarnated but the Americans do. The only thing that has any possibility of fact is the second language. Napoleon was born on the island of Corsica and Napoleon spoke French and Corsican. The Corsican language is obscure."

"Are you saying a man insane would not speak two languages?" one of the men asked in French.

"Precisely," Pierre answered in French. "The older woman delivered the envelope." He shrugged his shoulders. "If she is the only person who speaks Corsican, he had to instruct her in Corsican. He had to have the knowledge to communicate and that envelope is proof he can understand French." He paused. "The fact that she delivered the envelope, where the American soldier named Benson instructed him to, is proof he understands two languages."

Pierre stood. "How many men do you have?" he asked in French.

"Thirty-two," one of the men answered in French.

"Can you trust these men?" Pierre asked in French.

"Yes," the man answered in French. "Each man is a retired soldier. They are older but well trained and disciplined. I can get more."

"I want you to locate more men," Pierre said in French. "I prefer French military but we may not have time to recruit French soldiers. I want you to find men, good men."

The man looked puzzled. "Are you instructing me to raise an Army?" he asked in French.

"Raise an Army is not a good sentence," Pierre answered in French. "We may have a situation where a French national is being held illegally by the American military. I do not believe diplomatic channels are an appropriate response at this time. We must be prepared to use force to rescue this man."

The man nodded his head. "Do you believe this man is Napoleon?" the man asked in French.

"This is too curious a situation to ignore," Pierre said in French. "It is possible this man is Napoleon Bonaparte or one of his descendants. For now, we obey the written orders of Napoleon. We will raise an Army and prepare to attack the city of Washington. For now, we will wait and watch for additional orders."

"We need money," one of the men said in French.

"We have money," Pierre said in French. "I can authorize anything you need."

"We will prepare," one of the men said in French. "We should plan an escape."

"Why?" one of the men asked in French. "He is not going anywhere."

"They may move him," Pierre answered in French. "According to the American soldier named Benson, they moved him once. He was at the city hospital and they moved him to a more secure location."

The main door opened and a man walked into the office. He did not knock before entering. "Planning to rescue Napoleon?" he asked laughing in French. He walked to a chair and sat. "You had better hurry because an Army is being raised in New Orleans and New York and they will beat you to it!"

He laughed loudly.

Pierre laughed. "Benoit, what do you know of this curious affair?" he asked in French.

"Nothing," Amaury Benoit answered in French. He paused. "A man was brought to a New York hospital with a fever. When he recovered, he began speaking two languages. One language is French and he said he is Napoleone Bounaparte." He paused. "Four French history professors were brought to the hospital to interview him." He paused. "The story reached New Orleans and many drunkards are claiming Napoleon has been reincarnated and they plan to come to New York and rescue him."

He smiled slightly. "You do believe the story?"

Pierre smiled. "I do not know what to believe. Do you believe it?" he asked in French.

"Yes!" Amaury Benoit answered in French. "Napoleon Bonaparte has been reincarnated. The drunkards in New Orleans are not professional soldiers and they have no chance of rescuing him. The drunkards in New York have no chance to rescue him either, so the French Army must do it for them."

"I have come to offer my services!"

The six men in the room did not laugh. They looked at Amaury curiously. Amaury was a retired soldier and he was not the type to make the joke or to make the fun of others. Amaury was always serious.

Pierre smiled as he walked to his desk and sat in his chair. He leaned forward and folded his arms on his desk. "I do not believe this," he said in French. "Why do you believe this?"

Amaury smiled as he folded his arms on his chest. "One of the four college professors is Abner Sykes!" he answered in French.

Pierre narrowed his eyes.

"Who is this Professor Sykes?" one of the men in the room asked in French. "I have heard the name but I am not familiar with the person."

Pierre frowned slightly. "Abner Sykes is the world's foremost authority on Napoleon and the Napoleonic Wars," he answered in French. "The only person who knows more about Napoleon than Abner Sykes is Napoleon. He is currently teaching at La Sorbonne in Paris."

"No he isn't!" Amaury said in French. "Abner Sykes is currently in New York City."

The men in the room looked at each other curiously and one of the men in the room started to speak when Pierre motioned for him to be quiet.

"Where did you hear this?" Pierre asked in French. He leaned closer toward Amaury.

"When the man recovered from his fever," Amaury answered in French, "an American captain named Lawrence recruited a lady named Astrid Marcelle to interpret for him. He wrote questions in English and she asked the questions in French. He gave her the answers in French and she wrote them in English."

He shrugged his shoulders. "The captain took the questions from a history book and the man answered every question except four correctly. The captain took the questions and the answers to Abner Sykes who was, at that time, a guest lecturer at Harvard University. Professor Sykes confirmed every question was answered correctly."

Pierre smiled and leaned backward in his chair. "Why would that make you think this man is Napoleon?" he asked in French.

Amaury smiled. "The captain did not understand French," he answered in French. "The man who says he is Napoleon told Astrid to locate a French officer and tell the officer his emperor has been taken prisoner before the battle of Brienne and he has been injured. I am the only French officer she knows and she came to me."

Pierre smiled. "Is that all?" he asked in French.

"No," Amaury answered in French. "The captain recruited four French history professors to interrogate him." He leaned forward. "One of those professors is Abner Sykes. Professor Sykes would not leave his teaching position unless he believed the man's story. If Abner Sykes believes the man, so should I."

Pierre leaned backward and thought. "How do you know Professor Sykes came to New York?" he asked in French.

"Because Astrid saw him and she described him," Amaury answered in French. "She was present when Professor Sykes was brought to the hospital. The Americans no longer needed her services and they paid her for her time and her silence."

He leaned forward. "They paid her one hundred American dollars."

Pierre smiled slightly. "Did this young lady tell you anything more about Professor Sykes?" he asked in French. He motioned for the men in the room to be silent.

Amaury Benoit smiled. "She told me Professor Sykes is dressed as his servant," he answered in French. "He has been placed in the room to gather additional information. Professor Sykes would not pose as a servant unless he believed the story."

Pierre looked puzzled. "Interesting," he said in French. "I would like to speak to this young woman and ask her questions. She will have full diplomatic immunity. I would like to speak to her today. Tell her we will double what the Americans paid her."

"Can you bring her here?"

Amaury Benoit stood. "I wish I could but she is dead," he said in French.

Pierre stood abruptly as the men standing in the room moved forward toward Amaury. Their eyes were widely opened.

"Tragic event," Amaury said. "Astrid has been having emotional problems. She was in a state of distress and attempted suicide by throwing herself into the river. She could not swim and the outcome was obvious."

"Curious," Amaury continued. "She looked fine to me the last time I saw her. The only thing she seemed distressed about was her belief the Americans would kill her. She was afraid the Americans would kill her to hide the fact that Napoleon Bonaparte had been reincarnated."

Pierre's eyes widened. "You believe the Americans killed her?" he asked in French. His voice was loud.

"Kill is a very strong word," Amaury answered in French. "Pushing a woman who can not swim into the river is a more likely scene. I have never heard of a woman who would walk more than five American miles to a river to commit suicide. If they did, I do not think they would wear sleeping apparel."

"Yes, I believe they killed her!" he screamed in French. "It is because of what they did to Astrid, I am offering my services."

"The Americans would not kill a woman," one of the men in the room said in French. "Their leaders have morals."

Amaury smiled slightly. "The Americans will steal, lie and cheat. Their leaders are no different than any other country. There are rumors of a revolution in Mexico. Pancho Villa is a puppet of the Americans who has become a hero to his people. On the government's orders the American newspapers are portraying Villa as a villain. Once Villa has served his purpose, the American president Taft will send the American dandy Black Jack Pershing to eliminate Villa."

Pierre frowned. "I have no concern of a peasant uprising in Mexico," he said in French. "This is serious! Do you know Professor Sykes? Can you speak to him? Can you confirm this?"

"Yes," Amaury answered in French. "I was curious after Astrid was found floating in the river. I visited the hospital under the pretext of visiting a patient. I walked about and did not see him. I went two days. On the second day, I located him in an area where visitors meet. It is a grass area with many benches. We met and passed casual conversation. He asked me to join him for lunch."

"I think he wants to discuss some things. I have his address and he has mine. If he does not contact me in three days, I will contact him."

"Which hospital?" one of the men asked in French. He nodded toward the other men in the room. "He is no longer at the city hospital. The Americans moved him and no one knows where he is. Do you know where he is?"

"Binghamton," Amaury answered in French. "He has been moved to Binghamton. Astrid knew where they moved him and I believe that is one of the reasons she was murdered."

The man nodded his head. “He knows as much as we know,” he said in French.

Pierre nodded his head. “On behalf of the French government, I welcome you into our special operation,” he said in French. “I have something to show you that you may have an interest in.” He motioned for Amaury to come to his desk and he handed him several pages from the envelope.

Amaury’s eyes widened as he began to read the pages placed in the envelope.

Chapter Twenty-Three

"He says he is Napoleon Bonaparte."

The woman smiled slightly. She was sitting in the office of Kristof Becker, a representative of the country of Germany, in the German Consulate office in New York.

Lutz Hahn leaned close to her. He offered her a beverage of beer in a glass and she accepted the beer.

"Thank you," she said in German.

Kristof was sitting at his desk and smiled. "Why does the American military believe this man?" he asked in German.

The woman smiled. "He has answered every question correctly," she answered in German. She sipped the beer. "There are four college French professors at the hospital. They ask him questions and he answers the questions in French." She sipped the beer. "There is a young French lady who also asked him questions." She frowned. "I think the lady has been keeping company with him."

"Frau Helga Baur," a man said in German. "My name is Holger Kellner."

The woman turned to look at a man standing in the far corner of the room. "Herr Kellner," she said in German.

Holger smiled. "You stated the Americans moved this man from one room to another. Why?" he asked in German.

"They brought his parents to see him," Helga answered in German. "He was dressed in a woman's robe and they changed his clothes. I was instructed to clean his clothes and prepare his different room." She sipped the beer and turned toward Kristof. "The man does not know his own mother and father."

"What does this man look like?" Kristof asked in German.

"Evil, pure evil," Helga answered in German. She pointed toward her face. "He has no eyes! There is a belief at the hospital the spirit of Napoleon entered this man's body when he was ill with the fever." She sipped her beer and appeared frightened.

"What does this man physically look like?" Kristof asked in German.

"French," Helga answered in German. "He is not too tall, perhaps six American feet in height. Dark skinned; short black hair and cleanly shaven."

Holger moved close to her. "How do you know these things?" he asked in German.

"I hear people talk," Helga answered in German. "They do not know I understand and speak English. I pretend I do not know the language and they freely speak when I am present." She sipped her beer and turned toward Kristof. "The American general named Tate believes Napoleon has been reincarnated. He wants to use this man against us."

Kristof smiled. "Why would America dislike us?" he asked in German.

Helga smiled. "I overheard General Tate speaking," she answered in German. "He thinks Germany will declare war against France."

Holger smiled. "There is no war or talk of war," he said in German. "The general is mistaken."

Kristof stood and bowed toward Mrs. Baur. "Thank you for coming to see us and reporting what you have overheard and seen." He reached into his trouser pocket and removed a fold of money. He counted American currency and handed money to her.

Helga refused the money. "I do not want money," she said in German. "I wanted to report what I have seen and heard." She handed the glass of beer to Kristof and stood. "It is my desire to help Germany in any way possible. If I hear of any information, I will report."

The six men in the room bowed slightly.

"What is the number of his room at the hospital?" one of the men standing asked in German.

Helga walked toward the door as one of the men opened it for her. She stopped near the opened door and turned. "He is no longer at the hospital," she answered in German. "The Americans moved him."

"Why?" Kristof asked in German. He was puzzled.

"The French are going to rescue him," Helga answered in German. "I overheard General Tate speaking that men in the city of New Orleans are planning to rescue him. They moved him."

Holger seemed alarmed and he moved forward. "Do you know where he is?" he yelled in German. His eyes widened and he appeared to be controlling his temper. His first desire was to strike this old woman for withholding information.

"Binghamton Asylum," she answered in German. "The Americans moved him to Binghamton."

"How do you know this?" Holger yelled in German.

"I packed his belongings," she answered in German. "I overheard the soldiers speaking as I packed his belongings. They were taking him to Binghamton. The four professors went with him."

Holger appeared to control his temper. He walked to a small table and he poured beer from a flagon into a glass. "What else do you know?"

Helga smiled. "There will be four soldiers in his room at all times and two soldiers outside his locked door," she answered in German. "There is one sentry at the front gate."

Holger laughed. "Only one sentry at the front gate?"

Helga moved closer toward Holger. "I have visited Binghamton on more than one occasion," she said in German. "The asylum is enclosed with a stone wall eight American feet high. There is only one entrance and the asylum is surrounded by woods. The Susquehanna River Valley is filled with wild animals. No one has ever escaped from Binghamton!"

She walked closer to Holger. "They keep the real bad ones in the basement," she said in German. "They have placed this one on the first floor at the end of a long hallway. The general thinks this is the most secure section of the asylum and the section most easily defended against attack."

Helga walked closer to Holger. She laughed when she saw his right fist clinched as to strike her. "Do you know who Napoleon Bonaparte was?" she asked in German. Her voice was sarcastic and intended to demean Holger.

Holger relaxed his right hand and turned from her. He sipped his beer. "A general," Holger answered in German.

Helga laughed. "Napoleon Bonaparte was the greatest military genius who ever lived," she said laughing. "Every German school boy and German school girl knows who Napoleon was."

Holger shrugged his shoulders.

Helga grabbed Holger by his shoulders and turned him toward her. "Look at me!" she screamed in German.

Holger's eyes widened.

Helga's eyes flared as she looked at Holger. She turned and looked at Kristof. "Napoleon Bonaparte has been reincarnated!" she yelled in German. "When Germany declares war on the United States, they will use Napoleon against us! He will bring the American Army to Europe and crush Germany's Army like a dove's egg."

She was upset as she walked toward the door. "My advice is to you, men," she said sarcastic as she spit on the floor, "is to quit acting like spoiled school children and act like men."

"Napoleon Bonaparte has been reincarnated," she said in German. Her voice was shaking. Helga was not frightened, she was terrified. She was a charwoman at the city hospital; she emptied chamber pots, cleaned the rooms and served meals. She did not come to this office to give information; she came to this office for help.

"My advice to you is to kill him before he kills us!" she began to weep. She turned and walked out the door.

Holger walked to the opened door and closed it. He locked the door. "When do you want me to have her killed?" Holger asked Kristof in German.

"As soon as possible," Kristof answered in German. "She knows too much and she has a large mouth. Helga will not be silent."

He turned to one of the men in the room. "This is the third German national who has come to this office with the same story," he said in German. "The first two were not as outspoken as Helga but all three must be eliminated as quickly as possible."

One of the men stepped forward. "What are your orders?" he asked in German.

"Kill Napoleon Bonaparte," Kristof answered in German. "I will contact the main office and clear our orders first."

Holger smiled. "Do you really believe this story? Do you believe Napoleon has been reincarnated?" he asked in German.

Kristof stood. "No," he answered in German. "The Americans are an arrogant, grandiose society. The Americans are corrupt and the ladies fashions show too much ankle." He stepped from behind his desk. "This man in the locked room is obviously an actor. The Americans are putting on a theatrical performance and the reactions of Helga are the result. You saw her face; she is terrified of this man. They intend to strike fear into the German people that they have the greatest military genius in history at their disposal."

"How many soldiers do we have?" he asked one of the men in the room.

Reinhard Maier stepped forward. He was short and overweight. "Most of our soldiers have been dispersed throughout the United States to gather military information," he answered in German. "We currently have forty-four at our immediate disposal. I can call them in."

"That is not enough soldiers for an assault on Binghamton Asylum," one of the men said in German.

"Forty-four German soldiers is more than enough to kill one man," Reinhard said in German. "I will send twenty to Binghamton Asylum to scout the area. If the area looks clear, they will be given the power to make the decision to mount an assault and kill Napoleon."

Kristof nodded his head in agreement. "Before you send the soldiers to Binghamton to kill this American actor, I want these three people eliminated," he said in German.

Chapter Twenty-Four

"This does not make sense!"

Captain Lawrence was positioned between the chalk board and the chairs occupied by professors Lytle, Angle, Marlow and Sykes. Lieutenant Simpson was not present in the conference room; he left the room to get coffee. He stood and walked toward the board.

"There has to be a reason," Professor Lytle said.

"There are many puzzles to this case but perhaps, this one, is the most intriguing," Professor Angle said.

Professor Marlow nodded his head. "It is as if the world came to a complete end."

Captain Lawrence returned to his chair and sat down. He continued to stare at the board. "Nothing," he muttered.

---> June 1813 Vitoria ---> October 1813 Hanau --->
January 1814 ---> NOTHING <--- May 1821

"An estimated seven years are missing," Professor Lytle said. "He can tell us nothing after January 1814." He turned to Professor Sykes. "What month and year did he say it was?"

"February or March 1814 is his best estimate," Professor Sykes answered. "He is positive of the year but he is uncertain of the month and day."

"When did his fever break and he begin speaking in French?" Professor Sykes asked.

"His fever broke almost three months ago," Professor Marlow answered.

"What is the date of the Battle of Waterloo?" Captain Lawrence asked puzzled as he continued to look at the chalk board.

"June 18, 1815," Professor Lytle answered.

"What month and year did his mother say his great grandfather was born?" Professor Angle asked.

Professor Lytle thumbed through a large stack of papers. “October 18, 1814,” he answered.

“That date is nine months after January 1814 and eight months before June 1815,” Professor Angle said thoughtfully.

Captain Lawrence stared at the chalk board. “There is nothing there,” he whispered. “There is no pattern.”

Professor Angle made a loud grunt noise. His noise broke everyone's concentration and everyone turned to look at him. “There is a pattern but the pattern is more fantastic than the puzzle we are attempting to solve.” He paused briefly. “Plato!”

Professor Marlow looked amused. “What does Plato have to do with Napoleon? If I remember my history, they lived an estimated two thousand one hundred eighty-one years four months nineteen days six hours and fifteen minutes apart.”

Everyone in the room burst into laughter.

Lieutenant Simpson opened the door as everyone burst into laughter. He was carrying two pots of coffee. He did not know why everyone was laughing but he laughed also.

“Hurry up!” Professor Marlow yelled to Lieutenant Simpson. “Professor Angle is going to explain why we have seven missing years!”

“Those seven years are not missing,” Professor Angle said.

Everyone in the room stopped laughing and looked at Professor Angle.

Lieutenant Simpson was puzzled by Professor Angle’s comment. He placed the two pots of coffee on the conference table and he began to pour coffee into several empty cups. “We have seven years that are missing.”

“No,” Professor Angle said. “According to philosopher Plato, we do not have seven years that are missing; we have seven years that are yet to occur.”

Everyone in the room looked perplexed.

“Profound statement,” Professor Marlow said. He stood from his chair and he walked to the table and accepted a cup of coffee from the lieutenant. “I am familiar with the works of Plato but I do not recall anything he wrote that sounds even remotely to your statement." He sipped his coffee as a sly smile came on his face. "I think I know what you think, but you are wrong."

"What is it?" Professor Lytle asked excited. He walked to the table and accepted a cup of coffee.

"This is Angle's show," Professor Marlow answered. "Let him explain." He paused and sipped his coffee. "If he can!"

Professor Angle walked to the chalk board. "Everything we have shows that he can answer any question correctly prior to January 1814. He can not answer any question after January 1814. He claims he knows nothing about the Battle of Waterloo."

"I see," Professor Sykes said. "He knows nothing about the battle so he is pretending the year is 1814. If he attempted to answer our questions, we would know he has been faking."

"No," Professor Angle said. "He can't answer our questions because he knows nothing about the battle."

"You just said what I said," Professor Sykes said.

"No," Professor Angle said. "You said he was pretending the year was 1814. In his mind the year is 1814."

"He has blocked out everything that occurred after 1814?" Professor Sykes asked puzzled.

"No," Professor Angle answered. "He has not blocked out anything."

Lieutenant Simpson was listening to the conversation. "I am confused," he said as he poured himself a cup of coffee.

Professor Marlow laughed. "If you think you are confused now, wait until you hear his explanation."

Everyone in the room laughed.

Professor Angle smiled. "Plato had a theory he used to explain animal instinct. He could not understand how a bird had the knowledge to build a nest if the bird was never taught how to build a nest."

Everyone in the room shrugged their shoulders.

"Other birds taught the bird?" Captain Lawrence asked.

"No," Professor Angle answered. "Plato believed the bird knew how to build a nest because they had built a nest before."

"A female bird only builds one nest," Professor Sykes said.

"No," Professor Angle said. "According to Plato, every female bird knows how to build a nest because they have built hundreds, perhaps thousands of nests before."

Professor Marlow giggled.

"A bird only lives a few years," Professor Sykes said. "In their lifetime, they would only build one perhaps two nests. Birds do not live for fifty years. A female bird would have to live for fifty years to build one hundred nests."

"A single bird does not have to live for fifty years," Professor Angle said. "It is not necessary."

Professor Marlow was sipping his coffee when he stopped. "Now I am confused! I thought you were going to explain Plato's theory of selective breeding." He turned to the others. "Plato in *The Republic* theorized if you selectively bred the best horses and dogs; you would have a generation of the smartest and the most intelligent. The birds who knew how to build a nest survived and the birds who did not know how to build a nest did not survive. I am unfamiliar with what you are saying or the point you are attempting to make." He sat in his chair and appeared very interested.

Professor Angle smiled. "Plato noticed certain physical characteristics were somehow passed from the parent to the offspring. Baby birds aged and looked and acted like their mommy and daddy birds. Pups aged and looked and acted like their mommy and daddy dogs."

"This happened in all animals, fowl, reptiles and insects."

Professor Marlow was *very* interested in what Professor Angle was saying. "What does this have to do with our missing seven years?"

Professor Angle smiled. "Plato theorized in addition to the parents somehow passing physical characteristics of feathers, body shape and color; the parents' collective consciousness was also passed."

"That makes sense," Captain Lawrence said. "Birds pass knowledge of how to build a nest to their offspring."

Professor Marlow was *very, very* interested in what Professor Angle was saying. "You did not answer my question. What does this have to do with our missing seven years?"

"Plato theorized the same thing happened in humans!" Professor Angle answered.

Every person in the room, except Professor Marlow, burst into laughter. He did not laugh because he was intrigued.

The tension is the room was gone. The professors laughed and Captain Lawrence laughed. Lieutenant Simpson giggled as he motioned for everyone to take coffee. Everyone laughed as they stood and walked to the table and accepted coffee.

Professor Angle giggled. He looked at Professor Marlow. Professor Marlow's face was thoughtful. Professor Marlow looked at the chalk board and stood. He walked to the board and stared at it. "Impossible, totally impossible," he muttered.

"What is impossible?" Professor Sykes asked laughing. "I know many women who know how to build a bird's nest because their great grandmother taught them."

Loud laughter erupted in the room.

Professor Marlow turned from the chalk board. "It is impossible but Plato has explained our missing seven years. They are not missing!"

The laughter stopped.

"It is a joke," Professor Sykes said with a smirk. "Professor Angle just broke the tension. It is a joke."

Professor Angle was standing beside Professor Marlow. "Do you want to explain?" he asked Professor Marlow as he smiled and walked to the table to get coffee.

Everyone in the room sat down and looked at Professor Marlow.

"This is going to sound bizarre and impossible," Professor Marlow began. "If we accept philosopher Plato's theory as fact, every person in this room has sights, sounds, feelings, emotions and memories passed from their parents inside them."

Professor Lytle stood and he began to speak when Professor Marlow motioned for him to sit.

Professor Lytle shrugged his shoulders and sat.

"These memories are passed to the offspring at conception." He turned to the chalk board and pointed. "According to the man's history, if we accept it as fact, Napoleon conceived the man's great grandfather in the year 1814."

Lieutenant Simpson was standing by the table. "How does that explain the missing seven years?"

Professor Marlow turned from the chalk board. "They are not missing because they have not yet occurred."

Lieutenant Simpson was to speak again when Captain Lawrence motioned for him to stop. "No more questions! That's an order!"

Lieutenant Simpson nodded his head.

"Fair question and asked at the appropriate time," Professor Marlow said. "In this room, everyone should have the opportunity to ask questions and offer suggestions."

He looked at the captain irritated. "I respectfully request you rescind that order!"

The professors all agreed and nodded their heads.

"Forget that order," Captain Lawrence said.

"If we accept Plato's theory as fact," Professor Marlow continued, "only those sights, sounds, memories, feelings and emotions, prior to conception, are passed. Napoleon passed the combined knowledge from his childhood and adulthood, up to the year 1814, to his son. Who in turn, passed it to his son? Who in turn, passed it to the man in the locked room?"

He paused and took a deep breath. "The seven years we think are lost are yet to occur."

The professors began to whisper to each other.

"That would explain why he knows nothing about Waterloo and how Napoleon died," Professor Marlow added. "In 1814,

Waterloo has not yet occurred and he has not been imprisoned and died."

"How did Napoleon die?" Captain Lawrence asked.

"We really do not know," Professor Lytle answered. "There is a belief he had some type of stomach illness such as an ulcer or he was poisoned."

"How could he answer a question we don't know?" Lieutenant Simpson asked.

Everyone in the room laughed.

"If we accept this as fact," Professor Sykes said. "If the parent can pass memories in addition to physical traits to their offspring, what activated these memories?"

"Yes?" Captain Lawrence asked. "What activated them?"

Professor Marlow shrugged his shoulders. "I have no idea. The only thing that has happened is the high fever."

"A high fever could not activate another person's consciousness," Professor Sykes said. "Many people have high fevers. They do not last for several weeks but many people have high fevers."

"I agree and I have no solutions," Professor Marlow said. He looked to Professor Angle. "Any ideas?"

"None," Professor Angle answered. "The theory explains the man's partial knowledge and the missing seven years but how his great-great grandfather's consciousness was activated, I do not know."

"What you two are proposing is some sort of reincarnation," Professor Sykes said. "The correct term is metempsychosis; the passing of the soul from one body to another. The man did not die. There is no way the soul of Napoleon could have been reincarnated in a living body."

"Interesting theory but impossible to believe," Professor Lytle said. "I do not believe it. Gregor Mendel proved mathematically physical traits are carried from generation to generation. How did Plato theorized these physical traits and memories were transferred?"

"Plato's pupil Aristotle theorized the male passed his collective consciousness in the sperm at conception," Professor Angle answered. "The female passed her collective consciousness during development."

"Interesting theory," Professor Sykes said. "There is no scientific proof that physical traits are contained in the body and there is no scientific proof these physical characteristics could be contained in male sperm and passed to the offspring. If science could prove such a thing, which is impossible, science could not prove memories were also contained in the body and transferred at conception and gestation."

"Plato's theory is without prior basis and current scientific confirmation. He proposes the body is filled with remnants of past lives and these current and past remnants were purged by a high fever, leaving only those of Napoleon Bonaparte."

"I cannot accept this theory because if I do accept it, it means I have to accept the fact that the man in the locked room IS Napoleone Bounaparte; the greatest military genius who ever lived!"

Captain Lawrence was sitting and he stood. "What are you talking about? This man is insane."

"We have been unable, so far, to prove that," Professor Lytle answered.

"What are you saying?" Captain Lawrence asked. His eyes narrowed and he appeared angry.

"It is possible, the man in the locked room IS Napoleone Bounaparte," Professor Sykes said. "If he is, he is the only hope we have of defeating Germany."

Captain Lawrence laughed. "Napoleon was defeated at Waterloo! He was no military genius!"

"Napoleon lost the confidence of his country," Professor Sykes said. "He wanted to continue on but others did not. The entire world was against him."

"He did what he could with what he had," Professor Marlow said.

"He would not make these mistakes again," Professor Lytle said. "Napoleon was not a six star general; he was a one thousand star general."

Captain Lawrence laughed as a knock was heard on the closed door. Lieutenant Simpson opened the door to see a soldier standing outside. The soldier saluted and presented a letter for Captain Lawrence.

Captain Lawrence took the letter. He opened and read it. He looked curiously at the soldier standing at the door. The soldier nodded his head and stepped backward.

"I must leave," Captain Lawrence said. "I will be back and I want to continue this conversation."

Captain Lawrence followed the soldier. They walked out of the front door of the asylum to see a parked military vehicle. The car was a closed Cadillac. It was night time. Captain Lawrence had not noticed the time. Professor Sykes drugged his wine at 10:00 P.M. and joined the group. He looked upward and estimated the time at 1:00 A.M. The soldier opened the rear door where General Tate was sitting. He motioned for Captain Lawrence to enter the car.

Captain Lawrence saluted and sat inside but the driver did not start the engine.

General Tate smiled slightly.

"We have heard no news from the French in New Orleans for several days," the general said. "It appears the rumor of a rescue was just that, a rumor."

"The French in New Orleans have abandoned their idea of a rescue?" Captain Lawrence asked excited.

"It appears so," General Tate answered. "However, there is a rumor this story has reached Germany."

Captain Lawrence frowned. "Is everyone insane?"

"Sanity is no longer an issue," General Tate answered. "The French do not have the stomach for a rescue but the Germans do."

"What do we do?" Captain Lawrence asked.

"It has already been done," General Tate answered. He reached downward to an electric lamp. The lamp was tubular in shape and made by Eveready. A small bulb was placed on the end and when a switch was moved, a light came from the end. He moved the switch and held upward a map of the asylum. On the map were many Xs. The map was of different floors. The Xs marked rooms.

"In these rooms we have placed soldiers," the general said. "Each room has five soldiers."

"When?" Captain Lawrence asked surprised. "I have seen no soldiers!"

"They arrived today," General Tate answered. "They were disguised as patients."

Captain Lawrence looked at the map. "How many soldiers?"

"Forty," General Tate answered. "They are to stay hidden, in case." He frowned. "No one is to know. You are to tell no one not even Lieutenant Simpson."

"I do not like this," Captain Lawrence said.

"What you like and what you dislike is not an issue," General Tate said. "These men have their orders and you have yours."

"What are their orders?" Captain Lawrence asked.

The general leaned closer. "If anything happens, their orders are to surround and protect the man in the locked room," he answered. "Nothing, nothing is to happen to him."

"The French?" Captain Lawrence asked.

"The French are a non-issue," General Tate answered. He laughed. "This rumor of the French rescue was just a rumor. There is no rescue. We can easily handle French civilians. We have no concern with the French. Our concern is with the Germans." He leaned backward in the seat. "They may want him but they are not going to get him."

Captain Lawrence looked puzzled. "How did the Germans know?"

General Tate shrugged his shoulders. “I do not know,” he answered. “We moved him because of talk at the city hospital. No one knows where he is but someone may have leaked information to the German Embassy. There has been a lot of activity at the German Embassy the last few days.”

“Any activity at the French Embassy?” Captain Lawrence asked.

“No more than usual,” General Tate answered. He leaned forward. “Everything will remain the same for a few weeks. There are four soldiers in his room, two outside his door and one sentry positioned at the front gate. They will be relieved as usual.” He leaned backward. “If nothing has happened in a few weeks, we will remove the additional hidden soldiers.”

Captain Lawrence nodded. “The professors were discussing he may really be Napoleon.”

General Tate laughed. “They can believe what they want. I think he is a German spy.”

“It is a strange case,” Captain Lawrence said. “You have read my reports?”

“Yes,” General Tate answered. “It is a strange case, but nothing to be alarmed about.” He smiled. “In a few weeks we will move him and everything will be over.”

He leaned toward Captain Lawrence. “You and Lieutenant Simpson have done an excellent job. Your reports are very concise.” He narrowed his eyes. “They are very concise!”

“Do you really think Germany wants him?” Captain Lawrence asked.

“No,” General Tate answered. “It is just a curious case. I think there is curiosity, nothing more.”

Captain Lawrence saluted as he exited the car. General Tate returned the salute as the soldier entered the car and closed the door.

The driver drove the car to the front entrance and turned right, away from the city. As the car was driven past the far stone wall, the man lying at the edge of the forest stood.

The man was standing in the dark, near the forest. He was wearing black trousers, a black shirt and a black hood. The black hood covered his head and his chin, leaving a section for his neck and his eyes. He replaced the field glasses in its case and turned.

Behind him were standing eight to ten dark shadows.

The man removed his hood. When he removed his hood, his face and hair could be seen. The man was young, under the age of thirty. "You were ordered to wait at the road," the man said in German.

The eight to ten shadows appeared to expand. The eight to ten shadows gradually became twenty.

"Where is Eric?" the man yelled in German. "He had explicit orders to wait at the road!" He shook his right hand at the shadows. "It is I who will give the command to attack!"

"I do not understand German," one of the shadows said in French.

The man's eyes widened as a hand covered his mouth from behind and a knife's blade was pulled across his throat.

The man fell to the ground.

The forest was suddenly alive as numerous dark shadows stepped forward. There appeared to be more than forty French soldiers hidden within the darkness.

Amaury Benoit stepped forward from the large group of shadows and he looked at the dead German soldier. "Place him with the others," he said in French.

Chapter Twenty-Five

Knock! Knock!

"Enter," a man's voice said in German.

The interior door to the German Consulate's office opened slowly as a short man entered the room. He closed the door slowly and locked it. Shrugging his shoulders, he walked to a chair and sat.

There were eight men standing in the room. One of the men prepared a drink and offered it to the man who entered. The man waved the drink away.

"The two men are late by eight hours," the man said in German.

Kristof Becker was sitting in the chair at his desk. He shook his head. "These men were trained professionals," he said in German.

"Apparently not trained well enough!" one of the men said in German.

The man who entered the room was sitting and he stood. "There is no better soldier than the German soldier!" he said angered in German.

One of the men standing stepped forward. "No one doubts their loyalty," he said in German. "We have doubts of their skills in battle."

The man who entered the room was angered. "These soldiers are the best Germany has!" he screamed in German. "They were trained as young boys and their skills are beyond belief."

"Then Germany needs to produce better soldiers!" the man yelled in German. "Their orders were simple, kill Napoleon Bonaparte!"

"Enough!" Kristof yelled in German. He slapped his hands on top of the desk. "The Americans did not do this!"

"They had to!" one of the men yelled in German.

"Seven American soldiers could not kill forty-two trained German soldiers!" one of the men yelled in German.

"Forty-four," Kristof said in German.

The man who entered the room was angered. "Twenty-four hours!" he yelled in German. "We give those soldiers twenty-four hours to report!"

Kristof frowned. "I appreciate your loyalty to your men," he said in German. "Eight hours, ten hours, twelve hours; it makes no difference. They are not coming back."

One of the men standing approached the desk. "My original plan was an assault on Binghamton Asylum," he said in German. He turned to the eight men. "It would have been simple. Forty-four German soldiers attack the asylum and kill everyone!"

One of the men laughed. "We discussed your plan and dismissed it. Who would the Americans blame the carnage on?" he asked in German.

"The patients," the man answered in German. He turned toward Kristof who was sitting at his desk. "My plan was to leave many American manufactured rifles and pistols in the hands of the patients."

Kristof smiled. "And where did these patients get these American weapons?" he asked in German.

"That question is for the Americans to answer," he answered in German.

Eight men in the room laughed. One of the men did not laugh. "This is not a humorous situation," Holger Kellner said in German. "We send forty-four trained German soldiers to kill one man and they themselves are killed."

"There is no evidence these soldiers were killed," the man who entered the room said in German.

"They were killed," Kristof said in German. "The question is who killed them?"

"The forest is clear," one of the men said in German. "There is no one in the forest. They had to have been killed when they assaulted the asylum."

"There was no assault," one of the men said in German. "The stone wall is eight feet tall. It would take a ladder to scale that wall. There is only one entrance. This entrance is at the front and there is only one soldier. One American soldier did not defeat forty-four of Germany's elite."

"What are our orders?" one of the men asked in German.

"The same," Kristof answered in German. "Attack Binghamton Asylum and kill Napoleon Bonaparte."

"How many soldiers do we have left?" one of the men asked in German.

"One hundred forty," the man who walked into the room answered in German. "I can order my soldiers to attack at dawn. There is an old road to the south of the asylum. The soldiers will be transported in trucks to this road. At dawn, they will kill every person in the asylum." He paused. "The first person they will kill is the man who says he is Napoleon Bonaparte."

"How will they traverse the eight foot stone wall," one of the men asked in German.

"Ladders," the man who entered the room answered in German. "We will bring ladders to traverse the south stone wall."

"Good plan," Kristof said in German. He stood. "Tomorrow we will enjoy a German victory; the first of many!"

One of the men prepared beverages. He gave to each man a glass.

"To Germany, the rulers of the known world!" Holger said in German.

The men nodded and drank from their glasses.

"Do you believe Napoleon has been reincarnated?" one of the men asked in German.

"No," Kristof answered in German. "It is a falsehood the Americans will use in war. It is their belief the idea the greatest military genius in history is commanding the Americans will strike fear in the hearts of German soldiers." He smiled. "Tomorrow morning, we will destroy that falsehood by killing the American actor named Napoleon Bonaparte."

The six trucks moved slowly on the old road. It was accessible from a road within the edge of the river valley. Four of the trucks contained twenty-five German soldiers. Two trucks contained twenty soldiers each with ladders. Each soldier was armed with an American manufactured rifle and an American manufactured side arm. The German soldiers wore black trousers with a black shirt. A hood of black covered their head, descending to their chin, with an open section for their neck and eyes.

The road was passable for a period of three American miles when the road narrowed into a path. The trucks could not pass and the soldiers were ordered from the trucks. They proceeded west on the path for a distance of ten American miles. As they approached the asylum, the lead soldier stopped the long column.

"What is wrong?" the commander asked in German.

"Horses, I hear the sound of horses," the lead soldier answered in German.

The commander listened but he did not hear a noise. "I hear nothing," he said in German.

"I heard the sound of horses," the lead soldier said in German. "It sounded like many horses."

"There is no one in this forest," the commander said in German. "The forest is clear. There is no one here."

"I heard the sound of horses," the lead soldier said in German. He pointed forward. "It sounded like many horses were moving from the south of the forest to the north toward the asylum."

"There is nothing," the commander said laughing in German. "Forward!" he yelled as he motioned for the long column to move forward.

The column followed the path to the south section of the asylum. They were positioned an estimated five hundred American yards from the south wall when the commander ordered the soldiers to form a single line and turn north. Many soldiers held ladders and awaited further orders.

The soldiers stood silently for more than one hour as the commander watched the eastern horizon. The sun began to break in the east and the night sky slowly became light. As the sun was rising, the commander ordered the soldiers to advance north.

The soldiers moved in formation forward, side by side. The woods were not thick and the underbrush was thinned. They moved slowly, without caution.

The eastern sky was beginning to lighten but the northern sky and forest was still in the shadows of night. As the soldiers moved forward, the forest suddenly came to life!

The ground in front of them suddenly rose. As far as the German soldiers could see, a solid wall of underbrush had risen upward in the darkness from the forest floor. The raised underbrush was of a height of six feet and was composed of French soldiers. There were more than one thousand.

The knives were thrown with such skill and precision; the German soldiers did not see them. The soldiers were struck in their throat and their chest. One hundred forty German soldiers fell silently to the forest ground.

Amaury Benoit moved from the long column of French soldiers to the fallen line of German soldiers. He was dressed in a grayish shirt and trousers. Brush, in varying stages of decay, covered his head, arms, chest and legs. Amaury wore a side arm. The gun and holster was covered with water soaked dirt to conceal the silver color.

He walked along the line of dead soldiers, surveying. One soldier was still alive and moved slightly. Amaury bent downward toward the soldier and he removed the man's hood. The man was not a man, he was a boy!

The boy appeared to be under the age of eighteen. The boy was gasping for breath from the knife stuck in his throat. A second knife was stuck in his chest. The boy's shirt was too large for him. The knife was thrown perfectly, striking where the heart should have been. Because the shirt was too large, the knife struck below the heart.

Amaury removed the knife from the boy's throat and plunged it into his heart. The boy's eyes widened and closed.

He removed the boy's pistol from its holder. The pistol was a Colt .38 revolver. The silver plating reflected in the morning light as Amaury sniffed the barrel; the pistol had never been fired. The boy's rifle only contained one round. He checked the boy's belt; there were ten rifle cartridges in a single pouch. The boy carried six rounds in the pistol, one in the rifle and ten rifle rounds in the pouch on the belt.

Amaury looked at the boy with sadness. The boy's face was not the face of a young boy. The face he was looking at was a killer, an inefficient killer, but a killer. He dropped the pistol and threw the boy's hood to the ground and continued walking along the line of dead soldiers. He stopped and removed various hoods. Each hood covered the face of a young German boy. He continued to walk and stopped at the commander. The commander was wearing a very ornate uniform; multiple ribbons and brass medals were attached to a black shirt.

He removed the man's hood to see the face of an old man. The man appeared to be the age of sixty plus. This man was short and overweight. One knife was stuck in the man's throat and two knives were stuck in the man's heart. The two knives stuck in his heart were so close together; it appeared they were thrown as one not two.

Amaury reached downward and removed the man's pistol from its holster. The pistol was a Colt .38 caliber revolver. The pistol was a gold color and reflected in the morning sun as he held it upward. The pistol looked like it had been plated with gold. He sniffed the barrel of the pistol; it had never been fired.

He dropped the pistol and hood in disgust.

"This is the German *Grande Armée*," he said in French. "Young boys blindly following the delusions of old men. Place them with the others!"

The clock hands had long moved past 12:00 noon. The men in the office of the German Consulate were prepared to celebrate their victory. Many bottles of champagne were placed in iced containers. The ice melted in the containers and turned into water.

"How is this possible?" one of the men asked in German. "How could seven American soldiers defeat Germany's best?"

"Seven soldiers could not defeat these soldiers," one of the men said in German.

"That is the only explanation," one of the men said in German. "There are only seven American soldiers guarding Napoleon." He paused. "Do you think Napoleon caused our defeat?"

"No," one of the men answered in German. "This man who claims he is Napoleon only has seven soldiers."

"What are we going to do?" one of the men asked in German. "These soldiers were the future of Germany. After their victory, they were to be promoted as generals."

Kristof Becker was sitting at his desk. His face was solemn as he leaned forward and placed his hands over his face. "Nothing, we do nothing," Kristof answered in German.

"We are going to lose this war!" Holger Kellner said in German. "I believe Napoleon trained those seven soldiers." He was standing and he sat in a chair. As quickly as he sat, he stood. Holger was angered as he walked to the table where the bottles of champagne had been placed.

The table top held champagne bottles, in ice containers, and tall fluted glasses. Sweeping his arm across the top, the bottles, containers and glasses were pushed to the floor. Two bottles of champagne broke when they struck the wooden floor as several bounced off of the floor and rolled to the edge of the wall, making a clank-type noise.

The men in the room did not flinch when the glasses shattered. They remained in their positions.

Holger picked up one of the bottles of champagne that did not break and he hurled it toward the wall. The bottle struck the wall and shattered with a loud pop sound.

He turned to look at the men in the room. Their faces showed fear, great fear.

"Napoleon Bonaparte has been reincarnated and the Americans have him!" he screamed in German. His voice was shaking. Holger was frightened.

He sat in a chair and shook his head in disbelief. "If Napoleon Bonaparte can defeat one hundred eighty-four elite German soldiers with seven soldiers; what could he do with one million?"

"We are going to lose this war!" he said in a frightened voice as he covered his face with his hands.

Chapter Twenty-Six

"There is no other explanation."

Professor Marlow sat beside Professor Angle on a bench in the south west section of the asylum. This section was reserved for guests visiting patients. The area was composed of a walking path with a series of wooden benches arranged for private conversation. The wood benches were placed at a distance from each other to prevent normal conversation from being overheard. The two professors met in this area frequently to discuss the mystery they could not solve. They spoke to each other in French.

"Plato's theory explains everything," Professor Marlow continued. "The only person who could answer those questions is Napoleone Bounaparte."

The tobacco in Professor Angle's pipe was never lit. He packed his pipe with tobacco as they sat together on the bench. The conversation was so astounding, he never lit his pipe. He puffed on it, not noticing it was not lit.

"I am still not convinced," Professor Angle said. "We are missing something. There has got to be a rational explanation."

"What could be more rational than God, in all of his glory, passing memories, emotions and thoughts from both parents to their offspring?" Professor Marlow asked.

"Reincarnation?" Professor Angle asked. "I can not accept reincarnation as rational."

"This is not reincarnation," Professor Marlow said. "It is something more basic and rational."

"Duplication is the same thing as reincarnation," Professor Angle said.

Professor Marlow took a deep breath. "Look at those pigeons." Professor Angle looked toward the path. Pigeons were walking on the path a short distance from where they sat. As they watched, a visitor sitting on another bench threw bread crumbs onto the grass. The pigeons moved quickly toward the food and pecked at the food.

"Simple observation shows us that each pigeon has differences in the color of their feathers," he continued. "There are seven pigeons waiting for food. There are not two pigeons that look alike. They all have slight differences. They all have exact similarities, they are all pigeons. Each pigeon has two wings, two legs, one head and two eyes."

"If we could observe the two parents, we would observe color similarities in the parent's feathers and color similarities in the offspring's feathers. We would also observe two wings, two legs, one head and two eyes."

He turned toward Professor Angle. "Those pigeons are not reincarnations; they are duplicates of the parents. Because there are two parents, not one, the physical characteristics are mixed."

"Plato's theory is the parents pass their physical traits to their offspring. This we can easily observe. He also theorized memories are passed. In essence, the parents duplicated themselves."

Professor Angle giggled. He noticed his pipe was not lit and he lit it with a match. He took several puffs and laughed. "Rober does not physically look like Napoleone."

"Exactly," Professor Marlow said. "Those pigeons do not physically look like their great grandparents either. Many generations have been mixed and the results can be seen on the outside. We can only speculate what is on the inside."

"If we accept this as fact," Professor Angle said thoughtfully, "Rober is not Rober. He is Napoleone Bounaparte. But how can we prove it?"

Professor Marlow leaned close to Professor Angle. He looked upward to see if anyone was close. "We already have."

Professor Angle's eyes widened.

"We have been unable to prove the man insane," Professor Marlow said. "If the man is not insane; the man must be sane. If we can not prove the man is not Napoleone Bounaparte; the man must be Napoleone Bounaparte."

Professor Angle smiled. "We have not solved the mystery because there is no mystery. The man in the locked room is exactly who he says he is… Napoleone Bounaparte."

"Yes," Professor Marlow said. He leaned backward into the bench and removed a cigar from his coat pocket. He lit the cigar with a match. "I have imagined what Napoleone could teach us… if he was free!"

Professor Angle frowned. "Free? Do you know what he would do if he was free? He would raise an Army and conquer the United States. Napoleone Bounaparte was a brilliant soldier and tactician. He brought chaos to Europe. He would do the same to America."

"He also brought order," Professor Marlow said. "Out of chaos came order. The Napoleonic law is still in effect. While Napoleone did much damage, he also did much good."

"Rebuild America?" Professor Angle asked.

"Everything could use a little polishing," Professor Marlow answered. "If he was free, he would build a new society and we could be a major part of that society."

Professor Angle stood. "Those are his words, not yours. He told me the same thing. What did he promise you if you help him to escape?"

Professor Marlow smiled. "The title of duke," he answered.

Professor Angle smiled. "He promised me the same title. Do you think he promised Professor Sykes and Professor Lytle the same title?"

"The world is a big place," Professor Marlow answered. "There is plenty of room for three new dukes."

"Three?" Professor Angle asked surprised. "Who is out?"

"Professor Lytle," Professor Marlow answered. "He has been approached but exhibited no interest. Nathan Lytle is a fool! He has the opportunity to follow the most famous general in history. We will live in splendor while he will live in squalor."

"How do we rescue him?" Professor Angle asked. "I am too old to fire a gun and I do not know how."

Professor Marlow smiled slightly. He removed the cigar from his mouth and carefully extinguished the lit end on the wood bench. He removed another cigar from his coat pocket and lit it with a match. "When you need a professional to do a job, you locate a professional."

He puffed several times on the cigar and blew a large whiff of smoke into the air. "Professor Sykes knows a retired French officer. They met accidentally at this asylum a few days ago and Professor Sykes suggested lunch. He thinks he can interest this French officer in a military action."

Professor Angle sat down on the bench. Both men leaned backward on the bench and laughed.

Chapter Twenty-Seven

"Do you know how insane this sounds?"

"Yes," Professor Sykes answered. He leaned closer to Amaury Benoit. "If we are incorrect, no one is harmed. If we are correct, this man could save France."

Amaury looked thoughtful.

The two men were sitting in a French restaurant in New York City speaking in French. Amaury was associated with the French delegation to the United States. He was a retired officer in the French Army and served as a consultant to the French ambassador. The two men met more than six months ago. Amaury was a scholar of Napoleon Bonaparte and they met when he attended a dinner hosted by Harvard University. Professor Sykes was a guest speaker. He lectured on Napoleonic Code.

"How is this possible?" Amaury asked.

"Science is just discovering what nature has already known," Professor Sykes answered. "Louis Pasteur discovered a small organism in cow's milk. This organism can cause illness. A simple heat treatment destroys the organism which makes the milk harmless."

Professor Sykes leaned backwards in his chair. "He also discovered a treatment for anthrax. I am not familiar with the treatment but it prevents cows from contracting the illness."

"Memories?" Amaury asked.

"You can test it yourself," Professor Sykes said.

"How?" Amaury asked. He was not interested in what Professor Sykes had been saying until now. "How can I test it?"

"Close your eyes and think of someone you know who is deceased," Professor Sykes answered. "This person should be a blood relative."

"My mother is deceased," Amaury said. "I can think of her." He closed his eyes and he began to think. The expression on his face changed several times. His face showed the expressions of happiness and sadness. His eyes remained closed for several minutes then he opened his eyes. "What was I supposed to see?"

"What did you see?" Professor Sykes asked. "What did you hear?"

"My mother's face," Amaury answered. "I remembered a time when I was a young boy. We were dining and my mother was speaking."

"How old were you in your memory?" Professor Sykes asked.

"I was the age of ten," Amaury answered.

"How old are you now?" Professor Sykes asked.

"Sixty-two," Amaury answered.

Professor Sykes smiled. "Plato theorized memories are somehow recorded in the body and passed from the parent to the offspring. This memory of your mother was somehow recorded somewhere in your body fifty-two years ago. It is still there. Just as this one memory is recorded, so are others."

"We believe, for whatever reason, the thoughts, emotions and memories of Napoleone Bounaparte have been passed to this man and somehow activated. In your memory, you witnessed your mother. You could see her face and you could hear her voice. The memories of that ten year-old boy are still there."

"Do you have children?" Professor Sykes added.

"One son," Amaury answered proudly. "He is in the French Army. Alexis is a French Legionnaire."

Professor Sykes smiled. "Does he look like you?"

"Yes," Amaury answered proudly. "He looks just like me! He is tall and strong."

"Plato theorized you somehow passed the memories of that ten year-old boy to your son at conception. It is possible your son could access your memory."

Amaury shrugged his shoulders. "If this man is a blood relation of Napoleon, how can he save France?"

Professor Sykes leaned toward Amaury. "There are rumors of Germany producing munitions. Some people believe Germany is making preparations to begin a war. In this war, they would seek to conquer Europe. The Germans and the French are not friends. It is only reasonable to conclude Germany would declare war on France."

"What could a blind man do?" Amaury asked.

"Napoleone Bounaparte is the greatest military genius who ever lived," Professor Sykes answered. "This man can not see, but he can think. He has an unbelievable memory; his intelligence can not be measured. This man has never physically seen Binghamton Asylum but he can repeat in detail what he has been told. If he could be told of the enemies movements, he could plot a defense or an offense."

Amaury laughed. "I do not know one soldier who would follow a blind man into battle."

Professor Sykes laughed. "How many men can you guess are in the French armies?"

Amaury laughed. "Two hundred thousand is a guess. It is not accurate but it is a guess. I could not find one man out of those two hundred thousand who would follow a blind man into battle."

Professor Sykes laughed. He reached for his wine glass and sipped from it. He placed his wine glass on the table and he took a small bite of a crape. As he was wiping his mouth with the napkin he grinned slightly. "Do you think you could find one man out of those two hundred thousand soldiers who would follow Napoleone Bounaparte into battle…to defend their country?"

Amaury stopped laughing. "I could find more than one, I could find two hundred thousand."

Professor Sykes nodded his head. "Out of those two hundred thousand soldiers do you think you could find one or two to rescue Napoleone Bounaparte from the Americans?"

Amaury was not laughing. He looked very serious. "I could find more than one or two, I could find two hundred thousand."

"We only need one or two," Professor Sykes said.

Amaury smiled slightly. "Why is the American Army interested in this man? Why is he guarded?"

"They are afraid someone will rescue him," Professor Sykes answered. "If there is war with Germany, they will use his military genius to protect the United States."

"Why the urgency?" Amaury asked. He leaned backward in his chair and sipped from his wine glass. "He is not going anywhere."

"They moved him once," Professor Sykes answered. "There were no soldiers at the city hospital. Something frightened the captain and he was moved. Where he is currently held there are soldiers. We are afraid they will move him again and we will not know where he is imprisoned. We do not know when they will move him. Time is of the essence."

"How many are you?" Amaury asked.

"Three," Professor Sykes answered. "Professors Marlow, Angle and myself."

"You said there were four of you, why is there only three?" Amaury asked.

Professor Sykes shrugged his shoulders. "Professor Lytle is not convinced. We have made some suggestions but he has indicated no interest. We have not told him anything."

"If you can give me the plans to the asylum and information on the soldiers who guard him, I will seriously consider the mission," Amaury said.

Professor Sykes was carrying a cloth bag when he entered the restaurant. The bag was a white covering from a bed pillow in his room. He reached to the cloth bag placed on the floor and he held it upward. "Floor plans, guard change schedules and placements."

He lowered the cloth bag to the floor of the restaurant. "I am your inside person. I can drug the four soldiers inside the room and open the door from the inside. There is one sentry at the front entrance and three to four soldiers outside the room. I can also drug those soldiers outside the room."

"We count a total of one soldier who will need to be dealt with."

"Do you have access to an automobile?" Amaury asked.

"That may frighten him," Professor Sykes answered. "It will take time to acclimate him to automobiles. Our suggestion is a horse drawn wagon. There are many in the city and the country. The best method of escaping from a city filled with horse drawn wagons is in a horse drawn wagon."

"From your description, Napoleone Bounaparte is a very visible person. He will be noticed," Amaury said.

"The best method of hiding a general surrounded by the enemy's Army is if the general is dressed as one of the enemy's soldiers," Professor Sykes said. "We will both change our clothing before we leave. We will appear as two American soldiers."

Amaury smiled. "Where do we take him?"

"French New Orleans," Professor Sykes answered.

Amaury frowned. "Why New Orleans? It makes more sense to take him to the harbor and then board a ship to France."

Professor Sykes smiled. "The first place they will look is the harbor. The best method of hiding a Frenchman is in a city filled with Frenchmen."

Amaury smiled and he leaned backward in his chair. "I am impressed! It is a brilliant plan." He sipped from his wine glass. "You three men thought of this plan? You three should be generals not college professors."

"We did not plan anything," Professor Sykes answered, as he sipped from his wine glass. "It is his plan!"

Chapter Twenty-Eight

"Everything is ready," Professor Angle said in French.

The four guards were listening to the conversation and observing. They did not speak or understand French and the conversation appeared as one of hundreds.

"How many soldiers?" the man asked in French. He sat at the end of the long table. He was dressed in a very ornate robe. The robe was made of velvet, blue in color, and extended to the floor.

He reached for his glass of wine but his hand missed the glass and it tipped over. The glass was not full and the spill was small.

Professor Sykes moved quickly to clean the spill. He wiped the spill with a cloth.

"Wine?" he asked in French.

The man nodded his head no.

Professor Sykes righted the glass and walked to the food preparation area. He placed the wine soaked cloth in a basin.

Professor Angle waited for Professor Sykes to clean the wine spill and answered his question. "I am not sure," he answered in French. "Fifty to sixty."

The man nodded his head and raised his hand. Professor Sykes approached the table and he bowed. He presented an envelope to Professor Angle.

"What is this?" Professor Angle asked in French. The envelope he was given was sealed. It was smaller than a post and there was no writing on the outside.

"A final communiqué," the man answered in French. "It is to be presented to the commander."

Professor Angle nodded his head. "I will deliver it tonight," he said in French. "The rescue will take place in three days. It will begin at night after eleven o'clock."

The man nodded his head and stood. "I am well pleased," he said in French. "Deliver the communiqué tonight. I have faith in my soldiers. They will carry out my orders." He presented his right hand.

Professor Angle stood and he bowed. He approached him, kneeled, and kissed his right hand.

He stood and began to walk toward the door. The man listened carefully to the sound of his steps. As he approached the door, the man smiled. "Before you leave me," he said in French.

Professor Angle stopped walking and turned.

"I am well pleased by your loyalty and devotion," the man said in French. "You will be well rewarded. I request you and the man named Marlow to join my soldiers on the other side of the south stone wall before the mission begins. It is my wish you wait for them and provide assistance if needed."

Professor Angle bowed. "The mission is to begin after eleven o'clock at night," he said in French. "What time do you request we arrive?"

The man smiled. "French soldiers have no concept of time," he answered in French. "They may arrive early."

"Before nine of the clock."

Professor Angle bowed. "Before nine o'clock," he said in French. He turned and nodded toward the soldier near the door. The soldier unlocked the door. The man could hear the sound of locks and a chain. Professor Angle exited the room and the soldier locked the door and replaced the chain.

The man turned to his servant. "I am tired and I wish to retire," he said in French. "Wine."

Professor Sykes nodded. He motioned for the soldiers to come to the food preparation area. "Brandy?" he asked in English. The four soldiers smiled as he poured each soldier a small portion of brandy.

The man smiled slightly. He was waiting for a particular sound. The sound he was waiting for was the sound of a small vial being opened.

The vial with the sleeping powder was contained in a glass tube with a metal top. The metal top made a particular sound when it was opened. The vial was placed in the food preparation area on the third shelf. It was placed to the right of food seasonings. He felt the vial many times when he moved about the area touching, feeling and smelling. He recognized the smell and he had smelled the vial, on more than one occasion.

Professor Sykes presented each soldier with a small portion of brandy. He poured a small portion of wine, opened the vial, and he placed the sleeping powder in the wine.

He could hear his servant's steps approach him. He held his right hand outward and accepted the wine.

The four soldiers laughed as they enjoyed the brandy. He heard the steps of his servant walk away from him and he turned and smelled the wine; it was a sleeping potion. He frowned slightly as he reached into his gown and touched a cloth.

He poured the wine onto the cloth and moved his gown to cover it.

As the soldiers laughed he walked to his bed and lay down. It was many minutes before he heard his servant leave the room. The sound of locks being turned and a chain being moved was distinct; four locks and one bolt with chain. The four locks did not require a key.

He lay on the bed pretending to be asleep. It was many minutes before he heard the soft breathing of sleep. The four jailers were asleep at their post. The sleeping potion he had placed in the brandy had taken effect.

He arose quietly and walked to the door. He felt carefully of the locks. Satisfied he could open them; he walked to the food preparation area where he removed the wine soaked cloth from underneath his robe and placed it in the basin with the cloth his servant used to clean the wine spill.

He poured himself a small portion of wine and walked to his settee. He sat quietly, listening to the sounds of his jailers sleeping at their post.

Chapter Twenty - Nine

"Is this the final order?" Amaury Benoit asked in French, as he read the communiqué.

"Yes," Professor Angle answered in French. "What is it?"

Professor Angle met Amaury near the asylum. He walked from the main entrance to a wooded area to the east. This area faced the Susquehanna River Valley and this area was very rugged. He met Amaury in this location twice. On both occasions, they were alone.

Amaury was not alone. Professor Angle counted five men. He could not see well into the wooded area because of the darkness but there appeared to be more men in the shadows. He guessed thirty to forty.

"Don't you know?" Amaury asked in French.

"No," Professor Angle answered in French. "The letter was sealed. I have not opened it."

Amaury presented the letter to Professor Angle. It was dark and one of the men standing beside him lit a match.

Accomplissez l'élimination, deux heures de vers l'avant
Fourragere – Croix de Guerre

"I do not know what it means," Professor Angle said in French. "It appears to be a command when we have safely escaped."

The match stopped burning and the light was gone. Before the match burned out, Professor Angle could clearly see the man who lit it. He was very large and powerful. The man who lit the match wore a grayish color shirt and trousers. The man's face was blackened. Amaury's face was also blackened. The men in the shadows were difficult to see. He would not have noticed them if they had not approached him when he called for Amaury.

"Did he give you final orders?" Amaury asked in French.

"Yes," Professor Angle answered in French. "Professor Marlow and I are to meet you on the other side of the south stone wall before nine o'clock. We are to provide any assistance you may need."

"What are your orders for Professor Lytle?" Amaury asked in French.

"Away from the asylum," Professor Angle answered in French. "He will be sent to the city library for research. He is concerned Professor Lytle may reveal the plan. On his orders, Professor Lytle is not to be at the asylum during the rescue. He knows nothing!"

Amaury nodded his head. "When does the mission start?" he asked in French.

"After eleven o'clock," Professor Angle answered in French. "Are you practicing?"

"No," Amaury answered in French. "It is customary for final orders before a mission. Sometimes the date and time of the mission may change. We were prepared tonight for any change in the mission."

"No change," Professor Angle said in French. "The mission starts after eleven o'clock in three days." He pointed toward the asylum. "You will place the milk wagon on the other side of the south wall. Professor Marlow and I will be waiting for you. If there are any changes in the guards we will inform you."

"Professor Marlow and I are in complete command until we have safely left the city. After we have left the city, he will take command."

"How is his health?" Amaury asked in French. "Is he well?"

"His health is fine," Professor Angle answered in French. "I think he is concerned because he has been spilling wine. Professor Sykes reports he spills a glass of wine toward the late evening before he retires for bed."

"He should not be concerned," Amaury said in French. "We have our final orders and we will carry them out, exactly!"

"How many men will participate in the rescue?" Professor Angle asked in French.

"On his orders, four," Amaury answered in French. "The remaining soldiers will be positioned to the south of the city. We will rejoin and proceed south."

"Where are you taking him?" Professor Angle asked in French.

"That information is being kept a secret at this time," Amaury answered in French.

"I agree," Professor Angle said in French, "the less people who know of our final destination, the better." He looked toward the wooded area. It appeared the men were gone. They were there and then they were not there.

"This should be simple," he continued. "Professor Sykes will drug the guards and him at ten o'clock. You will enter the asylum from the south wall one hour later. The guards in the hallway will also be drugged. Professor Sykes will open the door from the inside. Two of the four men will help him carry him to the milk wagon."

He paused. "No one should get hurt. We will have more than one hour before someone discovers he is gone. The guards change at six o'clock A.M."

"We have our final orders and we will carry them out, exactly!" Amaury said in French.

Amaury and the five men began to move backward. As they moved backward, they appeared to melt into the darkness.

Chapter Thirty

Professor Angle shrugged his shoulders. He was alone on the north east section of the asylum at the edge of the woods. He turned and walked west toward the stone wall. The stone wall was eight feet in height and it enclosed the perimeter of the asylum. He was standing on the outside of the east wall. He walked to his left, headed toward the south side.

The walk was not difficult. The area near the stone wall was flat. It was night but he could see the stone wall to his right. The walk seemed to take almost one hour when he approached the south section of the stone wall.

Professor Angle began to calculate the time and distance. Professor Marlow and he were over the age of fifty, much over. He calculated it would take a minimum of two hours to walk from the front gates of Binghamton Asylum to the south side.

He was out of breath but he continued walking. He walked another ten minutes when he stopped. He heard the sound of a horse.

The horse made a type of noise horses' make. A horse will snort and strike their front hoofs against the ground. He listened carefully. There was more than one horse.

Two things happened. The two things were almost simultaneous and occurred as one not two.

A hand was placed over his mouth and a knife blade was positioned against his throat; simultaneously "Release him!" a voice ordered in French.

As quickly as the hand and knife blade appeared, they disappeared.

The voice he heard was Amaury Benoit.

"Why are you here?" Amaury asked angered in French.

Professor Angle was surprised. He turned to see Amaury standing behind him. Amaury was alone.

"Practicing," Professor Angle answered in French. He reached to his throat where he had felt the knife blade. There was no cut.

"It is not safe to walk in these woods at night," Amaury said in French.

"I was judging time and distance," Professor Angle said in French. "If Professor Marlow and I leave the asylum before seven o'clock, we will arrive before nine o'clock."

"Why are you still here?" Professor Angle added.

"Practicing," Amaury answered in French.

"Where is the milk wagon?" Professor Angle asked in French. He could see the woods and the clear area near the wall but there was no milk wagon.

"There is a path not far from here," Amaury answered in French.

"Where is it?" Professor Angle asked in French. "I would like to see it. I would like to determine if the milk wagon is acceptable."

Amaury laughed. His laugh was not a funny laugh. Amaury Benoit's laugh seemed sinister. The laugh was out of place and it frightened Professor Angle.

"A milk wagon is a milk wagon," Amaury said in French. "It is not here. It has been moved."

Professor Angle nodded his head. "Are you finished practicing?" he asked in French.

"Yes," Amaury answered in French. "We have our final orders. I briefed my men and we were in the process of leaving when you approached. My apology. In the darkness we could not tell who you were. My soldier acted appropriately and there will be no punishment."

He paused. "You will have no difficulty returning to the asylum or difficulty returning to this location in three days. It is not safe to be in these woods at night. I advise you to restrict your practice to the daytime."

Professor Angle nodded his head. "Professor Marlow and I will meet with you in three days," he said in French.

He turned and followed the direction he had walked from.

The sentry reported to Amaury Benoit when Professor Angle entered the front entrance to Binghamton Asylum. Amaury gave his men the order to mount their horses. The men mounted their horses and rode them south.

The woods near the south section of the asylum were not thick. The area dropped slightly toward the Susquehanna River Valley and leveled off one quarter of a mile from the stone wall. The river valley encompassed more than four thousand square miles. This area was a lush hunter's paradise filled with deer, hare and fowl and the valley slopes was dotted with small streams that flowed into the Susquehanna River.

Amaury led the column as they rode past an old road. This road was not used. Nothing had passed on this road in more than ten years.

The woods were thick but the column of horses and men moved easily through the woods. Amaury and his men were familiar with the woods; they practiced both directions they would take. They practiced in daytime and nighttime.

They rode for more than one hour. Their ride was not fast. The ride was an easy gallop. As he approached the river valley floor, Amaury Benoit turned toward the west. The column of horses and men followed him. The men on horseback were silent as they rode. The only sounds in the night were the hoofs of the horses striking soft forest ground. The saddles were tightly packed with weapons and ammunition. Each saddle contained a rifle scabbard. The rifles were covered with a grayish cloth to prevent noise. Each man wore a sidearm. The sidearm was blackened to prevent a reflection of the metal.

The long column of riders proceeded south west. There was no moon at this time of the month. The rescue had been planned to coincide with the new moon.

Amaury Benoit rode for an additional one hour and stopped at their camp.

The camp was composed of tents. There was an area prepared for the horses and the men dismounted their horses and led them to the fenced area. The fenced area was composed of tree trunks that were placed in sections.

Forty-two soldiers began to remove the weapons, saddles and blankets from the horses as thirty-six soldiers prepared water and feed.

Amaury dismounted his horse and walked to a large tent. This tent was larger than the others and he was met by six soldiers who guarded the entrance. The six soldiers saluted as he walked inside.

The tent inside was lit with kerosene lanterns and a large table had been prepared near the center. On the table were a series of maps. Two men were reviewing the maps as Amaury placed the final order before the two men.

When Amaury Benoit entered the tent, the two men did not offer, or give, a salute.

The two men nodded their heads as they read the final order.

"His horse, his saddle and his saddle blanket arrived," one of the two men said in French. He motioned toward his right.

Amaury nodded his head as he walked toward his left. Near the edge of the tent was placed a saddle and blanket. The saddle was placed on an upright. The saddle was made of the finest leather and the stirrups were positioned for his height, an estimated American measurement of five foot eight inches.

The saddle blanket was also placed on an upright. It was made of black wool. Emblazoned in gold threads was the First Consul Seal of Napoleon Bonaparte; a large N encompassed by a laurel wreath. An eagle, emblazoned in gold thread, grasping three lightening bolts, was placed above the large N.

Amaury nodded his head in approval.

"What color is his horse?" he asked in French.

"We have two," one of the two men answered in French. "One is solid white and one is solid black. They are both gentle and we have prepared an extra lead on the harness."

Amaury nodded his head in approval. He walked to the table and he began looking at the battle maps. The battle maps were of the city of Washington; in the District of Columbia.

Chapter Thirty - One

Professors Marlow and Angle awoke early. Their plan was to practice the route they would take in two days. They ate a leisurely breakfast and began their walk at nine o'clock in the morning.

This was their first full practice. They walked to the front entrance of the asylum on two prior occasions and turned to the right. They walked a short distance and returned.

During their practice they spoke of different things. They did not speak of him or their plans for the future. They talked of their classes and French history. They did not speak of Napoleone.

Their walk this morning was leisurely. They walked the length of the stone wall, staying far away from the woods. On two occasions, they stopped to rest. The Susquehanna River Valley was beautiful and wild. The spring season had begun and the trees were beginning to bud. There were large sections of bare branches and large sections of green. As far as they could see were woods.

Professor Angle frequently checked his pocket watch. They arrived at the south section of the wall in less than two hours. They guessed at the measurement of the distance of the south wall and walked to an area they believed was the center. The wall was made of stone and eight American feet in height. They could not see over the wall and estimated the distance from the wall and the kitchen area was three hundred American yards.

"How will they scale the wall?" Professor Marlow asked in French.

"Ladders," Professor Angle answered in French.

They walked along the length of the wall looking toward the woods. "There is a road not far from here," Professor Angle said in French. "The milk wagon was here last night and they moved it after the practice."

They walked toward the woods and entered them. The woods were not thick. There was undergrowth but it was easily passable. They walked a short distance and the woods cleared. As they exited this section of the woods they could see a path.

They looked puzzled. The path was a path; it was not a road. The path looked like it had not been used in many years. There was plant growth on the path; separated by sections of stone.

"It must be to the left," Professor Angle said in French.

They walked to the left on the path. The path began to widen and it became a road. The road appeared to have not been used in many years. They looked for the tracks of wagon wheels but they could not find them.

"Curious," Professor Angle said in French. "There was a milk wagon here last night but there is no sign of wagon wheels or horse hoofs."

They continued to walk on the road. They walked a short distance and stopped. They could see disturbances in the road where horses crossed the road. The horse came from the direction of the stone wall, north, and the horse was ridden south.

The section of disturbed earth was not very wide. It looked like two or three horses crossed the rode, side by side.

"Where were you last night when you heard the horses?" Professor Marlow asked Professor Angle in French.

"Near the south wall," Professor Angle answered in French.

He pointed north and they began to follow the horse trail toward the south, now north, stone wall of the asylum. They walked a long distance. The horse trail seemed to move in directions of left and right. The horse trail they followed was not straight. The trail of the horses they followed moved around large trees. It appeared the horses stayed together and did not separate.

They came to a section of the woods that had recently been cleared. Trees were chopped down and underbrush removed. The area was very large. It appeared to be almost fifty yards square. In the cleared area were multiple horse droppings. The area smelled of horse feces and urine.

In the cleared area, with horse hoof prints were wagon wheel tracks.

"This must be it," Professor Angle said in French. "They brought the milk wagon here. This is where we will meet them in two days."

Professor Marlow nodded his head. They walked through the cleared area north. They walked a short distance and stopped at the south wall.

"Brilliant plan!" Professor Marlow said excited in French. He pointed south. "They will bring the milk wagon to the cleared area. Four soldiers will use a ladder to scale the wall. They will rescue him and return the same way. One of the four soldiers will drive the milk wagon and three soldiers will follow on horseback. You, I and Professor Sykes will be in the milk wagon with him. The milk wagon will be taken to the docks. We leave that milk wagon and enter another milk wagon and head south. When we successfully leave the city, we will be met by additional soldiers."

"I agree!" Professor Angle said in French. "It is a brilliant plan." He pointed toward the south. "I want to see the area where the milk wagon will be placed again."

They walked south to the cleared area. It was larger than they recalled. They had estimated the cleared area at fifty yards when they first discovered it but the area was larger, much larger. It was in a square and a rope was tied to trees, forming a type of barrier. They ducked under the rope when they passed through this area but they did not recall ducking under the rope. One section of the square had no rope as a barrier. A long section of rope lay on the ground. It was as if the barrier had been removed to allow the horses to pass.

The horse dung formed a pattern. It appeared the horses had been placed side by side. The square had an inner square of horse dung. The horse dung was in a square and there was no break.

There was another square within the square. A series of troughs had been placed. The troughs were in a square and contained water. Larges patches of straw were placed near the water filled troughs.

It looked like the cleared area had been prepared for horses; many, many, many horses.

"How wide is a horse?" Professor Angle asked Professor Marlow in French.

Professor Marlow raised his hands and moved them outward. "Difficult to say," he answered in French. "There are large horses and there are small horses."

Professor Angle kneeled to the ground and carefully observed a large pile of horse dung. "This was a large horse!" he said in French.

He stood and held his hands outward. "If we estimate the distance from pile of dung to pile of dung," he said in French, "this horse is three feet wide!"

"How many horses were here?" Professor Marlow asked puzzled. "Let us count the piles of dung. It appears that each horse left a pile of dung."

They began to walk along the perimeter of the large square. They counted and completed the square.

"My count is nine hundred forty-two," Professor Angle said in French.

"My count is one thousand sixteen," Professor Marlow said in French.

"You counted seventy-two too many," Professor Angle said in French.

"You counted seventy-two too few," Professor Marlow said in French.

"If we average," Professor Angle said in French, "nine hundred seventy-nine horses were here last night."

Both professors looked puzzled.

"This is a puzzle," Professor Marlow said in French. "Why would four soldiers bring nine hundred seventy-nine horses here? They only need four horses. One horse to pull the milk wagon and three horses to ride as the three soldiers followed and guarded the milk wagon."

"Amaury was not alone last night," Professor Angle said in French. "There were five men with him and I estimated twenty to thirty were hiding in the woods. That would be thirty-six. He said there would be four men to perform the rescue and the remaining soldiers will be positioned south of the city. He also said they would rejoin and head south."

"Is that all he said?" Professor Marlow asked in French.

"No," Professor Angle answered in French. "He said it is customary for final orders before a mission. Sometimes the date and time of the mission may change. He said they were prepared last tonight for any change in the mission."

"Thirty-six minus four is thirty-two," Professor Marlow said in French. "We must have counted incorrectly. Thirty-two soldiers would not need nine hundred seventy-nine horses. They only need thirty-two."

Chapter Thirty-Two

"Where is everyone?"

Professor Sykes entered the conference room and closed the door. He expected to find professors Angle and Marlow waiting for him but there was no one there. He was alone and he began to remove his servant's coat. The coat was made of blue velvet and heavy. He removed it and placed it on the back of a chair.

He looked at his watch, the time was 11:12 P.M. "Where are they?"

Professor Sykes began looking at one of the reports. As he was reading, the door opened.

"Is everything ready?" Professor Marlow asked. Professor Angle followed him into the room and locked the door.

"Where is Professor Lytle?" Professor Sykes asked.

"Not interested," Professor Angle answered. "I threw some more suggestions and he thought I was making a joke."

"Did you talk to him?" Professor Sykes asked.

"No," Professor Angle answered. "I did not want to press him. He's out. He knows nothing."

Professor Marlow sat in one of the six chairs. "How is he?"

Professor Sykes shrugged his shoulders. "Asleep. I drug his wine about ten o'clock. It takes about thirty minutes to take effect." He looked at his watch. "I have about eight hours until he awakes."

"How many guards?" Professor Angle asked.

"Awake or drugged?" Professor Sykes asked smiling.

Professors Angle and Marlow laughed.

"The guards are replaced at six o'clock A.M.," Professor Sykes said. "There are four in the room and two outside in the hallway."

"How are you going to drug them?" Professor Angle asked.

"Simple," Professor Sykes answered. "I have made it a habit of giving the guards a small portion of his brandy. They like it. Napoleone has good taste in brandy!"

Professor Marlow smiled.

"I am not sure of the time," Professor Angle said. "I was told it would be after eleven o'clock P.M. The date is one day from today."

"How do we get him out of the city?" Professor Sykes asked.

"Milk wagon," Professor Angle answered. "He will be taken from the asylum and placed in a milk wagon. From here he will be taken to the harbor."

Professor Sykes was standing and he leaned toward Professor Angle. "That's a stupid plan! The first place they will look is the harbor. They will check every ship."

"Yes," Professor Angle said. "They will go to the harbor and find the empty milk wagon. Then, they will organize a search of every ship in the harbor. While they are searching every ship, he will be in another horse drawn wagon headed south."

"That's a brilliant plan!" Professor Sykes said excited. "Who thought of that?"

"He did," Professor Angle answered. "You will help him change clothes with one of the drugged soldiers. You change clothes also. The two of you will look like two drunken soldiers on leave."

Everyone laughed.

"Where is he being taken south?" Professor Sykes asked.

"I do not know," Professor Angle answered.

Professor Sykes looked puzzled. "You do not know?"

"No," Professor Angle answered. "He is keeping that to himself. When we are out of the city, he will take complete command."

Professor Sykes turned slowly. He walked toward the end of the room and looked outward. From the window he could see the grounds of the asylum. It was night and there were no lights. In the far distance he could see the entrance. There was a single lantern near the opened gate and one sentry. The sentry stood at attention.

He looked toward his right and his left. From where he stood, he could see nothing but darkness. "How many soldiers?"

"I am not sure," Professor Angle answered. "I think as many as fifty or sixty will be waiting outside the city. Four will perform the rescue."

"Sixty-four soldiers," Professor Sykes said to himself. "There is only one sentry at the front entrance." He turned from the window. "Why so many soldiers?"

"They are not coming through the front entrance," Professor Angle answered. "They are coming over the back wall from the south. They are coming through the loading area in the back, through the kitchen area."

Professor Sykes looked worried. "Why?" he asked slowly.

Professor Angle smiled. "The front area is too easily accessible. By coming in through the back, it will be easier to escape. They will think he was taken through the front."

"Who thought of that?" Professor Sykes asked.

"He did," Professor Angle answered.

"When did he tell you that?" Professor Sykes yelled. "I was present at every meeting."

"He slipped me a note," Professor Angle answered.

"What note?" Professor Sykes yelled. "He can not read or write!"

"He slipped me a note," Professor Angle answered laughing. "It appears he can write."

Professor Sykes frowned. "This was going to be simple. There is only one sentry at the front. With the guards drugged we will be out of here before anyone knows. We will have more than one hour's head start."

"It is his plan," Professor Angle said. "They come through the back, through the kitchen and into the hallway. They leave the same way."

"What about the people? Does he know about the people?" Professor Sykes asked.

"What people?" Professor Angle asked.

"Nurses, orderlies and doctors," Professor Marlow answered. "They gather in the kitchen area."

Professor Sykes narrowed his eyes. "There are usually a minimum of three to four. What are they going to do with the people?"

"I do not know," Professor Angle answered. "Gag and tie them, I guess." He stared at Professor Sykes. "What's wrong?"

Professor Sykes frowned. "Does it not bother you that he has changed the plan? Does it not bother you that he slipped you a note? Does it not bother you that it appears he can write? Does it not bother you that one or two soldiers are now sixty-four?"

"Are you afraid?" Professor Angle asked.

Professor Sykes walked away from the window. He smiled slightly as he sat in one of the chairs. "Why are you doing this?" he asked Professor Angle.

"Money and power," Professor Angle answered. "He promised me the title of duke when he is freed."

"Hum," Professor Sykes muttered. "Why are you doing this?" he asked Professor Marlow.

"The same reason," Professor Marlow answered, "money and power. He also promised me the title of duke when he is freed."

Professor Sykes smiled slightly. "He promised me the same thing but I am no longer doing this for money or power."

Professor Angle smiled. "A place in history?"

"To save my neck," Professor Sykes answered.

"Are you afraid of him?" Professor Marlow asked.

"Aren't you?" Professor Sykes asked.

Professor Angle laughed. "Why would he harm the people who rescued him? He has promised us power and wealth. Our names will be in the history books as the men who rescued Napoleone Bounaparte!"

Professor Sykes smiled. "I thought you were a scholar of Napoleone. A soldier will risk his life for a piece of ribbon; he will die for a piece of brass."

Professor Marlow laughed. "You did not answer Professor Angle's question. Are you afraid of him?"

"I am not afraid of him," Professor Sykes answered. "I was afraid of him when I was told he had two soldiers. I became terrified of him when I was told he slipped Professor Angle a note and he has sixty-four soldiers. He does not need sixty-four French soldiers to escape from this asylum, he only needs one."

Professor Angle frowned. "He will not harm you. When he is freed, he will make you a duke! You will have all the money you will ever need and live in a big grandiose house."

Professor Sykes frowned. "Where will he get all of this money?"

"From them," Professor Angle answered. "When he is freed, he will conquer the United States. All who stand in his way will be put to the sword. He will create a new aristocracy in the United States. Because we helped him to escape, he will reward us. You should not be afraid of him."

Professor Sykes stood. He walked to the window and looked outward. "Absolute rulers rule absolutely."

Professors Angle and Marlow looked at each other strangely. "What does that mean?" Professor Angle asked.

"Exactly what it says," Professor Sykes answered. "He can give and he can take."

"Exactly," Professor Marlow said. "You help him and he helps you!"

Professor Sykes laughed. "You are correct! I should not be afraid of him. It is the others who should be afraid." He turned from the window. "Excellent plan! Where does he want you and Professor Angle to be during the rescue?"

"On the other side of the south wall," Professor Angle answered. "Professor Marlow and I are to meet his soldiers there and give them any additional information they may need."

Professor Sykes frowned. "What information? They have everything they need. We gave them the floor plans to the asylum. They know everything about it, guard changes, staff changes. What could we tell them that they do not already know?"

Professor Angle shrugged his shoulders, "Anything that has changed. If nothing has changed, there is nothing to tell them. We wait in the milk wagon and help them if they need help."

"Excuse me for asking so many questions," Professor Sykes said. "I was unaware the plan was changed. I was unaware he could write and he slipped a note to Professor Angle. What happens to us?"

"We go with him," Professor Angle answered. "He has told me everything except where we go after we leave the city. The original plan was to travel to the French section of New Orleans. However, he has not confirmed it."

"What about Professor Lytle?" Professor Sykes asked. "Where will he be?"

"In the city," Professor Angle answered. "He has given strict orders that Professor Lytle is not to be here. He thinks Professor Lytle will reveal the plan. We will send him into the city under the falsehood of research."

Professor Sykes was standing by the window and he turned toward it and looked outward. He was terrified of what he thought could happen. He wanted out but it was too late. He had to go through with it and hope for the best.

"I'm in," Professor Sykes said. "We all need some sleep. I am going to stay and review some notes."

Professors Angle and Marlow smiled. They walked to the door and Professor Angle unlocked it. "Goodnight," they both said as they exited the room and Professor Marlow closed the door.

Professor Sykes stood at the window looking outward. He wondered what his plan really was. "If he slipped a note to Professor Angle, how many notes has he slipped to someone else?" he asked himself. "He does not need sixty-four French soldiers to escape from this asylum."

Professor Sykes lowered his head. He was afraid of what could happen. It was too late to back out. He had a job to do and he would do it.

Chapter Thirty-Three

"You are early!"

Thump. Thump.

Professor Angle's murder was swift and complete. The hair on his head was grabbed and used to pull his head downward. As his head was pulled downward, the knife blade sliced his throat, severing the jugular vein and cutting muscle and nerve to the lower body. He fell to his knees and then forward.

Professor Marlow's murder was also swift and complete, but more brutal. A knife was plunged into his chest as the hair on his head was grabbed and used to pull his head downward. As his head was pulled downward, a different knife blade sliced his throat. He collapsed onto the ground.

The four men moved to the right and effortlessly scaled the eight foot stone wall. They dropped silently to the other side and surveyed the darkness.

The only light seen was an electric bulb located inside the asylum. The light was inside the kitchen area.

The men moved carefully in the darkness to the outside door to the kitchen. Looking through the single pane of glass in the door, from the outside, they could see three women and one man sitting at a table. The four people were drinking a beverage from cups and speaking to each other. The women wore a white nurse's dress uniform and the man was wearing white trousers and a white shirt. From the outside, the four men could smell coffee.

Tap. Tap.

The four people stopped speaking when they heard a noise at the door. The noise sounded like someone knocking but the noise was not a knock. It sounded like metal being lightly tapped on the glass pane in the door.

The man stood and walked to the door. It was dark and he could not see anyone standing outside. He unlocked the door.

"Hello?"

No one answered. He opened the door and stepped outside.

Thump.

The three women heard the thump noise. It was not loud but a noise. Two of the three women stood and walked to the opened door and looked outward.

There was nothing to see. The outside was dark.

"Wayne?" one of the two women whispered. The woman's voice was not loud.

As the two women peered outward from the opened door, something grabbed the two women by their white uniform dresses and pulled them outside.

Thump. Thump.

The third woman began to stand when something struck her in the throat.

The knife was thrown professionally and expertly. The knife was thrown from outside the opened door. It was thrown with such speed, the woman never saw it.

She slumped into her chair as her hair was used to pull her head downward. The knife blade stuck in her throat was pulled to the left and pushed to the right. She slumped onto the table as the three men joined the fourth.

The four men nodded their heads. They paused, listening for noise. The asylum was quite, according to schedule, patients were prepared for sleep at 8:00 P.M. The time was a few minutes after nine. Professor Sykes had not yet placed the drug in his wine.

The original plan was to begin the rescue after 11:00 P.M. That plan was changed. He did not trust his servant Rober and he was of the belief the man, named Professor Sykes, would become afraid and reveal the plan. To counteract that possibility, he moved the time forward.

He did not trust any one of them. They demonstrated no loyalty to their country or their president. Their loyalty to him was purchased very cheaply, a title. Such men are no more than women who sell their personal goods for personal gain. Such men disgusted him!

He wanted everyone punished for his treatment. Two of his four questioners were first. Professors Marlow and Angle were to be eliminated before the rescue began.

His servant Rober, Professor Sykes, was third. He had no intention of leaving his prison wearing the uniform of one of his jailers.

On his specific orders, the questioner named Nathan was not to be harmed. He was the only one whose loyalty could not be purchased. The man named Nathan Lytle was the only questioner who treated him with respect. For these actions, Napoleone would spare his life.

The last communiqué Professor Angle delivered was the most confusing. It was dictated in French and contained one sentence: Accomplissez l'élimination, deux heures de vers l'avant; translated into English - Complete elimination, two hours forward.

There was one additional series of words dictated that also made no sense. The words were not a sentence; Fourragere – Croix de Guerre.

To a nonmilitary person, the sentence appeared a command that was to be followed after they had safely left the city. To a military person it was a standard order: the time for the attack had been moved forward two hours and they were to kill everyone.

Fourragere – Croix de Gerre was known to every French soldier. It is a decoration instituted by Napoleon Bonaparte for units which distinguished themselves in battle.

One of the four men crouched and slowly opened the far door to the kitchen. This door allowed access to the hallway. They paused and checked their weapons. Each man wore a leather belt. Attached to the belt was a stiff, cotton gun holster. Their guns were the new Colt .45 caliber Army Automatic Model of 1910. Attached to the belt were buttoned pockets that contained additional ammunition. Each man carried two hundred rounds of ammunition. Additional ammunition was placed on the far side of the south wall. The milk wagon also contained additional ammunition, pistols and rifles.

One of the four men carried a shortened stick of dynamite. The dynamite would be used to blow the door. The charge was small. It was small enough to damage the locks.

They began to slowly move down the hallway, staying close to the wall in the darkness.

Their first objective was to free him. Their second objective was to kill everyone who held him prisoner.

Mama Leon was awakened in the night to the sound of guns being fired. There were screams in the asylum and additional guns being fired. She rose from her bed and opened the door to be pushed backward into her room. An armed soldier pushed into her room and he locked the door from the inside. He motioned for her to hide behind the bed and positioned himself between the bed and the locked door. He pointed his rifle toward the door and removed his pistol from the gun belt and placed his pistol on the bed.

Mama Leon hid behind the bed. She could hear many sounds. People were running and yelling. The sound of guns being fired appeared to have left the inside of the asylum. The sounds were now outside. After a few minutes, the sound of guns being fired stopped.

It was many minutes before Captain Lawrence came to her door and yelled, “Everything is OK! Is Mama Leon safe?”

“Yes Sir!” the armed soldier answered. “What are your orders?”

“Stay where you are,” Captain Lawrence answered. “You will be relieved in six hours.”

“How many dead?” Captain Lawrence asked.

“Twenty-two of us, four of them,” Lieutenant Simpson answered.

"Did we get them all?" Captain Lawrence yelled.

"I do not know," Lieutenant Simpson answered.

"How! How! How!" Captain Lawrence yelled.

Captain Lawrence and Lieutenant Simpson were in an unused patient's room. The room was in use as a command center for the operation. They were surrounded by soldiers as they attempted to sort out what had happened.

The door to the room was opened abruptly as two armed soldiers pushed the servant of the man in the locked room into the room. "Here is the source of the breech!" one of the soldiers yelled, as he saluted.

Captain Lawrence's eyes widened as he stood from the chair. "Professor Sykes?"

Professor Abner Sykes was pushed into a chair. His hands were handcuffed behind his back and his servant's uniform was torn. There were bruises on his face. Above his left eye was a cut and blood had flowed from the cut into his eye.

He began to laugh.

"Is he the only one?" Captain Lawrence asked.

"I don't know," the armed soldier answered. "We can not locate Professor Angle and Professor Marlow. They did not report today and we can not locate them. Professor Lytle is in the city. It is possible all four conspired together."

Another armed soldier entered the office and saluted. "We have the men. All four are dead and we have identified them."

Captain Lawrence saluted. "Where are they?"

"We have placed them in a patient's room," the soldier answered. "General Tate has requested you join him."

Captain Lawrence walked toward the opened door. He paused to look at Professor Sykes. "Do you know what you have done?"

Professor Sykes laughed. "Yes," he answered. "And I would do it again."

Captain Lawrence followed the soldier down the hallway. "How did they do it?"

"They came from the south end of the asylum's property," the soldier answered. "They used their knives to cut the throats of four sentries." He stopped walking. "Three nurses and one orderly were found murdered in the kitchen area. Their throats were also cut."

"What four sentries?" Captain Lawrence asked puzzled.

"General Tate's orders," the soldier answered. "Four sentries were placed in the stairways."

He continued walking. "They made their way to the corridor. I think their plan was an all out assault. The gun fire erupted when they neared the hallway. I do not think they were told exactly how many soldiers were positioned. Eighteen of our men were killed before our gun fire drove them back. They were killed outside as they attempted to escape."

Captain Lawrence followed the armed soldier down the corridor to a different section of the asylum. This area was sectioned off and protected by armed soldiers. They entered a patient's room where four men were placed on the floor. Sheets covered their bodies and the sheets were blood stained. General Tate sat in a chair looking at the four dead men.

The patient's bed had been moved to the side and multiple weapons were placed on the bed. The bed held several pistols with large packets of bullets. One item looked like a small stick of dynamite. There were multiple knives and an object that looked completely out of place – a crown! On the bed was a crown. The crown looked like a ring of laurel leaves. It was made of solid gold.

Captain Lawrence saluted General Tate but General Tate did not respond.

Captain Lawrence reached to the sheets that covered the four men and removed them. The four men were large and physically fit. They were dressed in grayish color shirts and trousers. Their faces and hands were blackened with a type of actor's paint. In the light of the room, the four men looked like shadows. Each man wore a belt. The belt had multiple pockets and one belt held a type of rope that was thin and looked metallic. The soles of their boots had been altered to add small metal spikes.

"What the hell have we gotten ourselves into?" General Tate muttered. "These men are not civilians," he said in disbelief. "It appears our information on the French was incorrect."

General Tate covered the men with the sheets and he looked upward at Captain Lawrence. "These men are French Legionaries. Why in the hell did four French Legionaries attack Binghamton Asylum?"

"Professors Marlow, Angle, Lytle and Sykes can answer that question," Captain Lawrence answered.

Chapter Thirty-Four

"What is your best estimate?"

General Tate was sitting on his horse as numerous soldiers, on foot, combed the area searching for clues.

"Difficult to tell," one of the soldiers answered. He pointed to the large cleared area.

This area in the Susquehanna River Valley was positioned in the high ground surrounded by four small hills. A stream flowed from the largest of the four hills and descended to a level section. The entire area had been cleared of trees and underbrush. The entire area cleared looked larger than three hundred square yards.

Near the stream, a long line of firewood had been placed. The firewood was cut in varying lengths and the wood was stacked higher than the height of a man and extended a distance of more than one hundred yards.

The firewood was doubled and more than half of one section had been removed. The cleared area was dotted with sections where the firewood had been placed and burned. Many wood fires smoldered as light whiffs of white smoke flowed upward.

From the position he was sitting, on his horse, General Tate could easily see large sections of crushed grass and bare earth where tents had been staked. The ground showed remnants of where the tent pegs had been placed, and removed.

As he sat observing, Captain Lawrence rode from the north through the woods. He was followed by sixteen soldiers on horseback. When they entered the cleared area, the soldiers separated into groups of four and rode away from the area in different directions.

He rode his horse to the general, saluted, and stopped. "There is at least one more like this one."

He dismounted his horse and stretched his legs. "They could have killed every one of us." He pointed toward the hills. "We counted the sentry posts. There appears to have been a minimum of forty. They were positioned in every direction."

"How many?" General Tate asked.

"I have no idea," Captain Lawrence answered. "There is no indication. A lot of men were here but we cannot tell how many."

"Take a guess," General Tate said irritated. "How many?"

"More than one thousand," Captain Lawrence answered. "That number is based on the best estimate of the temporary horse corrals. The corrals of the two areas combined could easily contain one thousand horses." He pointed toward the north. "There were at least nine hundred horses near the south wall of the asylum three to four days ago; where we found the bodies of Professor Angle and Professor Marlow last night."

He pointed toward the west. "The men on horseback left the area near the south wall and entered the cleared area there. The horse tracks show at least two horsemen side by side. We can tell how many were side by side but not how many were in the column."

General Tate nodded. He moved his horse to the left and began a slow gallop. He completed one pass of the cleared area and returned to where Captain Lawrence was standing.

"This was a temporary camp," General Tate said. "It appears to have been setup for a specific purpose."

A soldier approached General Tate and Captain Lawrence on foot. He saluted as they returned his salute. "Everything is clean," the soldier reported. "They cleaned up after themselves. We cannot locate one cigar, one stub, or a chaw of tobacco that was spit out. Either these men did not smoke or chew or they took it with them."

"Is the other cleared area the same?" Captain Lawrence asked.

"Yes Sir," the soldier answered. "Nothing. This area is clean just like the area near the south wall near Binghamton Asylum where the two men were found with their throats cut.

Everything is clean. They even took the horse dung. We have no way of knowing how many men or horses were here."

Captain Lawrence pointed toward the south. "We cannot tell how many left because the horse tracks' moving away from the two areas is in a double column." He shrugged his shoulders. "There could have been more than one thousand."

"Where are the wagons?" General Tate asked. "They would need wagons."

"Difficult to tell," Captain Lawrence answered. "The horse tracks may have covered them." He pointed toward one of the trails that led outward from the cleared area. "If the wagons left first, the horses following the wagons covered the tracks." He shrugged his shoulders. "It is possible everything was brought here and removed by horse."

"If each man rode a horse, which is one thousand men," General Tate said. "Where are they?"

"They could be anywhere," Captain Lawrence answered. "There are more than four thousand square miles of wilderness in the Susquehanna River Valley."

Tweet! Tweet! Tweet!

One of the soldiers was standing at the south east section of the cleared area. He was blowing a whistle. The whistle was used to communicate over long distances. Three blows was the signal that something had been found. Six blows was danger!

General Tate rode his horse to the soldier and the soldier saluted. Captain Lawrence and many soldiers followed the general on foot.

"We found something," the soldier reported. "Eleven dead men!"

General Tate dismounted his horse and followed the soldier. The woods were very thick and it was difficult walking through several sections of underbrush. Captain Lawrence and additional soldiers followed. Each soldier held their pistol as they proceeded cautiously through the woods. They walked an estimated four hundreds yards away from the cleared area. When they arrived at the location, General Tate paused.

This area was also cleared of trees and underbrush. The cleared area was small, an estimated thirty yards square. At one end were eleven men. The men were tied to trees with rope and they had been shot, execution style.

Three soldiers were examining the men and they saluted General Tate. General Tate returned the salute.

"Each man has been shot twice in his heart," one of the three soldiers said. "They appear to have been dead less than twenty-four hours." He leaned toward one of the men. "The bullets are from a pistol not a rifle."

One of the three soldiers was leaned forward and he sniffed the chest area of one of the dead men. "Gun powder! This man was shot at close range. Probably less than six inches."

General Tate frowned. "Assemble the men!" he ordered. "I want every soldier here, now! I want every soldier to see what we are up against!"

Tweet! Tweet! The soldier blew the whistle and paused.

Tweet! Tweet! The soldier blew the whistle two more times. Two whistle blows divided by a pause and followed by two whistle blows was the signal to assemble.

Two soldiers ran from this area to the larger cleared area.

Tweet! Tweet! The soldiers blew the whistle and paused.

Tweet! Tweet! The soldiers blew the whistle two more times.

The soldiers quickly assembled and stood in formation. There were sixty-two. When the men were assembled, Captain Lawrence led the men to the area where the eleven men were executed.

The men's eyes widened when they saw the eleven men. They began to whisper to each other when Captain Lawrence ordered the men to be quiet.

"Quiet!" Captain Lawrence ordered.

"I rescind that order!" General Tate screamed. "I order every man to look at these men and talk! I want every soldier to know what we are up against!"

The soldiers approached the eleven men and looked at them. These men were large and powerful. They were dressed in a grayish shirt with matching trousers. There were bruises on their face and they appeared to have been beaten before they were tied to the tree. Their faces were blackened with an actor's paint. Sections of the black had been removed, by a fist striking their face. It was difficult to tell what actor's paint was and what a bruise was.

Four soldiers walked to the back of the trees. The men's hands had been tied behind them. One of the soldiers looked at their hands. "There are no injuries or bruises on their hands. These men did not defend themselves!"

General Tate allowed the soldiers an adequate time to observe the men. As the soldiers moved away from the trees, Captain Lawrence approached the general and he saluted.

"Permission to remove these men from their bindings?" he asked.

"Not yet," General Tate answered. He did not return the salute. His voice was tense and he was controlling his anger. "I order every soldier to sit on the grass in front of these men."

The soldiers regrouped and sat in formation before the trees. Captain Lawrence sat near the edge.

"Every soldier knows what happened last night," General Tate began. He pointed toward the eleven men tied to the trees. "Four French soldiers attacked the Binghamton Asylum. They killed twenty-two American soldiers before we killed them!"

"Four American soldiers were killed when they were attacked from behind. Their throats were cut!"

"Four civilians, three women and one man had their throats cut while they drank coffee in the kitchen!" he screamed.

He walked toward the trees where the men were tied and he pointed toward the men. "These men are not farm boys! These men are not shop keepers! These men are professional soldiers and they will follow the commander who has the most money!"

"These men are hired killers!" he yelled.

"These men are mercenaries!" he screamed.

He pointed to a soldier who was sitting on the grass. "If I pay one of these soldiers five dollars to kill you, he will kill you! If you pay this same soldier five dollars and ten cents not to kill you, he will not kill you! They work for money! They work for the highest bidder!"

He frowned. "Our best estimate is there are one thousand of these professional soldiers somewhere in these woods and they will be back! These soldiers are disciplined and they follow orders exactly."

He pointed toward the men tied to the trees. "These eleven men did something wrong and their punishment was an execution. My guess is these eleven men were ordered to help the four men last night but they did not."

He paused. "They were executed because they demonstrated cowardice in battle. These eleven men were executed as a lesson to the other men."

"I want every soldier on high alert!" he screamed.

He looked upward to the trees and the forest. General Tate was frightened; Napoleon had a real Army! There were a minimum of one thousand trained French soldiers hidden in the forest and they could rescue him at any time.

"What are they waiting for?" he asked himself quietly. He continued looking in all directions. *Was this a test? Was this a test of our defenses and our response?*

He looked at Captain Lawrence. "These men are soldiers and although they have declared themselves as enemies of our country we will respect their remains. Respectfully remove these men from their bonds and place them on horses."

"We leave this area in five minutes!"

Chapter Thirty-Five

The three men observed General Tate and his soldiers leave the cleared area. They were positioned high into the tree and concealed with new green foliage. They were positioned where they could observe every soldier.

Two soldiers followed the small column north toward the asylum. One soldier rode to the far right and one soldier rode to the far left; looking for any indication they were being followed.

The three men were silent as the watched the soldiers leave. They counted each soldier who came to the area and they counted each soldier who left. There were six missing!

They remained motionless in the tree as six soldiers regrouped near the cleared area. The six soldiers were ordered to remain briefly behind and they were on horses. They spoke to each other and separated. The six soldiers followed the small column north. When the six soldiers crossed the far hill, the three men climbed down the tree.

They ran south, toward one of the small hills that encircled their temporary camp. They crossed the hill and continued south for almost ten miles. Near a clearing, tied to trees, were their horses. They mounted their horses and continued south.

They rode for more than two hours and stopped at a much larger camp.

They were greeted at the entrance by eight sentries. They dismounted and one of the sentries took their horses and led the three horses to a corral. The three horses joined more than two thousand others.

The three men walked to a large tent. Guarding the tent entrance were twelve armed sentries and one of the sentries allowed entrance.

They stood before Amaury Benoit and two additional men. They saluted and Amaury returned the salute. The two men standing beside him did not return the salute.

"General Tate and his soldiers have left the area of our temporary camp," one of the three soldiers said in French. "They responded with sixty-two soldiers and they were not prepared for battle. They located the disobedient ones and took them with them."

Amaury Benoit nodded. "You are dismissed," he said in French.

The three soldiers saluted and left the tent.

One of the two men standing beside Amaury nodded. "My best estimate is two weeks before he will contact us again," he said in French.

Amaury nodded in agreement. "We have the possibility of Professor Lytle but I do not think we can rely on him," he said in French. "I think they will replace the three professors and he will have three new opportunities."

"What about the old woman?" one of the men asked in French.

"We can not rely on her," Amaury answered in French. "She has served her purpose. Our best hope is another concerned soldier or another ambitious professor. I think it was a mistake to execute those eleven men. They were moving forward to help the four before they were ordered to stop. If they had rejoined, combined, they would have turned the tide of battle and completed the mission."

"Those were not their orders!" one of the two men yelled in French. "Their orders were to wait in the cleared area." He walked toward the front of the tent and turned. "I do not care if they believed they could help! A soldier must follow orders. We follow his and they follow ours! His orders were explicit and we can not allow soldiers to think."

His face was angered. "An Army must have discipline," he continued. "We can not conquer the United States if soldiers do not obey orders."

Amaury nodded. "You are correct," he said in French. "A soldier must obey orders. You must consider, if the eleven men were allowed to continue and succeeded, they would be rewarded." He looked to the other man. "We would all be rewarded."

The man stepped forward. "Yes," he said in French. His tone of voice was sarcastic. "He would reward them. If we allowed them to continue, we would all be rewarded. He would place the Fourragere – Croix de Guerre on our coats." He turned toward the front of the tent and waved his hands in the air. "He would make a grand speech about our heroism and lack of fear in battle."

He turned toward the two men. "First, he would reward us for thinking for our self and disobeying his orders, and second, he would execute us for disobeying his direct and explicit orders!"

"We would have an estimated ten minutes to bask in our glory before all fourteen of us would be executed."

"I do not think so," Amaury said in French. He took a stand and folded his arms. "I do not think he would do such a thing."

"Think! Think!" the man yelled in French. "You think when I tell you to think!"

He walked to Amaury and placed his right hand on Amaury's left shoulder. "You are an excellent officer and you have done an excellent job with these troublesome Germans. I allowed you to think for yourself because I was not there to think for you. I am your superior officer. You do what I tell you to do when I tell you to do it."

Amaury reluctantly nodded his head in agreement.

"We have supplies for eight months," one of the two men said in French. "We restock our supplies in three months and wait. He will contact us."

The two men nodded their heads. They walked to a table and looked at the battle maps. The maps were of the city of Washington located in the District of Columbia.

Chapter Thirty-Six

Professor Abner Sykes was handcuffed and placed in a chair. The room was filled with armed soldiers and General Tate ordered the professor to the room for questioning.

"Who did you contact?" General Tate asked.

"A friend of a friend," Professor Sykes answered.

"What did you tell him?" General Tate asked.

"The truth," Professor Sykes answered.

"And what is the truth?" General Tate asked.

"Napoleone Bounaparte has been reincarnated," Professor Sykes answered.

General Tate and every soldier in the room laughed. "The man is insane and he thinks he is Napoleon," General Tate laughed.

"If the man is insane, why are you afraid of him?" Professor Sykes asked.

The general stopped laughing and every soldier in the room stopped laughing. General Tate puffed his chest. "I am not afraid of him!"

"You are correct and I misspoke," Professor Sykes said. His hands were handcuffed behind his back and he leaned forward. "You are not afraid of him you are terrified of him!"

General Tate frowned and he leaned backward in his chair. "Why would I be afraid of an insane blind man who thinks he is Napoleon?"

"Because the man is not insane," Professor Sykes answered. "He is Napoleone and when he is released, he will kill every one of you! He will raise an Army and conquer the United States. He will create a new aristocracy in the United States and you will not be a part of it."

"When he is released?" General Tate asked. "That man will never be released. He is a danger to himself and others."

Professor Sykes leaned backward in his chair. "It is only a matter of time. The first attempt to rescue him failed but the second and third attempt may not fail."

General Tate was angered. He stood from the desk and walked to Professor Sykes. He snarled as he struck him on his face with his right fist. "I have twenty-two soldiers dead and four asylum employees dead. Three of the asylum employees were women!"

"A small price to pay," Professor Sykes said.

"Do you know what you have done?" Captain Lawrence asked. "We have twenty-two dead American soldiers killed by four French soldiers on American soil."

"Four? Four?" Professor Sykes asked surprised. "They sent three too many."

The soldiers in the room were angered at his remark and they began whispering to each other.

Tensions in the room were high and General Tate motioned for everyone to calm down. He returned to the desk and sat down. "What do you know about these four dead French soldiers?" General Tate asked.

"Nothing," Professor Sykes answered. "They are four of many. Many people in the French military believe Napoleone has been reincarnated. As we speak, an Army is being raised in France to free him!"

General Tate frowned. "The French are allies. They would never attack the United States."

"If you do not release their emperor they will," Professor Sykes said. "They will sweep through the state of New York like locusts; killing every man, woman and child who stands in their way."

Captain Lawrence laughed loudly. His laughter broke the tensions in the room. "Why do you believe he is Napoleon?"

"Obvious," Professor Sykes answered. "The man in the locked room correctly answered every question. He knows information only Napoleone would know."

"No he didn't," Professor Lytle said. He held upward a sheet of paper. "Mama Leon lied! The four steps to the birth place of Napoleon are made of wood not stone. There is no large tree near the house." He thumbed through several sheets of paper in his lap and he held upward a photograph of the house. The house was made of brick and was four stories. There was no front porch and the house appeared to be among a row of houses. There was a tree near the house but it was a small tree.

Professor Sykes laughed. "Napoleone was born in that house in 1769. That photograph was taken thirty years ago, one hundred eleven years after he was born. The four wooden steps were placed over the three stone steps because tourist broke pieces of the stone as a souvenir. That tree was cut down more than forty years ago because its height threatened the structure of the home."

He laughed and leaned forward. "Only the real Napoleone would know the real reason why the quarrel with the mayor of Corsica forced the Bounapartes to leave the island in 1793."

Professor Lytle frowned. "There was tension between Pascal Paoli and the Bounapartes. Paoli was afraid Napoleon would remove him from power."

"It had nothing to do with power," Professor Sykes said. "It was a woman! Paoli and Napoleone had the same interest in a woman. Paoli had more military power at the time and the Bounapartes were forced to leave." He laughed very hard. "It was a waste of time and effort because the woman died three years later. Paoli lost a potentially powerful ally."

"You can not verify that!" Professor Lytle shouted.

"You are too blind to see the truth," Professor Sykes laughed. "Check the original French writings of General Pascal Paoli. Page seventy-two, paragraph five."

Professor Lytle began rummaging through a large stack of papers. He located what he was looking for and he read a section. "I have never noticed this before." He looked upward. "What was her name?"

"Aleria Candorine," Professor Sykes answered.

Professor Lytle's eyes widened. "That's correct," he said as he held upward a sheet of paper. He looked toward General Tate. "Professor Sykes could not know what is in the French writings. They have never left my possession and I did not share with him the contents."

"Who told you that?" General Tate asked Professor Sykes.

"He did," Professor Sykes answered.

"Why did you not tell us?" General Tate screamed.

"You would not believe me," Professor Sykes answered. He motioned with his head toward the door. "The man in the locked room is the greatest military genius who ever lived. That man is not insane."

General Tate laughed. The laugh started loud and changed to a giggle. "This is a strange case but one the American military has solved," he said. "That man is insane because he is not who he says he is." He shuffled through a stack of papers, removed one and he held it upward. "One section of the Army has completed a separate investigation. They hired their own experts and they have confirmed the man in the locked room does not know what he is talking about." He paused and stood. "Napoleon's last name was never spelled Bounaparte. It was spelled Buonaparte! The u comes before the o not after."

Professor Sykes laughed out loud.

Professor Lytle narrowed his eyes. "What do you base that on?"

"History," General Tate answered proudly. "It has been confirmed with experts in the French and the Italian military." He placed the sheet of paper on the desk. "Sorry, but that man is insane. He is not who he says he is. He does not know how to spell his last name."

Loud chuckles and giggles erupted in the room. Captain Lawrence laughed out loud.

Professor Sykes laughed very loudly. He twisted his head and jerked in the chair. "Do you want to tell him or do you want me to?" he laughed out loud as he looked at Professor Lytle and licked his lips.

General Tate stopped laughing and everyone in the room stopped laughing. "Tell me what?"

Professor Lytle rummaged through a stack of papers and removed one. He stood and walked slowly to the desk and placed the sheet of paper in front of General Tate. "Your experts are incorrect. They did not go back far enough."

General Tate sat in his chair and looked at the sheet of paper. "What is this?"

Professor Lytle walked to his chair and sat down. "When Napoleon Bonaparte was ten years-old his father wrote a family history," he answered. "The family history was written in the year 1779. In the family history, the name Bounaparte is spelled with the u after the o not before." He paused. "Sometime in the late 1780s, the spelling of their last name changed. Early records show the name spelled both ways. The accepted historical spelling is Buonaparte but it is incorrect."

Professor Lytle lowered his head. "The earliest recorded history of Napoleon was written by his father. According to the family history, Napoleon Bonaparte was born August 15, 1769 and he was christened Napoleone di Bounaparte." He raised his head. "The man in the locked room did not make an error. Your experts made the error."

General Tate looked dumbfounded as he looked at both sheets of paper and compared dates. All the information he was given was dated after 1790 not before. The family history went backward more than three generations and the last names were spelled Bounaparte. The sheet of paper was very old and it appeared to have been torn from a printed book. The language looked different but one entry was easily seen.

1769 15 *August. Male child. Napoleone born to Carlo and Letizia Bounaparte. Ajaccio Corsica.*

General Tate's eyes widened. "Is this real?"

Professor Lytle had a solemn look on his face as he shrugged his shoulders. "I am afraid so," he answered.

Everyone in the room was silent. They looked at each other puzzled.

"What is it?" Captain Lawrence asked. He was sitting in a chair and he leaned forward. "What is it?" he asked again.

General Tate slowly held the torn page from a book upward. "It is a recording," he answered. "Napoleon's birth certificate!"

Everyone in the room froze as Professor Sykes laughed.

General Tate stood slowly, with a puzzled look on his face. He walked to the left and then to the right. He paused, thinking.

Slowly and very carefully, with great reverence, he placed the torn page from the book on the desk. "How is it possible that a twenty-nine year-old illiterate blind man would know the real, real name of Napoleon Bonaparte?"

"He IS Napoleone Bounaparte!" Professor Sykes screamed. "When he is freed, he will order his soldiers to kill every one of you!"

"He will never be freed or rescued," General Tate said angered.

"It's only a matter of time," Professor Sykes laughed. "Professors Angle and Marlow will see to that!"

"I am afraid they can no longer help him," Captain Lawrence said. "They are dead!"

"They are not dead," Professor Sykes laughed. "They are waiting with sixty-five French soldiers on the outskirts of the city. They will be back!"

"Professors Marlow and Angle are not coming back!" General Tate yelled. "They are dead! Their bodies were discovered on the other side of the south wall. Someone cut their throats."

Professor Sykes' eyes widened. "He would never betray us!" he screamed.

"Someone did," Captain Lawrence said. "It appears loyalty is one sided."

Professor Sykes laughed and laughed. His laugh was more of a scream than a laugh. His eyes widened and he licked his lips. He twisted his body to the left and the right and he rolled his head.

He jerked his body in the chair as the soldiers in the room moved backward.

Professor Sykes was insane!

"I know why you are terrified of him!" he laughed. His laugh was loud and maniacal. "You are the ones insane. You think he is possessed by an evil spirit?"

The charge was intended as a joke, to demean the general and the soldiers. No one laughed.

Professor Sykes stopped laughing. He licked his lips and rolled his head. "You really think he is possessed?"

"That is a possibility," Professor Lytle answered. "Any thing is possible. However, we have made plans to confirm or deny that theory."

Chapter Thirty-Seven

Several days passed and one morning Mama Leon and her son Victor were requested to attend a very special session with the man in the locked room. Captain Lawrence told her, through Victor, they needed her present in the event he spoke in Corsican. He seemed excited about the special session. Captain Lawrence was hopeful everything would soon be over and they could return to their home.

Professor Lytle joined them and they stood waiting at the end of the hallway for the special session to begin. Victor noticed the hallway was lined with armed soldiers; he counted thirty-three. As they stood waiting, Mama Leon and Victor noticed a smell in the air. The smell was sweet yet pungent.

They also heard a noise. The noise sounded like a swinging bell. The noise was faint and began to sound louder. The smell was light but became stronger. Something was coming down the hallway. It was out of their sight.

The sound became louder and the smell became stronger. Their eyes widened as a Catholic Bishop, flanked by four priests, turned the corner in the hallway and walked toward them. The Bishop was dressed in his vestments, wearing his miter and carrying his crosier; shepherd's staff. Two of the four priests were holding chains, swinging a censer thurible; incense burner. One of the four priests carried an opened Bible and the first priest, who led the procession, dipped the aspergillum into the aspersorium and sprinkled the hallway with holy water.

The special session was an exorcism!

Three days earlier…

"This does not meet the requirements for an exorcism by the Church," Bishop Clair said.

"Why not?" Captain Lawrence asked.

"There is no supernatural aspect to this case," Bishop Clair answered. "It is unusual but nothing supernatural has occurred."

"What is supernatural?" Captain Lawrence asked.

"Many things: levitation; foretelling the future; unusual markings on the body; a stench in the room; different voices," Bishop Clair answered. "Has this man exhibited any of these things?"

"No," Captain Lawrence answered.

"The Church can not help you," Bishop Clair said. "This case does not warrant an exorcism."

"There are elements to this case that do appear to be supernatural," Professor Lytle said. "He has answered every question correctly and his memory is beyond belief."

Bishop Clair laughed. "I have read your report and correctly answering the location of every chamber pot of the first floor of the Palace of Versailles does not qualify as a supernatural ability."

Professor Lytle stood. "What about the secret room on the third floor of the palace? That room was allegedly built by Napoleone and unknown until thirty days ago. There is no way that man could possibly know about that secret room unless he was Napoleone. He recognized and correctly identified the scent of the perfume. Only a few people in our lifetime have ever smelled that perfume."

"You have not presented any evidence that this man is possessed by the spirit of Napoleon Bonaparte," Bishop Clair said. "The Church can not help you."

Professor Lytle was standing. He shuffled through several papers. "Perhaps we are not presenting our case in an appropriate manner. Let us look at this case from a different viewpoint."

He walked toward the door and turned.

Professor Lytle was in the study of Henri Clair, the Bishop of New York. A request was submitted to the Catholic Church to perform an exorcism. Information was submitted to the

Bishop with a demand for an immediate answer. They received an immediate answer…no.

Professor Lytle and Captain Lawrence requested an audience with the Bishop to plead their case. They were told they had five minutes.

"There are several men in history who have been called the 666 Beast," Professor Lytle said. "February 10, 1798, Napoleone sent General Louis Alexander Berthier to Rome, Italy. He abolished the Papal government and forced Pope Pius VI to flee Rome. Many people claimed the combined Popes were the 666 Beast. Pope Pius VI claimed Napoleone was the 666 Beast as revealed by Saint John in the Book of Revelation."

Bishop Clair smiled. "Napoleon Bonaparte died in the year 1821 on the island of St. Helena. He was not the 666 Beast because he died."

"Everything we have uncovered indicates the man in the locked room is Napoleone Bounaparte," Professor Lytle said. "Apparently the 666 Beast did not die. Somehow, the spirit of Napoleone has been placed in this man's body."

"God didn't do it!"

He frowned at Bishop Clair. "It is the obligation and the duty of the Church to send him back to the hell from where he came."

Bishop Clair smiled. "Impressive argument but the argument is not impressive enough. This case does not meet the requirements for an exorcism by the Church."

Professor Lytle smiled. "There has been one attempt to free him. It failed but the second or the third attempt may succeed. In this first attempt, twenty-two American soldiers, three nurses, one orderly and two college professors were murdered. If you count the four dead men who did the killing, that is thirty-two people who died as a result of one, just one, of his orders. It is believed the four men were ordered to kill everyone in the asylum including the patients. That number could have been as high as one hundred and eighty. One hundred and eighty men, women and children could have died by his one, just one, order."

"During Napoleone's seventeen years of war, it is estimated six million Europeans died as a direct result of his orders. Do you know what the spirit of Napoleone will do when this man's body is released?"

Bishop Clair was startled from the question and he shrugged his shoulders.

"The man in the locked room will raise an Army and conquer the United States," Professor Lytle said, answering his own question. "When he gets to Italy, he will not abolish the Papal government; he will order his soldiers to burn the Vatican to the ground! Before he burns the Vatican, he will order his soldiers to hang the Bishop of Rome and every member of the College of Cardinals from the parapets of the walls."

Bishop Clair's eyes widened and he became angered as he tightly grasped the arms of his chair.

Professor Lytle leaned closer toward Bishop Clair. "We do not know for sure if this man is possessed by the spirit of Napoleone but we must eliminate all possibilities. Do you want to explain to Jesus Christ how you had the opportunity to stop the 666 Beast but didn't?"

Bishop Clair smiled brightly as he opened a notebook on his desk. "I will clear my schedule."

Three days later…

The Bishop chanted in French as he walked slowly toward the locked room. Captain Lawrence leaned toward Victor. "We must not say anything," he whispered. "Only answer if asked. The exorcism must not be interrupted."

Victor nodded and whispered into his mother's ear. Mama Leon nodded that she understood.

Captain Lawrence nodded toward an armed soldier positioned in front of the door. The armed soldier lightly tapped on the door and whispered. Victor and Mama Leon could hear the sounds of locks turning and the sound of a chain moving. The door opened slowly from the inside as the Bishop approached.

The procession stopped briefly before the opened door. The priest in front of the Bishop sprinkled holy water on the entrance. The Bishop continued to chant in French. The priest continued to sprinkle holy water as he led the procession into the room.

Captain Lawrence, Professor Lytle, Victor and Mama Leon followed the procession and sat in chairs positioned to the side.

The Bishop entered the room and stood in the center. He continued to chant as the four priests took their positions. The priest with the opened Bible moved to the left of the Bishop and he held the Bible toward him.

The man in the locked room had his back turned toward them as they entered his room. When every person was in the room, he could hear the sounds of locks being turned and the sound of a chain.

The Bishop was chanting in French but stopped speaking abruptly when the man in the locked room turned toward them.

He looked dead!

The man was dressed in a crimson gown that flowed to the floor of the room and ended in a white trimming. The man's eyes were without pupils and appeared to have sunk into his skull. There was no emotion on his face. The man stood motionless.

Bishop Clair had been startled by the man's appearance and lack of reaction. He had performed three successful exorcisms but he had never seen anyone like this. Two exorcisms were performed in Africa and one exorcism was performed in the state of Louisiana. In all three cases, the evil spirit reacted immediately when he approached the person possessed. The evil spirits were frightened of him but this evil spirit showed no emotion.

He began to chant in French.

The man in the locked room showed no emotion.

The Bishop performed the exorcism but nothing happened. He performed it again but nothing happened. He was in the process of performing the third exorcism when the man said something in Corsican.

The Bishop looked toward Mama Leon. "What did he say?" he asked in English.

Victor whispered into his mother's ear and she whispered in his ear.

"What is your name?" Victor answered.

"Bishop Clair," the Bishop answered in French in a loud voice.

Professor Lytle whispered in Victor's ear and Victor whispered into his mother's ear.

"Bishop Clair," Mama Leon answered in Corsican.

The man said something else in Corsican.

The Bishop looked toward Mama Leon. "What did he say?" he asked in English.

Victor whispered into his mother's ear and she whispered in his ear.

"What is your superior's name?" Victor answered.

"Cardinal Monteau," the Bishop answered in French in a loud voice.

Professor Lytle whispered in Victor's ear and Victor whispered into his mother's ear.

"Cardinal Monteau," Mama Leon answered in Corsican.

The man said something else in Corsican.

The Bishop looked toward Mama Leon. "What did he say?" he asked in English.

Victor whispered into his mother's ear and she whispered in his ear.

"What is the name of the church to which you perform Mass?" Victor answered.

"Saint Mary of the Seven Sorrows," the Bishop answered in French in a loud voice.

Professor Lytle whispered in Victor's ear and Victor whispered into his mother's ear.

"Saint Mary of the Seven Sorrows," Mama Leon answered in Corsican.

The man spoke several sentences in Corsican. There was no emotion in his face as he spoke. He turned his back to the Bishop and said something else in Corsican and waved his left hand into the air.

Mama Leon was visibly upset by what he said. She appeared frightened as she whispered into Victor's ear. She stood and turned toward the door. She rushed to the door and attempted to leave the room. Captain Lawrence nodded to the armed soldier and he unlocked the door and she ran into the hallway.

Professor Lytle and Victor followed her.

The Bishop said several prayers, made the sign of the cross and led the procession from the room. When the procession exited the room, the armed soldier locked the door from inside.

Mama Leon was standing in the hallway and she was visibly upset.

"What did he say?" Bishop Clair asked.

Victor also looked visibly upset. "Who is the man in that room?" he asked.

"I do not know," Bishop Clair answered. "What did he say?"

"His answer to your answer of the church you perform Mass was strange," Victor answered.

Bishop Clair removed his miter and one of the four priests held it for him. He handed his staff to one of the four priests. "I answered his question that I perform Mass at Saint Mary of the Sevens Sorrows. What did he say?"

Victor looked at the door to the locked room. "The man said I will add one more! When I am free, I will order my soldiers to burn that church to the ground and spread its ashes to the four winds of Egypt."

Bishop Clair laughed. "Is that all? I have heard worse during an exorcism. The evil spirit has threatened my mother and my father. I have never had an evil spirit threaten a stone church. What upset Mama Leon?"

Victor looked frightened. "When he turned his back to you, he said something strange."

"What?" Bishop Clair asked. He laughed as he looked toward the locked door. "I think the exorcism is working. I scared him!"

Victor frowned. "He said before he ordered the church burned, he would place Bishop Clair and Cardinal Monteau inside."

Bishop Clair laughed. "I have been threatened before. That spirit does not frighten me or Cardinal Monteau! The exorcism is working!"

"That is not all he said," Victor added. "You will not be alone."

Bishop Clair cocked his head slightly and he looked puzzled. "What did he say when he turned his back?"

Victor's throat was dry and he coughed slightly. "The man said I will add one more sorrow to the Saint Mary Church of the Seven Sorrows. When I am free, I will order my soldiers to burn that church to the ground and spread its ashes to the four winds of Egypt. Before I order the church burned, my soldiers will place Bishop Clair, Cardinal Monteau and every man, woman and child who ever entered that church inside."

Bishop Clair's eyes widened as a look of terror came over his face.

"When he turned his back to you he said I am not amused. You have my permission to leave," Victor added.

Captain Lawrence was listening to what Victor said. "Did the exorcism work?"

Bishop Clair was visibly upset. "No," he answered in a frightened voice. "There is nothing to exorcise. Those are not the words of an evil spirit. I do not know who the man in that room is, but he is not possessed by an evil spirit. The man in that locked room is made of flesh and blood!"

Chapter Thirty-Eight

President William Taft was sleeping when he was awakened. He dressed and entered his sitting room to see eight men waiting for him. The eight men were upset and frightened.

One of the men held upward a telegram. "Mr. President. We have positive confirmation! An Army is being raised in France to free the man who says he is Napoleon!"

"Mr. President. More than three hundred thousand French soldiers are preparing to sail to the United States and free their emperor," one of the men said. "We have thirty days before the flotilla leaves the harbors of France!"

President Taft laughed. "I can't decide who is most insane! The man who thinks he is Napoleon or the people who believe him. Have you spoken to the delegates from France? Surely there is someone who is French who has not lost their mind."

"Mr. President. They are gone!" one of the men answered. "Every French delegate has left the city of Washington and New York. They left two days ago."

"Mr. President. France is going to declare war on the United States!" one of the men said frightened.

President Taft looked frightened. "War with France? What are we going to do?"

"Mr. President. We have a plan!" one of the men shouted.

One of the men approached President Taft and he placed a document in front of him. "This man who claims he is Napoleon has initiated an insurrection against the legal government of the United States with a foreign power. In essence, he has declared war!"

"He is a traitor to our country and since he claims he is a military general, as Commander in Chief, you have the Constitutional power to incarcerate him in a military prison."

President Taft laughed. "How will placing him in a military prison stop French soldiers from attacking the prison?"

"Simple," one of the men answered as he approached the president. "This man's story is so bizarre as to be believable. No one has ever heard of such a thing. People believe Napoleon has been reincarnated and the French government is going to free him. We remove this false belief by incarcerating him for life."

President Taft laughed. "You did not answer my question! How will placing him in a military prison stop French soldiers from attacking the prison?"

"Simple," the man answered. "Which Napoleon are they going to rescue?"

President Taft looked puzzled. "How many Napoleons are there?"

"As many as we need, Mr. President," the man answered. "The easiest method to hide a single apple is in a barrel filled with apples."

One of the men approached President Taft. "Mr. President. We create a series of false stories that there are fifty men who are in mental asylums who believe they are Napoleon," he answered. "We create a false story that this one has committed suicide. That will leave a minimum of forty-nine."

President Taft laughed. "The simple thing to do is to kill him!"

"Mr. President. The Government of the United States would never do such a thing to an innocent man," one of the men said. "As Commander in Chief, you have the Constitutional power to incarcerate him for life as a threat to our national security. There is no need to have a trial and we can do every thing in secret."

"How do you incarcerate a man for life?" President Taft asked.

"Mr. President. Sentence him as a traitor to a military prison for one hundred and ninety-nine years," one of the men answered.

One of the men approached the president. "Mr. President. If you do not think that is long enough, we can add a charge of twenty-eight murders. Each charge can carry the sentence of ninety-nine years. Combined he will be sentenced to two thousand nine hundred seventy-one years."

"What twenty-eight murders?" President Taft asked puzzled.

"It was on his direct order the French soldiers attacked Binghamton Asylum, Mr. President," one of the men answered. "It is obvious he was in collusion and therefore, guilty of all charges."

"Ridiculous," President Taft said. "One hundred ninety-nine years is long enough."

He signed the document. "What happens next?"

"Mr. President. Tomorrow a series of stories will run in every major newspaper in America and Europe," one of the men answered. "One story will report the suicide of a man who believed he was Napoleon. The story will also include additional information about additional men who believe they are Napoleon. We have a prominent psychiatrist who has agreed to falsify a diagnosis." He turned to one of the men in the room. "What is it?"

"Inferiority complex," the man answered. "The men want to be someone important. Napoleon was a great military leader and they imagine they are him."

The men in the room laughed as the man placed his right hand into his coat imitating the painting.

President Taft laughed. "I will pretend I do not know anything about it and contact the French government and inquire why their delegates left Washington D.C."

The men smiled as they began to leave the room. "Mr. President, everything will be taken care of," one of the men said.

"Who is he?" President Taft asked. "I have been kept informed but no one has told me the man's name. Who is the man in the locked room?"

The eight men were leaving the room when each man stopped walking and turned. They looked at each other with solemn faces.

"Facts are facts," one of the men answered. His answer was slow and deliberate. His face showed no humor or attempt to dissipate the seriousness of the meeting; and the immediate emergency which faced the United States.

"Mr. President. The man in the locked room IS Napoleone Bounaparte!"

One of the men stepped forward. "Mr. President. If Napoleone Bounaparte is ever released or rescued, he will raise an Army and kill every one of us. He will order his soldiers to attack Washington D.C. and order his soldiers to kill every man, woman and child who lives here!"

President Taft had been amused by this story. The recent events, and this man's statement, removed all humor. "Where will he get this Army?" President Taft demanded.

"The poor," one of the men answered. "There are more poor people in the world than wealthy people. The Army being raised in France is composed of professional soldiers and the poor." He paused. "More than two hundred thousand impoverished Frenchmen have joined the French Army and they are preparing to attack America to free their emperor. These people have no idea what they are doing. If Napoleone is rescued, he will spark a second French Revolution that will leave Paris a burned out cinder."

"Mr. President, you did the correct thing!" he added. "We are going to imprison Napoleone Bounaparte where he can never be found!"

Chapter Thirty-Nine

Man Who Believes He is Napoleon Bonaparte Commits Suicide

New York: Forty-seven year-old Rupert Johnson committed suicide, by hanging himself with bed sheets, in his protective cell Tuesday June 14, 1910. Mr. Johnson gained notoriety among prominent psychiatrists with his belief that he was the reincarnation of Napoleon Bonaparte, the emperor of 1814 France. "Mr. Johnson would sit on the floor of his protective cell and play with a child's toy soldiers," Psychiatrist Nathan Lytle is quoted. "He would reenact battles and make sounds like firing cannon as he ordered the toy soldiers to advance and retreat."

Mr. Johnson was admitted to a local hospital with a minor infection, which resulted in a fever. He began to exhibit bizarre behavior and he was transferred to Binghamton Asylum for the chronic insane where he would play with toy soldiers, rant, rave, and beat his hands against the cement walls.

"This is a classic case of an inferiority complex," Psychiatrist Nathan Lytle stated. "The man was born blind and compensated his physical deformity with the irrational actions of an imagined notable figure from history."

Psychiatrist Nathan Lytle further stated, "This is not an uncommon form of a mental defect. There are currently forty-nine males in the United States who believe they are Napoleon. These men have been placed in protective cells to protect themselves and others."

A search of local asylums revealed two women who believe they are Josephine, the first wife of Napoleon; three women who believe they are Queen Cleopatra and a nineteen year-old woman who believes she is Martha Washington, the wife of the first president of the United States George Washington. On the male side, there are two Abraham Lincolns; six Julius Caesars; and three men who are of the belief they are Wyatt Earp, the gun slinging marshal, of the 1800s American west Dodge City.

"It is very sad," Psychiatrist Nathan Lytle further stated. "Each person has been diagnosed with an inferiority complex. Their lives have no meaning to them and they have withdrawn into a world to which we can not comprehend. Our medicine has not advanced to where they can be cured and our only option is to make them as comfortable as possible."

Psychiatrist Nathan Lytle is an expert of French history and teaches the Napoleonic Wars at Cambridge University. He received his doctorate in medicine from the University of Bern. Attempts were made to inquire further about the men who believe they are gun slinging Dodge City Marshal Wyatt Earp. Professor Nathan Lytle could not be contacted. He is on leave from his teaching position at Cambridge University and his current location is unknown.

U.S. News Association

Woman Who Believes She is Queen Cleopatra Drowns in Bathtub

San Diego, California: Sixteen year-old Patricia Norris drowned in a bathtub at the San Diego Children's Institute for the Insane Tuesday June 14, 1910. Miss Norris gained notoriety among prominent psychiatrists with her belief she was the reincarnation of Cleopatra, the Queen of Egypt. "Miss Norris would sit in the bath and pretend she was on a barge on the

River Nile," Psychiatrist Nathan Lytle is quoted. "She would shout commands to imaginary slaves. Row! Row! Row!"

Miss Norris was admitted to a local hospital at the age of ten. She began to exhibit bizarre behavior and she was transferred to the Children's Institute for the Insane where she would sit in a bathtub of water. She was of the belief she was Queen Cleopatra, on a barge in the River Nile, on route to meet Marc Antony.

"This is a classic case of an inferiority complex," Psychiatrist Nathan Lytle stated. "The young girl read a book about Cleopatra and she compensated her impoverished life with the irrational actions of an imagined notable figure from history."

Psychiatrist Nathan Lytle further stated, "This is not an uncommon form of a mental defect. There are currently three females who believe they are Cleopatra. These ladies have been placed in protective cells to protect themselves and others."

A search of local asylums revealed one woman who believes she is Josephine, the first wife of Napoleon; three women who believe they are Martha Washington, the wife of the first president of the United States George Washington; and a nineteen year-old woman who believes she is Mary, the mother of Jesus. On the male side, there are six Abraham Lincolns; one Julius Caesar; two Napoleons; one Daniel Boone; and two men who are of the belief they are Buffalo Bill.

"It is very sad," Psychiatrist Nathan Lytle further stated. "Each person has been diagnosed with an inferiority complex. Their lives have no meaning to them and they have withdrawn into a world to which we can not comprehend. Our medicine has not advanced to where they can be cured and our only option is to make them as comfortable as possible."

Psychiatrist Nathan Lytle is an expert of French history and teaches the Napoleonic Wars at Cambridge University. He received his doctorate in medicine from the University of Bern. Attempts were made to inquire further about the men who believe they are Abraham Lincoln. Professor Nathan Lytle could not be contacted. He is on leave from his teaching position at Cambridge University and his current location is unknown.

U.S. News Association

**Man Who Believes He is Billy the Kid
Looses Shoot Out with Himself**

Salt Lake City, Utah: Forty-seven year-old Robert Kane died when he attempted to outdraw and shoot himself in a full-length mirror at the Salt Lake City Institute for the Insane Tuesday June 14, 1910. Mr. Kane gained notoriety among prominent psychiatrists with his belief he was the reincarnation of Billy the Kid, a notorious outlaw of the American west. "Mr. Kane would stand in front of a mirror and practice his quick draw," Psychiatrist Nathan Lytle is quoted. "He would draw his imaginary gun and yell bang; and then shout Die Varmint, Die!"

Mr. Kane was admitted to a local hospital when he began to exhibit bizarre behavior. He would run about his home in the belief the marshal was after him.

Mr. Kane was given a child's metal gun and holster from a visitor. He was practicing his quick draw when the metal gun slipped from his hand and struck the full-length mirror. A shard of the shattered glass cut him on his right gun hand and he bled to death before the bleeding could be stopped.

"This is a classic case of an inferiority complex," Psychiatrist Nathan Lytle stated. "The man read a book about Billy the Kid and he compensated his impoverished life with the irrational actions of an imagined notable figure from history."

Psychiatrist Nathan Lytle further stated, "This is not an uncommon form of a mental defect. There are currently three males who believe they are Wyatt Earp. These men have been placed in protective cells to protect themselves and others."

A search of local asylums revealed one woman who believes she is Josephine, the first wife of Napoleon; three women who believe they are Martha Washington, the wife of the first president of the United States George Washington; and a nineteen year-old woman who believes she is Mary, the mother of Jesus. On the male side, there are six Abraham Lincolns; one Julius Caesar; eight Napoleons; one Daniel Boone; and two men who are of the belief they are Buffalo Bill.

"It is very sad," Psychiatrist Nathan Lytle further stated. "Each person has been diagnosed with an inferiority complex. Their lives have no meaning to them and they have withdrawn into a world to which we can not comprehend. Our medicine has not advanced to where they can be cured and our only option is to make them as comfortable as possible."

Psychiatrist Nathan Lytle is an expert of French history and teaches the Napoleonic Wars at Cambridge University. He received his doctorate in medicine from the University of Bern. Attempts were made to inquire further about the two men who believe they are Buffalo Bill. Professor Nathan Lytle could not be contacted. He is on leave from his teaching position at Cambridge University and his current location is unknown.

U.S. News Association

Man Who Believes He is George Washington Dies in Bizarre Accident

Memphis, Tennessee: Sixty-seven year-old Albert 'Georgie' Knox died in a bizarre accident when he lost his balance and fell from a table he was standing on at the Memphis City Institute for the Insane Tuesday June 14, 1910. Mr. Knox gained notoriety among prominent psychiatrists with his belief he was the reincarnation of George Washington, the first president of the United States. "Mr. Knox would stand on top of a table and pretend he was George Washington crossing the Delaware River during the American Revolutionary War," Psychiatrist Nathan Lytle is quoted. "He would shout damn the torpedo and full speed ahead; I only have one life to give to my country; and the British are coming!"

Mr. Knox was admitted to a local hospital when he began to exhibit bizarre behavior. He was a history instructor in the Memphis school system and believed he was the reincarnation of George Washington. One day, he accused all of his students of conspiring with the British; which caused him to loose the battle of the Alamo.

Mr. Knox was a favored of the patients of the asylum. Doctors, nurses and orderlies affectionately named him 'Georgie'.

"This is a classic case of an inferiority complex," Psychiatrist Nathan Lytle stated. "The man read numerous history books and his facts got mixed up. He compensated his impoverished life with the irrational actions of an imagined notable figure(s) from history."

Psychiatrist Nathan Lytle further stated, "This is not an uncommon form of a mental defect. There are currently three males who believe they are George Washington. These men have been placed in protective cells to protect themselves and others."

A search of local asylums revealed three women who believe they are Josephine, the first wife of Napoleon; two women who believe they are Martha Washington, the wife of the first president of the United States George Washington; and a nineteen year-old woman who believes she is Mary, the mother of Jesus. On the male side, there are six Abraham Lincolns; one Julius Caesar; eight Napoleons; one Daniel Boone and two men who are of the belief they are Buffalo Bill.

"It is very sad," Psychiatrist Nathan Lytle further stated. "Each person has been diagnosed with an inferiority complex. Their lives have no meaning to them and they have withdrawn into a world to which we can not comprehend. Our medicine has not advanced to where they can be cured and our only option is to make them as comfortable as possible."

Psychiatrist Nathan Lytle is an expert of French history and teaches the Napoleonic Wars at Cambridge University. He received his doctorate in medicine from the University of Bern. Attempts were made to inquire further about the six men who believe they are Abraham Lincoln. Professor Nathan Lytle could not be contacted. He is on leave from his teaching position at Cambridge University and his current location is unknown.

U.S. News Association

Mother and Son Die in Apartment Fire

New York: June 23, 1910 a mother and her son died in an apartment fire from smoke inhalation. Seventy-two year old Angelina Leon and her forty-two year old son Victor died when a fire erupted on the first floor of their building. Their apartment was located directly above the apartment where the fire started. Firemen are investigating the cause of the blaze.

Their apartment was the only one occupied in this building at this time. The residents of the building were recently evicted for non payment of rent. The Leon's recently paid all of their back rent and paid forward more than one year.

Victor Leon's twenty year old daughter Sophia, her husband Tommaso and their one year old infant daughter were not at the apartment at the time of the fire. Victor Leon recently purchased a small home for his daughter, her husband and their child.

Affectionately called Mama Leon, Angelina Leon's remains will be returned to the Italian island of Corsica where she was born in the year 1838. She will be buried beside her husband Serge in the Leon family cemetery in the town of Ajaccio. Ajaccio is the town where Napoleon Bonaparte was born in 1769. Mama Leon was born seventeen years after Napoleon died in exile on the island of St. Helena in the year 1821.

The Leon family cemetery is located near the birthplace of Napoleon.

New York Evening World

American Army Officers
Injured in Training Accident Expire

Dallas, Texas: June 25, 1910 Three American Army officers expire from wounds received in a training exercise accident.

Army officers Captain Russell Lawrence, Lieutenant Craig Simpson and Corporal Mark Benson died from wounds received in a bizarre accident. The officers were recently transferred from New York and were participating in a training exercise.

The officers were in the process of planning the exercise with new recruits when a recruit's rifle accidentally discharged. The bullet struck munitions placed near the area and the explosion resulted in life threatening injuries. The three officers never regained consciousness and expired within hours of each other.

The three officers were the only soldiers injured in the accident. The officers were never married and leave no family. Representatives of the Army are investigating the incident.

Larado Cronica

Search for Missing College Professor Halted

New York: August 22, 1910 The search for missing college professor Abner Sykes has been stopped. "There are no leads," New York City Police Captain Mark Anderson is quoted. "It is as if he simply disappeared into the air."

Professor Abner Sykes was last reported in Boston six months ago. Professor Sykes is a professor of French history at the University of Paris often referred to as La Sorbonne. One of his published books, *The Early History of Napoleon Bonaparte* is used as a text book in advanced college level French history classes. He was on a leave of absence from La Sorbonne as a guest lecturer at Harvard University when he suddenly disappeared. Before he disappeared, he is reported to have stated he had been recruited by the United States Army to travel to New York for a special assignment.

"He was last reported speaking to a United States Army military officer in his office in Boston," New York City Police Captain Mark Anderson continued. "A minimum of six students testified under oath they witnessed an Army officer speaking to him in his office. Representatives of the Army have no knowledge of the meeting or the officer."

An intensive search was conducted in the cities of Boston and New York but no one has reported seeing the professor in six months. The search halted because there are no leads. Foul play is not suspected at this time.

Long Island NY Daily Star

Chapter Forty

"How long has he been here?"

"Since 1914," General Tate answered. The two officers were walking toward a door located in the basement of the White House. The hallway was located below the lowest level and accessed by descending a series of stairs.

The two officers walked to the end of the hallway and stopped before a wooden door. The door appeared to be the door to a storage room.

"Here?" the officer with General Tate asked. He seemed puzzled.

General Tate tapped on the door, in code. A similar series of knocks, in code, answered.

The sound of locks being turned and a series of bolts moving could be heard. The door was slowly pushed open as four soldiers exited holding .38 caliber revolvers.

"Identification?" one of the four soldiers asked.

General Tate presented a photograph identification card. The soldier looked at the card. He turned to the officer standing beside General Tate. "Identification, please?" the soldier asked firmly.

The officer puffed his chest. "You know who I am!"

"Identification, please?" the soldier asked again. He raised his gun toward the officer. "Identification, please?"

"This is preposterous!" the officer yelled. He stepped backward and pointed his right hand toward the soldier. "You know who I am!" he screamed.

Three of the four soldiers held a small whistle in their mouth. One soldier blew the whistle once.

Tweet!

The sound of many boots running could be heard inside the partially opened door. The sound was of many soldiers running. The sound stopped as suddenly as it began and the sound of guns cocking could be heard in the hallway.

"Excellent!" the officer yelled. He reached into his coat pocket and removed a photographic identification card.

The soldier who asked for identification looked at the card, nodded, and he blew his whistle twice.

Tweet! Tweet!

The sound of boots moving into a position of attention could be heard from the hallway.

One of the four soldiers nodded as he opened the door.

The door was made of steel covered with thin strips of wood. The steel door appeared to be two inches thick. Behind the door was a large staircase eighteen feet wide. The stairs descended downward with three levels of landings. On each stair landing stood four soldiers. Each soldier on the landing held .38 caliber revolvers. The revolvers were cocked and pointed toward the opened door.

General Tate and the officer descended the stairs. At each level, they presented their photographic identification cards. One of the four soldiers looked at the two cards, nodded, and allowed them to descend to the next landing.

They walked a distance of three levels to come to an opening. This opening was composed of bars. The bars were a distance of six inches from each other and four armed soldiers stood behind them.

"Identification?" one of the four soldiers asked. The two officers presented their photographic identification cards. One of the soldiers nodded and four bolts were moved to open the gate from inside. The gate opened from the inside to the outside.

They entered this area to see a long hallway. The hallway looked to be thirty yards long and on each side of the hallway, armed soldiers stood. Each soldier held a .38 caliber revolver. The revolver was cocked and pointed toward them.

One of the four soldiers standing at the gate blew his whistle three times.

Tweet! Tweet! Tweet!

The soldiers in the hallway released the hammer on their pistol and replaced it in its holster. They stood to attention.

"Amazing!" the officer with General Tate said.

"They are ordered not to salute or to speak," General Tate said. He turned to the officer. "I was worried upstairs."

The officer smiled. "Just testing. I am fully aware if I was asked one more time for identification, their orders were to kill me!"

General Tate frowned. "This is not a game! Do not test these men; they will kill you!"

The officer smiled. "I am fully aware of their capability."

They walked to the end of the hallway to a single door. This door was made of steel and it looked like the door to a bank vault. They presented their photographic identification cards to one of four armed soldiers. One soldier looked at the cards and nodded. The soldier tapped on the metal door with a metal object. The sound of bolts moving could be heard as the door was slowly pushed open from the inside to the outside.

Laughter could be heard inside.

The inside room was very large. It appeared to be the size of the first floor of the White House and very ornate. A large table was placed in the center, with seating for forty.

The large room was divided into sections: food preparation, bathing, sleeping and setting. The long room ended in a darkened area. The darkened area was large but the officer with General Tate could not see what was in this section.

The setting area contained a very ornate settee. One man was sitting and another man was placed to the side, in a very ornate chair. The two men were laughing.

As General Tate and the officer entered the room, Professor Lytle stood.

"He is here as you requested," Professor Lytle said in French.

The man on the settee stood. He was almost six American feet tall and dressed in a military uniform. The man's hair was cut short and black. The man's face was clean shaven. The officer did not flinch when he saw the man's eyes. The officer had been prepared for the man's eyes.

The man looked dead!

His eyes were without pupils and they looked like they had sunk into his skull.

The man looked liked Napoleon Bonaparte. He was wearing a French military uniform as depicted in the 1812 painting by Jacques-Louis David, *The Emperor Napoleon in His Study at the Tuileries.*

The man said something in French.

"Your reputation precedes you," Professor Lytle said in English.

The officer bowed. "And your reputation has long been admired," he said in English.

Professor Lytle repeated what was said in French.

The man laughed as he pointed toward the darkened area of the large room. He said something in French as he began walking toward the darkened area.

"I have much to teach you and we have little time," Professor Lytle said in English.

"Can I ask a question?" the officer asked. "I have a question I want answered before we begin." The officer took a firm stance. He was not moving.

Professor Lytle repeated what was said in French.

The man was preparing to enter the darkened area when he stopped and turned. He said something in French.

"You can ask any question at anytime," Professor Lytle said in English. "What is your question?"

The officer nodded his head. "Why did you choose America over France? The French soldiers could have rescued you at any time but they did not."

Professor Lytle frowned and he repeated what was said in French.

The man smiled. He walked to the long table, reached for a carafe of wine and poured himself a glass of wine. The man was blind but he had memorized every step and every object in the room.

He spoke in French and sipped his wine.

Professor Lytle turned toward the officer. "A soldier must have discipline but the soldier must have the ability to think for themselves if needed," he said in English. "The French soldier is brave but the ability to think has been taken from them."

He spoke in French and sipped his wine.

"The French were tested and they failed," Professor Lytle said in English. "My orders were misunderstood. My orders did not include the killing of innocents."

He sat in one of the chairs at the table with a sad look on his face. He said something in French as he sipped his wine.

"The French soldiers' demonstrated cowardice when they murdered three women," Professor Lytle said in English. "The American soldiers demonstrated bravery when they knowingly pursued a superior force and the man named General Tate showed compassion when he returned the eleven men who were executed for thinking for themselves. If these men had been allowed to continue, I would have been rescued. My first act would be to execute those responsible for the deaths of the three women and the one man."

Suddenly, he struck his right fist on the top of the table. He began to scream in a language the officer had never heard. The man ranted as he struck his right fist, repeatedly, on the table. He pointed his right hand toward the officer as he continued to yell.

As quickly as his rant started, it stopped. He calmed himself and sipped from the wine glass.

"I know that language," Professor Lytle laughed. "It is Corsican. He taught me the language. I suspect he knows and can speak English but he refuses." He turned to the officer. "The soldier's first duty is to eliminate the enemy soldier. The soldier's second duty is to protect innocents. The Americans demonstrated this second duty when the man named Captain Lawrence ordered his soldier from the field of battle to protect my angel. The Americans demonstrated honor, courage and innovation. The French demonstrated nothing. I will not have my soldiers' murder women and children. I will kill those soldiers myself."

The officer smiled. He appeared to relax and he smiled. "Where are they?" he asked in English. "Where are the French soldiers in the Susquehanna River Valley? We searched for them but we could not find them."

Professor Lytle repeated what was said in French.

The man sipped his wine and said something in French. He stood and adjusted his coat. He placed his wine glass on the table and said something else in French.

"Those soldiers waited for orders that would never come," Professor Lytle said in English. "They were ordered to remain hidden for a period of twelve months. If they received no additional orders, they were to disperse. They are gone because they are incapable of thinking for themselves."

He smiled slightly as he pointed toward the darkened area.

"One more question," the officer said. "Who killed the Germans?"

Professor Lytle narrowed his eyes as he repeated what was said in French.

The man smiled slightly as he spoke in French. He moved his hands outward as he spoke and frowned.

"I do not have confirmation but it is my belief the French," Professor Lytle said in English. "It does not matter because the one man, whom I had trust, has been replaced. It was this one man who demonstrated the ability to think when needed. His superiors considered him dangerous and had him replaced. These French soldiers cannot defeat Germany."

The officer laughed. "I can give you that confirmation! Amaury Benoit is alive and currently in France. Benoit left the valley two weeks after the failed assault. When he left, he took more than one thousand soldiers with him. It was he who told us where to find the German soldiers. It appears he has the same view of the French as you do."

Professor Lytle repeated what was said in French.

The man laughed and said something in French.

"You are fortunate France has one soldier who can think for himself when needed," Professor Lytle said in English. "Perhaps he will be at your side in battle."

The officer laughed. "I certainly hope so. Benoit is an excellent soldier."

Professor Lytle repeated what was said in French.

The man said something in French.

"Have I answered your questions to your satisfaction?" Professor Lytle said in English.

"Not yet," the officer answered. "I have one more."

Professor Lytle repeated what was said in French.

The man smiled and said something in French.

"I know the question," Professor Lytle said in English. "I anticipated your question and I prepared your answer. Your question is of the actions of the American soldiers in my room, that night, during the failed French rescue?"

He was standing but he picked up his glass of wine and filled it. He walked to the end of the table, to the ornate chair, and sat. He motioned for the officer to sit beside him and sipped his wine.

The officer did not move. He took a firm stance and folded his arms.

The man leaned backward into his chair and he said something in French.

"The American soldiers performed their orders, exactly!" Professor Lytle said in English.

The officer was puzzled by what was said. He unfolded his arms and placed them behind his back. "No! They did not!" the officer said forcibly.

Professor Lytle's eyes widened. He looked at General Tate.

General Tate's eyes were widened. He looked to the officer. "This is not the proper place or the proper time!"

The officer smiled. "Yes it is!" He looked to Professor Lytle. "Repeat what I said in French."

General Tate nodded his head toward Professor Lytle and Professor Lytle repeated what was said in French.

The man smiled slightly and said something in French. He placed his wine glass on the table and said something in French.

"Your interpretation of their actions is incorrect," Professor Lytle said in English. "I was present and you were not. You are basing your interpretation of the soldier's actions on incorrect information."

The officer looked puzzled at the response. "There is nothing to interpret. The forty soldiers were ordered to surround and protect you. Thirty soldiers did not understand their orders and they disobeyed those orders when they left you!"

Professor Lytle repeated what was said in French.

The man laughed. It was a very loud laugh. He smiled as he said something in French.

Professor Lytle seemed puzzled by the man's response. "It is you who do not understand their orders," he said in English. "They understood their orders perfectly and they performed their orders with courage and distinction."

The officer frowned and shook his head. "Thirty soldiers left you. They disobeyed orders."

Professor Lytle repeated what was said in French.

The man smiled. He leaned forward and sipped from his wine glass. He motioned, again, for the officer to sit beside him. He turned his head, listening for the sound of footsteps. Hearing none, he placed his glass on the table and stood. He walked to stand directly in front of the officer.

The officer was surprised by the man's actions. He knew exactly where he was standing and walked to within three feet of him. The man, dressed at Napoleon Bonaparte, looked at him upward and downward and stood in the exact same position. He folded his hands behind his back and spoke softly in French.

"You have been misinformed," Professor Lytle said in English. "The soldiers were given two orders. They were ordered to surround me and they were ordered to protect me. The thirty soldiers followed both orders, exactly."

The officer appeared to be unnerved. The man's eyes were without pupils; he looked dead! He stood in a commanding position and his voice was mesmerizing.

The officer frowned. "It is you who misunderstand their orders. They were not ordered to leave you. In leaving you, they failed to protect you!"

Professor Lytle repeated what was said in French.

The man did not smile. He leaned his head slightly to the right and said something in French.

"In leaving me, they protected me," Professor Lytle said in English.

The man spoke softly in French. He paused and turned. He walked a distance of four feet and turned. He said something in French and he motioned with his hands as if telling a story. Returning to stand within three feet of the officer, he duplicated the officer's stance, exactly.

Professor Lytle shrugged his shoulders. He looked to the officer. "You know nothing of your soldiers and what they are capable of doing," Professor Lytle said in English. "If a soldier has accurate and timely information, they will make the correct decision every time. But that soldier must have the ability to think for themselves when needed. Those soldiers were ordered to protect me. When the gunfire erupted, they came to my room and surrounded me. The man named Professor Sykes attempted to open the doors from the inside and they stopped him."

"As more gunfire erupted, they made the correct decision to end the assault. Ten stayed as thirty left the room. If those thirty soldiers did not do what they did, when they did it, the assault would have been successful."

The officer looked puzzled by the response. “They disobeyed orders and left the safety of the room. Those thirty soldiers went into battle not knowing the numbers they faced or the possible outcome. They disobeyed orders and because they disobeyed orders; eighteen soldiers gave their life … for you!”

Professor Lytle’s eyes widened as he repeated what was said in French.

The man’s eyes widened in anger as he shouted in a language the officer heard him speak earlier. The man stepped backward and unleashed a barrage of angered words. He ranted as he shook his hand toward the officer, yelling. As quickly as the outburst began, it stopped. He took the same stance as the officer and glared at him.

Professor Lytle’s eyes widened. “The language is Corsican,” he said in English. “I will do my best to repeat what he said and how he said it.”

“Me! Me! You think this is about Me? It is about You and every Man, every Woman and every Child in the United States!”

“Those soldiers were told I was important in the defense of their country against Germany. Those soldiers believed the assault was from the Germans! They were not protecting Me they were protecting the United States!”

“Those eighteen soldiers did not die for Me they willingly gave their lives for America!”

“They decided amongst themselves to enter the battle to protect their country and every Man, Woman and Child who lives in it!”

“The French soldiers were battling for a piece of ribbon and a piece of brass. Those thirty American soldiers battled for something far greater, Liberty and Freedom!”

“Your information is incorrect! Those soldiers acted with courage and determination! They made the correct decision and they did not disobey orders!”

Professor Lytle paused. "This is the American *Grande Armée*; soldiers who can never be defeated because they battle for Liberty and Freedom!"

Professor Lytle paused again. "I will not have you speak of these thirty American soldiers in such a manner!"

The officer's eyes widened and he relaxed his stance. "You are correct! I misunderstood their orders," he said in a firm voice. "I misunderstood their actions and their goal. I have learned a valuable lesson today … I will not forget."

He turned to General Tate. "I want the records of these thirty soldiers corrected and I want to see those corrections on my desk tomorrow morning at zero eight hundred hours! In addition, I want the families of those eighteen soldiers who died in battle for their country taken care of."

He paused briefly. "This is not a request. As your superior officer, this is a direct order!"

General Tate's eyes widened. He had never seen the officer back down; this was the first time. The man was correct! These soldiers did not disobey orders, they followed them, exactly. He nodded his head.

Professor Lytle repeated what was said in French.

The man relaxed his stance and said something in French.

Professor Lytle smiled. "When a soldier has accurate and timely information, they will make the correct decision every time," he said in English.

"Exactly," the officer said.

The man said something in French.

"Have I answered your questions to your satisfaction?" Professor Lytle said in English.

"Completely," the officer answered.

Professor Lytle repeated what was said in French.

The man nodded his head. He spoke in French as he walked toward the darkened area.

"The Army and their leaders must have the respect and the admiration of the people they are fighting for," Professor Lytle said in English. "Without this respect and admiration, the Army and their leaders will fail."

The officer nodded his head in agreement as he walked toward the darkened area. The two men walked into the darkness as Professor Lytle followed the officer.

The large area was dark and the officer could not see. He could hear the man speak in French and the sound of something large moving.

"Our first step is to plan the defense of France," Professor Lytle said in English. "The Americans must win this war and I will teach you how to win it."

"Win what?" the officer asked in disgust. "I cannot see anything!"

Professor Lytle laughed as he repeated what was said in French. "He does not need lights but we do. Lights!" he yelled in English.

A click sound was heard as a large lever was moved. The room was suddenly bathed in bright overhead lights.

The officer covered his eyes from the lights. He could not believe what he was seeing.

The room was more than one hundred yards square and thirty feet in height. Large metal columns supported the roof. On the three walls of the room were large maps. The maps were of cities, towns and countries.

The man stood in a path that had been created as he walked toward a large series of tables. The tables held models of cities, towns and countries. The models were very ornate and held buildings, rivers, lakes and streams. Soldiers stood to the side and pulled handles, moving sections of the table, as the man walked toward one section. The section he walked toward moved outward, and under, one section to allow the man to walk.

He walked to a section and stopped. He said something in French as he held his arms outward.

"Eastern border of France and western border of Germany!" Professor Lytle yelled in English.

Soldiers pulled and pushed handles as the entire room seemed to change. A large three dimensional map of the eastern border of France and the western border of Germany began to move upward and outward to surround the man. A wide path allowed him to walk around and through the map.

The whole scene was bizarre. It looked like a giant man standing on the eastern border of France. The tables came to his waist and he moved his arms and hands outward and downward to feel the mountains, lakes and rivers.

He said something in French as he reached to his right and touched a large section of forest.

"The Argonne Forest is our problem," Professor Lytle said in English. "Both armies will be locked in a battle to control this section."

The officer moved backward in disbelief. "Washington?" he asked slowly. "We must plan the defense of Washington!"

Professor Lytle smiled as he repeated what was said in French.

The man walked toward the officer, through the path, and stood at the entrance to this section of the large room. He turned and said something in French.

"Washington in the District of Columbia," Professor Lytle said in English. "Complete!"

The officer's eyes were wide but they widened further. The entire room began to transform. Soldiers moved maps placed on the wall. Maps moved backward and maps moved forward as detailed maps of the city of Washington covered the walls.

Soldiers pulled and pushed handles as the table changed. The three dimensional maps on the tables moved sideways, and under, as three dimensional maps of the city of Washington took their place. The whole room seemed to move as a detailed model of the city of Washington emerged.

The model was very detailed. The officer could see the White House and the streets surrounding it. Buildings were in their proper place and the officer quickly recognized sections of the city. He could see bridges.

The whole scene was bizarre. It looked liked the entire city had been captured in detail and placed on a series of tables.

Small flags were placed on the model. He looked closely at one flag. The writing was Second Infantry – Captain Craig Johnson.

The man said something in French. He began to walk forward as soldiers pulled and pushed handles. The model appeared to expand allowing him to walk forward. He stopped at the model of the White House and turned.

"In the event the German Army breeches our defenses," Professor Lytle said in English, "the city of Washington is protected."

The man began to move his arms outward, pointing at different sections. He spoke rapidly in French.

"I am not familiar with all of the names but I will do my best to repeat what he said," Professor Lytle said in English. "The perimeter of the White House will be protected by infantry under the commands of Generals Burke and Townsend. .50 caliber automatic guns, mounted on muter cycle wheel carts, will patrol and protect the eastern and western sections."

Professor Lytle paused. "He spoke too fast. He is pointing at two buildings. The State-War-Navy Building, located on 17th Street NW, is to be moved to a new building that will be constructed on B Street. This building will hold munitions until a larger one can be constructed here."

Professor Lytle walked to a section of the model. The section was located in Virginia, across the Potomac River. "He designed this fort to protect the military leaders. The fort is designed to be defended from all sides. The design is a form with five angles and five sides."

The officer walked to a section of the three dimensional map that was very detailed. It was located near the Arlington National Military Cemetery. He knew the cemetery well. In 1899, Spanish-American War Soldiers were returned from the battlefields to be buried at Arlington National Cemetery. The building Professor Lytle was pointing to was odd shaped, there were five sides. It was a pentagon.

The officer was stunned. He looked under the table and there appeared to be multiple layers of tables that descended below the floor. The tables were moved by a series of pulleys. Eight soldiers operated the pulleys by pushing and pulling handles. Small electric lights bordered the table allowing the soldiers to see in darkness.

He had never seen such large, detailed maps. Everything could be seen. It was like looking at a battlefield from the height of an eagle in flight. He could see everything: buildings, railroad tracks, roads, trees, lakes and rivers.

General Tate had been standing in the first section and he walked slowly toward the officer. "It has taken us three years to prepare this room," he said. "He calls it the War Room and it is from here he will plan, and you will execute, the defense and liberation of Europe."

The officer stood staring in disbelief. He had never seen such a thing. As he looked, a door to the side opened and one man emerged. The man was elderly and he was holding a small building in his hands. A statue of a man sitting was placed in the front of the building. The image of the man was large, too large for the building. The statue of the man was not proportioned.

"It is complete," the elderly man said proudly.

Professor Lytle smiled as he repeated what was said in French.

The man smiled as he walked away from the White House. The table began to move as the soldiers pulled and pushed handles. An opening emerged, allowing the elderly man to advance and carefully place the building in the man's hands.

The man turned, felt the edge of the table and expertly placed the building in a location reserved for it.

The officer moved forward to observe. The building was placed near to the Washington Monument. Construction of the

Washington Monument began in the year 1848 and it was not completed until the year 1884.

There is no building near the Washington Monument. He looked closer and the statue of the man sitting was very detailed. He immediately recognized the man, it was President Abraham Lincoln.

The memorial to President Abraham Lincoln was begun in the year 1914; two years before he was sent to Mexico to capture Poncho Villa. He knew the designer Henry Bacon and the memorial was not to be completed for one more year. The monument was beautiful!

The man moved his right hand to a section under the table and he removed small flags. He placed the flags around the building slowly as he spoke in French. He touched the building gently, spoke softly, and he turned with a stern look on his face; and said something in French.

"I have been teaching him as he has been teaching me," Professor Lytle said in English. "He knows all about American President Abraham Lincoln. As he placed the flags, he repeated the Gettysburg Address." Professor Lytle paused. "When he touched the building, he said, 'Great words from a Great man.'"

He turned to the officer. "General Bradshaw will command the forty-fourth brigade to protect the monuments of this city."

The officer was astonished as he moved backward. The man knew every inch of the city of Washington. He knew the streets, roads and buildings. The man was blind but he could see, in his mind, everything!

"I have heard stories but I did not expect this," the officer said. He adjusted his uniform coat and stood straight to attention. "You know who I am and I know who you are but I want to hear it for myself."

"Who are you?" the officer asked in disbelief.

Professor Lytle laughed as he repeated what was said in French.

The man smiled as he placed his right hand into his coat.

"Je Suis Napoleone Bounaparte."

Chapter Forty - One

French Soldiers, in Retreat, Cheer as General John Joseph 'Black Jack' Pershing Advances

Paris, France: November 23, 1917 – French soldiers weary and in full retreat from multiple defeats from the German Army, cheered as General John Joseph 'Black Jack' Pershing and the American Army War Machine continued their advance.

"Since 'Black Jack' stepped foot on French soil in October, he has held complete command, defeating the German Army at every turn," French General Andre Bertrand is quoted as saying.

General Pershing's battle tactics were initially criticized by commanders of the French Army.

"His battle tactics were unusual," French General Bertrand is quoted as saying. "General Pershing would order his men to move to the left and move to the right. Advance. Retreat. Advance. Change the elevation of the guns and move them forward. Change the elevation of the guns and move them backward. While these commands seem unusual, they disoriented the enemy; causing their battle lines to split."

"General Pershing did not interrupt the enemy as they made mistakes and he took full advantage of those mistakes."

As the French Army retreats in disarray, with no clear commander or clear battle plan, the American Army War Machine under the leadership of General Pershing, continues their surge forward; moving the German Army backwards away from French soil toward the Argonne Forest. They will soon encounter a type of warfare that has never been fought in the history of mankind, trench warfare.

It was General Pershing who initiated the development of the masks to protect American soldiers from the mustard gas used by the German Army.

"The masks are a simple device used to protect allied soldiers from the mustard gas," French General Bertrand said. "I do not know where he got this idea; it is pure genius and the mask has saved the lives of tens of thousands of allied soldiers. It works!"

The American military has introduced new methods of warfare on French soil; mounting automatic guns on motorcycles and automobiles. This concept was first conceived in 1899 under the leadership of Major R.P. Davidson. It was not until 1910 the Secretary of State for War was convinced of the military necessity to develop new weapons.

In the year 1910, the United States military began to redesign their machines and implements of war.

"General John 'Black Jack' Pershing is executing a brilliant offense," French General Bertrand continued. "His battle tactics are currently being compared to the greatest military genius in history. It is almost like Napoleon Bonaparte is planning and directing every move of the American Army."

The Stars and Stripes

Chapter Forty-Two

"Bridges!"

General Roth turned to his right to Colonel Bragg. "I have never heard of such a thing. It has never been done."

Professor Lytle smiled slightly as he pointed to the scale model of the Argonne Forest. "The four trenches are close enough. He estimates six to eight hours to cross all four."

General Roth stood. He was in a conference room where Professor Lytle called a meeting to discuss his plan on how to break through the German defenses in the Argonne Forest. There were seven senior members of the American Army in attendance and General Roth frowned as he picked up a small bridge from the table.

"What are these arches?" General Roth asked. He turned the small bridge in his hand. The bridge had no supports above the top and several arches were below the top.

"To support weight," Professor Lytle answered. "The cathedrals of Europe use an arch to support the weight. They are called a flying buttress. There are many bridges, hundreds of years old, which use the same design. These bridges were built by the Romans. They are made of stone and the arch dissipates the weight."

"How many do we need?" General Roth asked. He placed the small bridge on the table and he looked at the model of the Argonne Forest. In one section, the model clearly showed four trenches converging almost as one. The general sat and looked at the small model of the Argonne Forest.

"Sixteen," Professor Lytle answered. He pointed toward the model of the forest and he placed the bridge within the first trench. "He estimates a minimum of four per trench."

"Why four?" Colonel Bragg asked.

"The attack must be swift," Professor Lytle answered. He pointed toward the model. "There is not enough time to construct more than four. The German Army must not be allowed time to regroup."

General Tate was sitting and he stood. He walked closer to the model and he picked up the bridge. "The armed motorcycles and automobiles will provide cover as our soldiers take the first trench. Once that trench has been taken, the armed vehicles will move to the edge of the trench while the first four bridges are being constructed."

He placed the small bridge in the first trench. "Once the four bridges are constructed, the armed vehicles will move across the bridges, over the first trench, and provide cover as our soldiers take the second trench."

He placed the small bridge in the second trench. "The same thing will occur at the second, third and fourth trenches." He removed the small bridge from the second trench and he placed it in the third and the fourth trench.

"The sixteen bridges must be strong enough to allow more vehicles and soldiers to pass. They must remain in place until a sufficient force has taken this section of the forest. Once this area has been secured, permanent bridges will be constructed to allow the armored tanks and the big guns to cross."

Colonel Bragg frowned. "This has never been done in the history of warfare."

General Roth nodded. "What is his estimate of time to construct one bridge?"

"One hour," Professor Lytle answered.

Colonel Bragg laughed. "That bridge can not be constructed in one hour!"

"I agree!" General Bates said. He was sitting but he stood and pointed toward the bridge. "Forty-five minutes!"

Colonel Bragg frowned. "It is impossible to construct a bridge in forty-five minutes, one hour or three hours. It would take one week to construct that bridge!"

General Bates smiled. "Are you an engineer?"

"No," Colonel Bragg answered. "Are you?"

"Yes!"

General Calvin Bates was in command of a section of the Army composed of engineers. The corps main function was to provide assistance in demolition. They outlined how to blow up bridges but they have never constructed one.

General Bates smiled as he picked up the bridge and examined it. “It is very basic in design,” he said. “The function is to support weights under two thousand pounds and this structure could possibly support twice that weight.”

Colonel Bragg smiled. “You really think you could build that bridge in forty-five minutes?”

“Nothing to build,” General Bates answered. “It will already be built, we just put it together.”

Colonel Bragg laughed. “A portable bridge? The main problem is making it fit. We do not really know the exact length and depth of those trenches.”

“He has already thought of that,” General Bates said as he enclosed the bridge in his hands. He placed the bridge in the first trench and it did not fit, the bridge was too small. There was distance to the sides and to the top. A vehicle could not move from the ground level to the bridge.

“It does not fit,” Colonel Bragg said.

“Watch and learn,” General Bates said. He reached to the model and slowly pulled the sides. The bridge expanded to both sides of the trench. He reached to the top and bottom and slowly pulled, the bridge expanded upward to meet the ground level.

“How did you do that?” Colonel Bragg asked. The other officers stood and looked at the bridge, it fit the trench perfectly.

General Roth did not stand with the others. He leaned forward, puzzled.

“I noticed the model adjusts when I held it,” General Bates answered. He picked up the model. “There are four sections. The main sections are the two uprights. Pieces of the sections fit inside the other section, allowing it to expand and to contract upward and outward. The center braces allow displacement of weight and support the sides. The top area slats can be moved closer or farther apart."

He smiled as he placed the model in the second trench and adjusted it. "The bridge is wide enough and strong enough to support two vehicles side by side. There are no railings. In the event a vehicle is damaged, it can be pushed off the bridge, to allow another vehicle to continue."

"The idea is to construct all four simultaneous," he added. "The soldiers constructing the four bridges are protected inside the trench. Once they are ready, eight vehicles will cross with guns blazing! Once those eight have crossed, eight more will follow."

Colonel Bragg leaned backward in his chair and smiled. "How soon can you have the first one ready?"

"Twenty-four hours to design and construct the first one and twenty-four hours to clean up any design flaws," General Bates answered.

"It will work!" Colonel Bragg said. "The only problem is getting the sixteen bridges to France. It will take weeks."

"He has already thought of that," Professor Lytle said. "The portable bridges will be constructed in France. There are two foundries in Paris that can make the parts. The dimensions can be sent by cable."

General Roth stood. "Done deal!"

American Army War Machine 'Breaks Through' German Army Argonne Forest Defenses

Paris, France: November 11, 1918 – The American Army War Machine, under the command of General John Joseph 'Black Jack' Pershing, breaks through the German Army defense in the Argonne Forest.

Since 1915 the Argonne Forest has been a strong hold for the German Army. The German position was impregnable, or so it was believed. A weakness in the German defense was discovered, and an unusual offense was initiated in the Meuse-Argonne Offensive September 26 to November 11, 1918.

"We could not see it until more detailed maps was completed," United States General Martin Tate is quoted as saying.

Rumors surfaced American topographers were sent from the United States to the battle lines to make detailed models of the forest in an effort to end the stalemate. General Tate denies those rumors. "This is absurd," General Tate stated. "This type of mapping is standard military procedure in times of battle."

The German Army's defenses were composed of four trenches in Belgium, Artois, and Champaign. The first, second, third and fourth trench lines were a great distance apart but merged closer together in the south east section of the Argonne Forest. "When the new, more accurate maps were complete, we could see a weakness in the German defense. In one section of the Argonne Forest, these four trenches were almost one," General Tate continued.

"The German Army made a mistake in their defenses and General John 'Black Jack' Pershing took full advantage of that mistake."

Automatic guns mounted on motorcycles and automobiles provided cover as American soldiers charged the first of four German trenches. Many German soldiers, surprised and overwhelmed by the superior force and fire power, dropped their guns and surrendered.

In an unusual maneuver, American soldiers constructed portable bridges to traverse the first trench, allowing the armed motorcycles and automobiles to pass. As each trench fell,

American soldiers constructed additional portable bridges to continue the surge forward.

"It was like stacked playing cards falling," General Tate stated. "The four trenches were close enough to be seen. When the first trench fell, the other three followed."

French citizens in Paris cheer and French soldiers salute as the American Army War Machine, under the command of General John Joseph 'Black Jack' Pershing, continues through Belgium toward Germany and the city of Luxembourg.

The Stars and Stripes

Chapter Forty-Three

Supreme Tactical Commander of the United States Army Buried in Arlington National Military Cemetery

Arlington, Virginia: June 20, 1947 – Sixty-seven year-old Rober Maurice Montpere was buried in Arlington National Military Cemetery, with full military honors, June 19, 1947. The service was closed to the public and attended by senior ranking officers of the United States Army.

Mr. Montpere was born June 14, 1880 in New York City and he died of natural causes on June 16, 1947 in Washington D.C.

Although Mr. Montpere was born blind, he was awarded a military commission in the year 1914, which allowed him to serve in the United States Army in a special capacity. Mr. Rober Montpere was commissioned Supreme Tactical Commander of the United States Army in 1914, and served with honor and distinction, during World War I.

Commander Montpere held this commission for thirty-three years.

Failing health, due to a sugar imbalance in his system, prevented his participation in World War II. The Commander has been bedridden for several years and he passed quietly in his sleep. His long-time friend, Professor Nathan Lytle, age ninety-six, was at his side.

Commander Montpere's commission allowed him to be buried in the Arlington National Military Cemetery with full military honors.

by Norris Anderson, Virginia Times

Tourist Visiting Arlington National Military Cemetery Claims Soldiers Confiscated His Camera

Atlanta, Georgia: July 12, 1947 - James Etheridge claims American soldiers confiscated his camera as he took photographs of a soldier's burial at Arlington National Military Cemetery on June 19, 1947.

"I have never seen so much brass," Mr. Etheridge is quoted as saying. "I saw the funeral and I setup my camera on the tripod. As I took photographs, four soldiers approached me. I was questioned and they took my camera."

"I swear the President and the First Lady were there," Mr. Etheridge continued, "and I want my photographs to prove it!"

Representatives of the United States Army state no such funeral occurred in the month of June and they have no knowledge of the event or Mr. Etheridge's claim. A newspaper article in the *Virginia Times*, stating such, is currently under investigation by representatives of the United States Army.

Mr. Etheridge states he is a professional photographer and he has an interest in military history. He was visiting the cemetery for genealogical research and he photographed several sections of the cemetery. "I know what I saw," Mr. Etheridge stated. "I am a scholar of military history and what attracted me to the event was an unusual flower arrangement. During the service, the President of the United States placed a flower arrangement in the design of the First Consul Seal of Napoleon Bonaparte on the soldier's grave."

"The flower design was vertical in shape and composed of black, gold and yellow flowers," Mr. Etheridge continued. "Gold and yellow flowers in the design of a laurel wreath enclosed a large N. A large gold and yellow eagle was positioned above the laurel wreath. The eagle's wings were outstretched and its beak opened; prepared for battle. In the eagle's talons it held three lightning bolts."

"A second flower arrangement was placed on the soldier's grave by the First Lady. Emblazoned in blue, white and red flowers was the 1812 flag of France. Inside the center white vertical stripe; the First Consul Seal of Napoleon was repeated."

"The flag of 1812 France was surrounded by black flowers. The use of black flowers symbolizes the death of a person of royalty. "

As erroneously reported in the *Virginia Times* on June 20, 1947, a search of military cemetery records did not reveal a burial on June 19, 1947. There is no record of a person buried with the name Rober Maurice Montpere in the Arlington National Military Cemetery. The section of the cemetery, where Mr. Etheridge claims the burial took place, is currently under the process of renovation; more than five hundred graves are having new sod placed.

"Mr. Norris Anderson wrote the article," publisher Lewis Sanders of the *Virginia Times* stated. "He is a very trustworthy reporter and I have no doubts the story of the military funeral was accurate. However, I want to speak to him concerning his sources. I have been unable to speak to him because Norris has not been seen since the article was published June 20, twenty-two days ago."

by John Woods, Atlanta Prospect

List of References

Anderson S, Bankier AT, Barrell BG, de Bruijn MHL, Coulson AR, Drouin J, Eperon IC, Nierlich DP, Roe BA, Sanger F, Schreier PH, Smith AJH, Staden R, Young IG. Sequence and organization of the human mitochondrial genome. Nature, 1981, 290- 465.

Aristotle. Generation of Animals, 350 B.C.

Aristotle. God from Metaphysics, 350 B.C.

Arnold, Edward Ronny. Plato's Dream. Nashville: Computer Classics, 2005.

Barbujani, Guido, Bertorelle, Giorgio. Genetics and the population history of Europe. Proceedings of the National Academy of Sciences of the United States of America , 2001, 98(1), 22-25, 2001.

Cann RL, Stoneking M, Wilson AC. Mitochondrial genome variation and the origin of modern humans. Nature. 1987, 325, 31-36.

Cott, Jonathan (in collaboration with Hanny El Zeini). The Search for Omm Sety - Reincarnation and Eternal Love. New York: Doubleday and Company, Inc., 2001.

Mendel, Gregor. Experiments in Plant Hybridization, Read at the February 8th, and March 8th, 1865, meetings of the Brunn Natural History Society, 1865.

Plato. Studying Death, 360 B.C.

Plato. Studying Death:II - Ways to Hades, 360 B.C.

Sykes, Brian. The Seven Daughters of Eve, New York, NY: W.W. Norton & Company, Inc., 2001.

Watson, James D., Crick, Francis. A Structure for Deoxyribose Nucleic Acid, Nature, 1953, 171, 737.

Watson, James D. The Double Helix: A Personal Account of the Discovery of the Structure of DNA, New York: Atheneum, 1968.

www.ingramcontent.com/pod-product-compliance
Lightning Source LLC
Chambersburg PA
CBHW030358310726
48979CB00001B/349

* 9 7 8 0 9 8 3 6 0 1 9 0 6 *